The Other (Secret)

Space Program

Presenting compelling evidence in support of the existence of a covert space program, operating outside of the mainstream of government and NASA and funded through a black operations budget.

Table of Contents

Chapter 1

Introduction

During my research into ancient civilization anomalies within our Solar System I kept stumbling upon evidence that possibly indicated a secret space program that was being operated outside of the mainstream NASA program. Further investigation has revealed a clandestine program funded through a mysterious "black budget" which is fully legal and approved through Congress.

I must admit that I was initially skeptical. It didn't seem possible because of the incredible amount of people required in keeping such a secret. But after reviewing the amount of credible and expert testimony, the actual possibility of this occurring based on the location, operations schedules and launch azimuths at various facilities on Earth, and government documents, there appears a strong possibility that such a program may have existed, and may currently still be in operation.

The Other (Secret) Space Program connects the dots and unravels the most expensive, secret and influential covert program hidden from society in the history of this planet. I will shine new light on our hidden ancient past, present and future, where human society is going, who is the driving force behind it, how a breakaway in-world civilization is imminent and insights into coming Earth changes.

What is not known is when this secret space program started, how long it has been going on, and its scope and magnitude. In other words how far have we traveled into space? Has it been restricted to exploration within our Solar System? Or has it gone beyond, perhaps into another star system, galaxy, or even another dimension?

Predictive Programming

Predictive programming allows governments to prepare their citizens for a forthcoming event by a controlled gradual release of information, so that when the event occurs the public is already prepared for it. It is a conditioning of the masses. This is accomplished through the use (manipulation) of the media, official government pronouncements and respected people in their particular field of discipline.

Over the past couple of years, we have had the Vatican announcing that they now believe it is possible alien life exists elsewhere in the universe and Stephen Hawking making a declaration that alien life may be malevolent, and should be avoided if at all possible. NASA and the other space agencies have been making non-stop announcements concerning new planets (exoplanets) that have been discovered, and also discovery of water on Mars and the Moon, which hints at the possibility of some form of basic life existing within the water.

THE OTHER (SECRET) SPACE PROGRAM

There have been a plethora of sightings of UFOs across the globe with strange craft being reported over major areas of population, many being videotaped and appearing on YouTube or other internet sites.

It would seem to me that we are being prepared for something involving extraterrestrial beings and it may just be an official pronouncement that life has been found somewhere other than Earth – perhaps amoeba being found on Europa (one of Jupiter's moons) or something similar. Yet what we see broadcast in films and on television indicates a far bigger proposition and actual official contact with intelligent beings, which is portrayed as not necessarily a pleasant experience for the human race, as they allude to hostile alien visitation or an outright invasion of Earth.

Former Apollo 14 astronaut Edgar Mitchell claims that he is aware that various world governments (United States, Canada, France, England, Italy, Belgium, Germany, Netherlands, Mexico, Russia, Spain and Brazil among them) have been exchanging and sharing evidence of UFOs for some time. Furthermore, Mitchell believes that these same governments are mounting towards full disclosure.

Certainly the public awareness of it is increasing and public acceptance is increasing as well. In the United States well over 70 percent of the people now accept this as fact. While they do not know the entire true story, they do know there has been – or accept the fact – that there has been extraterrestrial visitation and see UFOs in the skies all the time that are very likely alien craft.

Now, not all of these aerial craft being observed in our skies belong to extraterrestrials. In fact it is impossible to determine which belong to ETs and which are of Earthly origin. You may be surprised to learn that many of them are "home-grown". I strongly believe that in the past sixty years or so there has been a considerable amount of reverse-engineering of alien technologies taking place – a black budget program operated on a massive scale. This top secret program has resulted in the development and creation of many of the unidentified aircraft which are reported as appearing in our skies. However, our copies – these UFOs of domestic origin – are not nearly as advanced as what the visitors have.

"We learn from history that we learn nothing from history."

– George Bernard Shaw (1856-1950)

Chapter 2

Black Budgets

A "black budget" is a budget that is secretly collected from the overall income of a country, a corporation, residents of a society, a national department, and so on. A black budget usually covers expenses related to military research. The budget is kept secret for national security reasons. The black budget allows intelligence activities, covert operations and classified weapons research to be conducted without Congressional oversight on the grounds that oversight would compromise the secrecy essential for the success of such "black programs".

Those billions of dollars earmarked for black budgets have created a secret world of advanced science and technology in which military units and federal contractors push back the frontiers of warfare. In the past, such handiwork has produced some of the most advanced jets, weapons and spy satellites, as well as notorious anti-gravity spacecraft.

Official budget documents tell very little. In 2008, for instance, Pentagon documents explained that Program Element 0603891c was receiving $196 million but would disclose nothing about what the project did. Private analysts believed it was aimed at developing space weapons.

It is alleged Dulce Base (a secret underground facility under Dulce Mountain, New Mexico) is operated by such a budget. Other programs such as Area 51 in Groom Lake, Nevada, and many experimental or covert military programs as well are said to be run by black budgets.

The United States Defense Department has a black budget it uses to fund expenditures it does not want to disclose publicly. Such an expenditure is called a "black project". The annual cost of the United States Defense Department black budget is sustained by funds funneled from other government agencies to the defense and intelligence community.

In February 2010 the Defense Department (DOD) released an enormous $708 billion budget for the 2011 fiscal year. Much of the proposed spending was fairly detailed – noting exactly how many helicopters the Pentagon planned to buy and how many troops it planned on paying. But about $56 billion was scheduled for simply "classified programs," or to projects known only by their code names, like "Chalk Eagle" and "Link Plumeria". That's the Pentagon's black budget.

Cobbling together this round figure for the military's hush-hush projects is easier than it seems. The Pentagon's separate ledgers for operations, research and procurement all contain line items for classified programs. Add those to the nonsensically-named programs, and you've got yourself an estimate for the Pentagon's secretive efforts.

The budget grew to more than $50 billion from the previous year – "the largest-ever sum," according to *Aviation Week*'s Bill Sweetman, a longtime black budget observer. A few more billion were added for wartime operations, for a total of $54 billion. 2011 total would be $2 billion higher, a 3.7 percent increase.

"The philosophy of the schoolroom in one generation will be the philosophy of government in the next."

– Abraham Lincoln (1809-1865)

Chapter 3

Why the Need for a Secret Space Program?

What reason would NASA or a government have for starting up a secret space program?

Because of an ongoing series of disasters on Earth (Japan nuclear reactor, BP oil spill, earthquakes, volcanic disturbances), there is more of a sense of urgency to look for another home. Theoretical physicist Stephen Hawking estimates that humans have only 1,000 years left on planet Earth, growing ever-closer to extinction as a result of their actions on the planet. Somewhere nearby, perhaps the Moon or Mars would be suitable.

We are in the midst of a natural cataclysmic cycle. According to the U.S. Geological Survey earthquakes, volcanic eruptions, tsunamis and geological disturbances have been on a dramatic increase for the last several decades. Magnitude 6.0 earthquakes are now common. NASA data indicates planetary changes across our Solar System are part of a huge natural cycle that has to do with alignments. Planet Earth has limited resources, limited energy, limited environment, living space, etc.

Another reason for developing a secret space program is due to the threat of an asteroid impact. The possible approach of Hercolubus (Tyche) – a gas giant planet which lurks in the outer reaches of our Solar System is another reason. Tyche is located in the Solar System's Oort cloud, first proposed in 1999 by astrophysicists John Matese, Patrick Whitman and Daniel Whitmire of the University of Louisiana at Lafayette. It orbits our Sun in a far elliptical orbit, is four times the size of Jupiter, with a helium and hydrogen atmosphere and is most likely to have many moons.

On February 13, 2011 NASA officially confirmed that it was tracking Hercolubus, which scientists called Tyche. The NASA Wide-field Infrared Survey Explorer (WISE) telescope showed a giant planet next to our Solar System. This planet fits the exact description of Planet X or Nibiru of ancient Sumerian mythology. The realization that an inevitable global cataclysm is imminent could have lead to the creation of a fast-tracked space program to save a select few of an endangered species – *Homo sapiens*. Why not announce this intention to the public? The answer is simple: to avoid creating and inciting mass panic and hysteria. It could all be part of a long term plan to "cherry pick" people to privately colonize a new planet.

To further investigate anomalous evidence on the Moon and Mars such as buildings, structures and various other sites. Off-world civilization records may contain libraries, maybe even translatable libraries. This would provide access to incredible new and advanced technological and medical discoveries. The first government or organization to find this information would be sitting in a great bargaining position with the rest of the world.

Perhaps the intention is to even destroy some of this evidence before the public becomes aware of it.

What better way is there to investigate the presence of alien civilizations on another planet without alarming the general public? A clandestine military space program could conduct exploration with impunity and with very little accountability.

Probably the most important reason to develop a behind-the-scenes military presence in outer space is to counteract a growing alien threat. Mounting evidence indicates that an increased amount of extraterrestrial activity has been monitored within our Solar System. In 1987, U.S. President Reagan in a speech before the United Nations established the tone and seriousness of this endeavor when he deliberately, or inadvertently, let slip the remarks that the world may one day unite to fight a threat from outer space.

This was followed by a series of subsequent remarks during the latter days of his term of office. The best way to refine and experiment with new, advanced technologies and/or weapons systems, which sometimes fail miserably and produce disastrous results, is to do it without anyone knowing. This eliminates political posturing, emotional public reaction and criticism, and media scrutiny.

The reason for this perceived alien threat was allegedly due to a fleet of UFOs which flew over the White House, Capitol Building and the Department of Defense on July 19th, 1952 and, again, on July 25th, 1952 (photo below). The world was electrified by large newspaper headlines and photos of squadrons of UFOs flying repeatedly over the nation's Capital in Washington, DC.

Fearful of an alien attack, President Truman ordered the military to make contact to arrange the release of a captured alien in the possession of the United States. Truman, in 1952, asked the CIA and later the NSA to broadcast a message to the extraterrestrials that we wanted to discuss a treaty. This became known as Project Sigma and it was successful. In 1953, the military formed "Alpha Teams" to find and retrieve crashed discs and any aliens found at the crash site. This was called Project Pounce.

The same month President Eisenhower took office (January 1953), the CIA's Office of Scientific Intelligence (OSI) was ordered to determine if UFOs were interstellar vehicles. OSI convened the Robertson Panel of scientists, which recommended expansion of an Air Force study of UFOs – Project Blue Book.

President Eisenhower came aboard in 1953 and realized the threat was real, so he contacted the Soviets, British and a few other trustworthy heads of state. They met to discuss the threat and decided to work on weapons to bring down these alien entities. In 1954 President Eisenhower allegedly met with a delegation of extraterrestrials. Subsequent meetings with other extraterrestrial races (another one on April 16, 1954) occurred resulting in a signed treaty. The treaty allowed for the return of captured ETs, in exchange for permitting the abduction of a few thousand humans for an exchange of technology. A permanent ET base here on Earth would also be allowed to be established. A list was to be kept, so that these abductions could be tracked and once the abductees were returned, the military would de-brief them.

On February 20-21, 1954 President Eisenhower allegedly made a secret trip to Muroc Field (now Edwards Air Force Base), in the California desert, accompanied by generals, reporter Franklin Allen of the Hearst Newspapers Group, Los Angeles Catholic Bishop James McIntyre, and others. The President had previously arranged to be in nearby Palm Springs, CA, supposedly for a golfing vacation. He was spirited over to Muroc one night, while reporters were fed the cover story that the President had a toothache and needed to see a dentist.

While at Muroc Air Field, Eisenhower was present while an extraterrestrial disc landed. Several extraterrestrials emerged to converse with the President and the generals (photo of meeting below).

Leaked photo of an alleged meeting at Muroc Field (now Edwards Air Force Base) between one extraterrestrial group and American officials.

The extraterrestrials requested that Eisenhower make the public aware of extraterrestrial contact with Earth forthwith.

The President protested that humans were not ready, and needed time to be prepared for adjusting to this stupendous reality. By the end of the following month, May 1954, President Eisenhower's CIA Director, Walter Bedell Smith, Prince Bernhard of Netherlands, David Rockefeller and other top world financiers, later-Secretary of State Dean Rusk, later-British Minister of Defense Denis Healey, and other Western power leaders convened the inaugural meeting of the Bilderberg Group, 'a means of Western collective management of the world order".

One of the early items on the Bilderberg agenda was extraterrestrial contact. Shortly after establishing itself, the Bilderberg Group collaborated with the Council on Foreign Relations (CFR), another international policy body devoted to world management. They discussed the problem of adjusting humankind to extraterrestrial presence. Bilderberg and CFR decided jointly in the mid-1950s to enter into an arrangement with the extraterrestrials: The ETs were given an island in French Polynesia as a base on Earth. This arrangement afforded them an opportunity to monitor closely Earth cultures and behavior; and it permitted Earth governments a way to monitor extraterrestrial culture and behavior. "It became an on-going experiment," as one former-NSA informant put it.

I provide a complete detailed account of this historic 1954 meeting between President Eisenhower and an extraterrestrial delegation in Chapter 6 of this book. This helps to explain many questions.

By 1955 it was realized that a group of the ETs had broken the treaty. Tens of thousands of people had been taken, some, multiple times. Others were not returned or found mutilated along with an increase in cattle mutilations. They continued to interfere with our military installations and missile tests.

As incredible as this story seems, it was the primary motivation behind the development of a secret space program, using technology retrieved from crashed alien spacecraft. This would allow us to deal with the ET presence (or threat depending on your opinion) on a level playing field. They would hold no advantage or superiority over us. Back when it all started, in 1953, President Eisenhower believed the only way to defeat the alien technology was to play along with them until we were capable of defending ourselves against them.

While this does not definitively prove the existence of a secret space program it does provide a clear motive for embarking on the development of such a program – especially if you have the ability to reverse-engineer spacecraft. What country or civilization would pass on such an opportunity if your survival depended on it?

Suspicion or interest in life on the Moon grabbed public attention when the inventor of the radio Marconi publicly reported his experiments in transmitting radio signals to the Moon and attempting to receive answers, which he believed took place. After that, American, British, and French astronomers reported glowing and moving and sometimes even blinking lights on the Moon during the 1920s and 1930s, often reported in local newspapers and scientific journals of those years which can often be found in public libraries.

This interest peaked when a respected expert in aerial phenomenon, Pulitzer Prize winning astronomer John O'Neill, publicly reported observing the "bridge" on the Moon that appeared artificially constructed by intelligence. There were other witnesses to the twelve mile long "bridge" which was erected because it was not seen in the same place before, and was later dismantled for unknown reasons (was it too conspicuous?). The bridge sighting occurred in the early 1950s.

During the 1950s many UFOs seen over Earth were tracked back to the Moon by government tracking stations in secret complexes in deserts in Arizona and Nevada and inside underground mountain bases. There is one photo of a saucer shaped craft hovering over the Moon, taken by a civilian astronomer. Sergeant Willard Wannail, who investigated UFO landings on Ohio while in Army Intelligence, provided an 8x10 clear glossy detailed photo of a silvery spaceship hovering directly over a huge Moon landscape, estimated to be several miles long, and said to be a "city-ship" designed to transport thousands of people who could live for extended periods of time in self-sufficient orbiting communities.

Through the 1950s and 1960s more moving, flashing, and stationary lights were seen on the Moon by civilian astronomers, usually inside craters, along with a mysterious glowing cross. Soviet and American spacecraft in orbit over the Moon began to photograph mysterious structures on the Moon which were censored by NASA, yet were obtained by scientific researchers who demanded the evidence from this so-called "civilian agency." It is amazing how NASA released these photos without comment. Many of the structures can only be seen when these photos are blown-up to a much larger size.

Most of the Gemini and Apollo astronauts admitted that they saw UFOs while they were in orbit, particularly Gordon Cooper who publicly admitted he believed they were intelligently controlled craft. James McDivitt also took UFO photos while orbiting Earth. One Soviet astronaut mission in the 1960s, designed to set a new record for time in orbit, was mysteriously aborted right after their craft entered space. Private researchers with powerful receiving radio equipment claimed the Soviet cosmonauts were followed into orbit by UFOs, which surrounded them and began bouncing them back and forth as if they were playing a pinball game with the Soviet craft. The cosmonauts reportedly panicked and were immediately sent back to Earth.

The U.S. spacecraft Ranger II took over 200 photographs of Moon craters with domes inside. These domes are nothing new. They were reported in the news media by French astronomers about 48 years earlier. There were 33 Moon dome photos from Lunar Orbiter 2 released without comment, in Washington D.C., in 1967. On June 1, 1966, NASA had admitted to the news media that astronauts had seen UFOs, then later on contradicted themselves by denying it. Anyone who saves all official releases on UFOs from agencies will find many contradictory statements to prove a cover-up. That did not stop Astronaut Gordon Cooper from his public statement "I believe in extraterrestrial life because I saw a spacecraft" (on his 16th Gemini orbit).

There are also the photos in of the "Blair cuspids", taken by satellites on the Moon showing strange spires that have been found to form perfect geometric patterns. Tall white spires resembling the Washington monument were photographed on the lunar surface, along with mysterious straight roads or tracks that cut through craters, hills, valleys, and rock piles without a twist. Some of the domes had flashing lights. Several NASA photos showed long cigar-shaped objects parked on the Moon, which later departed in other photos. Another photo of a pyramid-like object appeared on the dark side.

The lunar dark side is always hidden to our eyes and telescopes on Earth, an obviously perfect place for extraterrestrials to construct secret hidden bases. A lack of atmosphere is no problem to enclosed domes with artificial environments, which even NASA admits our scientists have the technology (but not the billions of dollars) to construct, and underground bases with artificial air-conditioning like our military now has on Earth. Astronaut Edgar Mitchell privately told Farida Iskiovet, of the UN Department of Interplanetary Affairs, that he saw a UFO on the Moon.

There is an unconfirmed report that when Buzz Aldrin opened the door after landing on the Moon, he immediately saw a transparent etherical being staring at him outside. Welcome to the Moon? NASA Director Christopher C. Kraft added that there was a public and a secret private A.S.A. radio frequency between the Moon and Mission Control.

Soviet radio operators also picked up these transmissions. One mysterious radio message from the Moon was broadcast on French public television only one time before it was censored after it leaked out. That transmission appeared to be a mysterious clearly spoken alien language. The famous French historian and author Robert Charroux published the transmission which has been suppressed in the United States. It came from Apollo 15 astronaut Alfred Worden.

Worden, who was in charge of telecommunications, had his attention drawn by a breathing sound and a long whistle. A sentence was constantly repeated on one note, varying from a small to a shrill tone, and from lightly stressed sounds to raucous exclamations. Luckily the transmission was recorded on LEM's tape recorder, and Worden transmitted it to NASA. Here are the 8 separate words:

"MARA RABBI ALLARDI DINI ENDAVOUR ESA COUNS ALIM."

Linguistic experts have been unable to translate this message. However, some public radio broadcasts from the Moon were not censored. Following is one example:

> "The dome-ical structures are partially filled up. Breach has either flowed into these structures before they were built or the domes are younger than the floor. The area is oval or elliptical."

What are these domes and structures that were referred to? Apollo radio public broadcasts from the Moon also used terms and phrases "Flashes of Light", "Buildings", "Roads", "Tracks", and "Huge Blocks." When news reporters asked space program officials what these terms were all about, they were absurdly told that these are metaphors for geological formations.

However, the scientist responsible for teaching geology to the astronauts admitted he was totally baffled by those terms. This geology expert, Dr. Farouk El-Baz, admitted the clincher when he said, "Not every discovery has been announced." When news reporters asked him about the flashes of light, Mr. El-Baz replied, "There is no question about it. Not natural."

Apollo 15 astronaut James Irwin radioed back to Earth, "that's the most organized structure I've ever seen." How could the most organized structure Irwin had ever seen be a natural formation? How can geological formations flash on and off?

NASA tried to distort the truth by replying volcanic action could cause the flashes, yet in other contradictory statements said there was no volcanic activity observed in those areas. Domes up to 1,500 feet high, taller than our skyscrapers were too high to deny that they were bigger than any building on Earth (miles wide). A radio tower appearing object was photographed, along with sequences of large moving vehicles leaving tracks in the lunar soil.

A huge clearly photographed lake was photographed by Apollo 8 hidden on the back side of the Moon with a spaceport near it, with what appears to be a long road in the distance.

Why do some of the craters photographed on the Moon have the exact same walls, floors, rims, and other details as atomic bomb craters and do not geologically look like the other craters formed by meteor impact? The Lamont Observatory and other civilian experts have noted that fact.

The government agencies policy of keeping UFOs secret from the general public is well-known and has been well-documented in several books by famous astronomers like J. Allen Hynek (who investigated UFOs for the U.S. Air Force), Major Donald Keyhoe, Timothy Good (in his book *Above Top Secret*), and many other highly credible professionals. One unquestionably absolute expert Christopher C. Kraft, who was Director of the NASA tracking base in Houston during the Apollo Moon missions, when he revealed the following Apollo 11 conversation after he left his job at NASA:

- ASTRONAUTS NEIL ARMSTRONG and BUZZ ALDRIN speaking from the Moon: "Those are giant things. No, no, no .... this is not an optical illusion. No one is going to believe this!"

- MISSION CONTROL (HOUSTON CENTER): "What...what...what? What the hell is happening? What's wrong with you?"

- ASTRONAUTS: "They're here under the surface."

- MISSION CONTROL: "What's there? Transmission interrupted... interference control calling Apollo 11."

- ASTRONAUTS: "We saw some visitors. They were there for awhile, observing the instruments."

- MISSION CONTROL: "Repeat your last information."

- ASTRONAUTS: "I say that there were other spaceships. They're lined up on the other side of the crater."

- MISSION CONTROL: "Repeat...repeat!"

- ASTRONAUTS: "Let us sound this orbita ..... In 625 to 5...automatic relay connected... My hands are shaking so badly I can't do anything. Film it? God, if these damned cameras have picked up anything... what then?"

- MISSION CONTROL: "Have you picked up anything?"

- ASTRONAUTS: "I didn't have any film at hand. Three shots of the saucers or whatever they were that were ruining the film."

- MISSION CONTROL: "Control, control here. Are you on your way? Is the uproar with the UFOs over?

- ASTRONAUTS: "They've landed there. There they are and they are watching us."

- MISSION CONTROL: "The mirrors, the mirrors...have you set them up?"

ASTRONAUTS: "Yes, they're in the right place. But whoever made those spaceships surely can come tomorrow and remove them. Over and out."

The above conversation took place during a mysterious two minute interruption in public transmissions. To prove it is the truth, hundreds of independent civilian radio operators with powerful VHF equipment separately reported hearing the spaceship report from the Apollo moonwalkers.

It is logical that if government agencies keep the existence of UFOs from outer space secret from the public, if they discovered the home of the UFOs that would obviously be secret also, and they would have to release "cover stories" about the Moon to hide the truth. The problem has been that witnesses have "talked" to such agencies as the Department of Interplanetary Affairs.

Why did the NASA space program land a probe on the Moon, its batteries went out, and it stopped working supposedly forever, and then someone or something mysteriously turned it back on, repaired it, and it began working after a year of silence? When confronted with their photos of domes and roads and other artifacts, why do certain NASA spokesmen reply "no comment", "subject to further analysis", "not all the discoveries have been announced" and other double-talk to keep them looking clean if the bubble ever bursts big-time?

• Plate 115, Apollo 16, image 16-18918 has to be blown-up to clearly see the large oval-shaped object inside a crater. NASA has no scientific explanation for this object that does not fit into the natural terrain.

• Apollo 13 image 13-60-8609 shows a large circular glowing UFO hovering over a very dark Moon landscape, definitely not natural.

• Lunar Orbiter 5 image HR 1033, taken on the hidden side of the Moon, clearly shows a huge cylindrical shaped object appearing to be parked on the Moon with front section in an opening on the side of the crater at Mare Moscovience. There is no scientific geological explanation.

• Apollo 15 image 1512640 shows a reported mining operation at the Humboldt Crater. Three domes are shown inside the crater Archimedes.

Why did NASA suddenly change its public policy? Was it the Apollo orbit around the Moon that sent back photographs of mining operations, domes, roads, a pyramid, a spaceport (named Luna) and lakes on the hidden dark side of the Moon? Did they fear a possible alien invasion from that base and panic and fear the public would panic? Was it too embarrassing to admit that all the billions of taxpayers dollars spent on the space program was largely wasted because the main goal was to colonize the Moon and we were kicked off that world because "we are screwed-up?"

The ancient Babylonians, Sumerians, Egyptians, Chaldeans, Phonecians, Assyrians, Aztecs, Mayans, Hindus, and Tibetans all left written records claiming they were contacted by ancient astronauts who taught them the basics of civilization, but not technology that could be used against the ET's. Modern historians do not tell us that because they believe the ancients were not telling the truth with no documented evidence to prove the ancients made up the histories.

There is a lot more evidence the ancients were telling the truth, based on the astronomical knowledge no primitive cultures could have possibly attained, artifacts and ruins only a modern technology could create, and the sudden appearance of the Egyptian civilization at its cultural peak with no prior history of evolving. There is plenty of documented proof.

Many scientists in 1990, as well as thorough archeologists-explorers like Robert Charroux, Eugenes Savoy, Warren Smith, Peter Colosimo, Dr. George Hunt Williamson, and many others from the last few decades, say they've absolute scientific proof of ancient astronauts based on ancient writings, ruins, artifacts, and historical contradictions they have analyzed in painstaking investigations.

Farida Iskiovet of the United Nations UFO investigation and eight former Army, Navy or Air Force intelligence officers who had top secret security clearances, as well as former NASA officials and ex CIA agents who were interviewed all say they know there were ancient astronauts influencing earlier cultures and here is the bombshell – there is scientific proof of ancient nuclear warfare on Earth. Evidence is left by radiated ruins and skeletons, nuclear bomb craters on Earth from ancient times, and buildings and objects with that nuked look, as well as carbon-dating and radiation tests on these things.

And if ancient astronauts could get to Earth from other solar systems, it would be even easier for them to get to our Moon. Its thin atmosphere and absence of violent weather would make it much easier for construction and mining, not to mention its absence of environmental contamination and large empires of hostile locals.

Have any of you ever wondered why there have been no astronauts sent to the Moon since Eugene Cernan on December 13, 1972? Why was the Moon program suddenly terminated after so much publicized success? What sense does that make? Why did NASA scientists and spokesmen of the 1960s brag about how they were going to establish space bases, mining operations, and colonies on the Moon in the 1980s change their plans? The likely excuse is lack of money from Congress, but that was nothing more than a cover-up.

Contrary to popular belief the Apollo program only cost less than one percent of the budget. Considering the huge billions spent on defense, the military advantage of having a base on the Moon would be enormous. Why were the American space officials of the 1950-60s so publicly afraid that the Soviet military might beat America to the Moon to gain a military advantage? So why risk that serious threat by abandoning the Moon flights? And why did the Soviet cosmonauts never land on the Moon?

Could it be that the Moon already belongs to someone else? Could it be that the Moon (and Mars) are foreign countries and someone else's property, and the landlords (owners) do not want us trespassing (invading) their territory with our nuclear weapons, pollution, disease, and dismal track record of foreign imperialism?

This extraterrestrial activity observed by the Apollo Moon astronauts is exhibit #1 in the growing alien threat. Many other similar extraterrestrial activities have been observed on other planets within our Solar System.

Some researchers believe that a breakaway civilization has emerged within our society; that advanced anti-gravity technology, pollutionless technology, free energy, and the ability to be able to manipulate DNA to extend human lifespan is all currently available to an elite group on our planet. This group has created for themselves a completely different capability to go into space, to utilize resources and maybe even to settle on other planets. They would have the power to veto this new free energy form from entering the civilian economy and yet would keep on researching in energy, propulsion, quantum access, and artificial intelligence. In all of these measures the black budget world is "a breakaway civilization." This breakaway civilization may not be totally divorced from this world, and may be an "Alternative 3" type of separateness.

Is this a plausible theory? Could this really be happening? Could most of humanity have been kept in the dark all this time?

"Don't let schooling interfere with your education."

— Mark Twain (1835-1910)

Chapter 4

World Launch Facilities

According to NASA's official website primary launch sites for Expendable Launch Vehicles are Cape Canaveral Air Force Station in Florida (located adjacent to Kennedy Space Center), and Vandenberg Air Force Base in California. NASA's Wallops Island, Virginia flight facility, Kwajalein Atoll in the Republic of the Marshall Islands in the North Pacific, Kodiak Island, Alaska, and the Odyssey platform, Pacific Ocean (mostly used for communications satellite launches) are additional ELV launch locations.

However, that is the **official** list. There are other sites which a secret space program could easily operate from totally undetected. These other sites include Edwards Air Force Base in California, Area 51 near Groom Lake, Nevada, and the Naval Support Facility (NSF) at Diego Garcia, in the Indian Ocean.

And this assumes that a spacecraft would need to re-enter Earth's atmosphere at all to land. If it could remain in orbit or space for an unlimited amount of time any runway on the ground would become irrelevant.

The runway at Edwards Air Force Base is by far the longest in the world at 39,600 feet (7.5 miles); Area 51 runway at Groom Lake 23,270 feet (4.4 miles); and the NSF at Diego Garcia has two parallel 12,000-foot-long runways (2.3 miles).

Vandenberg AFB, located 55 miles northwest of Santa Barbara, California, has a 15,000-foot-long (2.8 mile) runway. Its location just a few miles from the northern Pacific Ocean makes it possible to easily launch satellites into polar orbit, unlike the Kennedy Space Center. This, along with its location relative to the jet stream, makes Vandenberg a good site to launch reconnaissance satellites.

Vandenberg is also used for the launch of non-military satellites into polar orbits. The space probe Clementine was launched there, using a recycled Titan II ICBM.

Details on military launches from Vandenberg are withheld until they are approved for public release. Prior to the launch of a classified payload, the exact launch time is kept secret until about T-18 to T-4 hours. The launch window is also secret and not made public. Instead of providing the launch window, the Air Force announces a launch period – a large block of time within which the launch window falls.

Vandenberg AFB is designated as a closed installation. Those without base access credentials may only enter the base when they are sponsored by authorized personnel. The visibility of rockets and missiles launched from Vandenberg AFB varies greatly. Some launches are difficult to see from relatively short distances while others are visible for several hundred miles.

With the exception of the Pegasus XL, all Vandenberg AFB launches take place from the base. Minuteman III missiles climb rather steeply and head due west (over Pacific Ocean). Launch vehicles include Delta II, Minuteman II and III, Athena, Taurus, and Pegasus XL. Delta, Taurus, and other satellite launch vehicles fly towards the south and climb more slowly.

Vandenberg AFB lists rocket and missile launches for the next six months and the status of pending launches on its official website. However, it does not list ballistic (non-orbital) launches (Minuteman III and missile defense tests).

In 1972, Vandenberg was selected as the West Coast Space Shuttle launch and landing site. Space Launch Complex 6 (SLC-6), originally built for the abandoned Manned Orbital Laboratory project, was extensively modified for shuttle operations. Over $4 billion was spent on the modifications to the complex and construction of associated infrastructure. I'm sure this money was spent with the expectation of using this facility and not having sit idle for 40 years. Furthermore, this wouldn't have been decided or planned at all if rocket booster stage separations were to have taken place over land (see trajectories for stage separations below).

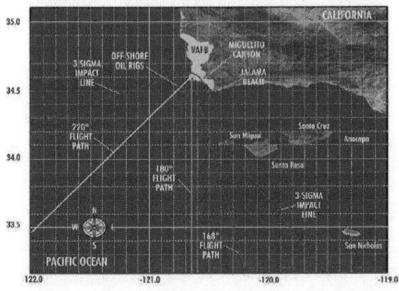

Vandenberg Spaceport Launch Azimuths

There has been an ongoing misinformation campaign being waged by those wishing to steer attention away from the Vandenberg facility as a possible launch site for a secret U.S. space program. Launches from Vandenberg travel due west over the Pacific, not over land. Therefore rocket booster stages would drop into the Pacific Ocean, much like launches from Kennedy Space Center in Florida where the rocket booster stages drop into the Atlantic Ocean.

Many debunkers claim it is impossible for Vandenberg to be used as a site for Saturn V rocket launches because the trajectory of launches result in rocket booster stage separation occurring over land, which is not the case. They obviously haven't done adequate research into the subject.

Vandenberg is responsible for west coast satellite launches for military and commercial organizations, as well as testing of intercontinental ballistic missiles, which today includes only the Minuteman III ICBM.

As of 2006 Vandenberg assumed a new role with the creation of the Joint Functional Component Command for Space (JFCC SPACE).

According to its founding commander, Lieutenant General William L. Shelton, the prime mission directive in JFCC Space is to ensure our freedom of action in space, while preventing adversary use of space against us. To do this, the component optimizes planning, execution, and force management, as directed by the commander of USSTRATCOM, of the assigned missions of coordinating, planning, and conducting space operations.

This definition, "to ensure our freedom of action in space, while preventing adversary use of space against us" appears to justify the use of any means to achieve the mission directive. One can only assume that this would include conducting secret space missions both manned and unmanned and Vandenberg would be a prime candidate from which to carry out such missions.

NASA's Glory spacecraft launched aboard an Orbital Sciences Corporation Taurus XL rocket from Vandenberg AFB on March 4, 2011, but failed to reach orbit. However, its planned launch timeline is typical of the sequencing events and stage separation schedule that occurs with other launches from Vandenberg.

Taurus/Glory Launch Timeline

• T+00:00 Liftoff – The first stage Castor 120 solid rocket motor is ignited and the Taurus rocket launches from pad 576E at Vandenberg AFB, California.
• T+01:25 Staging – After burning its solid-fuel propellant, the first stage is separated to fall into the Pacific Ocean. At the same time, the Orion 50SXLG solid rocket motor second stage is ignited.
• T+02:50 Second stage jettison – Having completed its firing at T+plus 2:45, the second stage separates from the rest of the Taurus rocket. **The spent stage falls into the Pacific Ocean**.
• T+02:52 Third stage ignition – The Orion 50XL solid rocket motor third stage ignites to continue the climb to orbit.
• T+02:58 Jettison payload fairing – The payload fairing nose cone that protected the spacecraft during the atmospheric ascent opens like a clam shell and falls away from the rocket.
• T+04:11 Third stage burnout – The Taurus rocket's third stage ends its burn after consuming all the solid-fuel propellant. A ballistic coast period now begins as the rocket heads toward the apogee of its final orbit.
• T+05:15 Third stage separation – The spent third stage is separated from the Taurus rocket's upper stage in preparation for the final push to orbit.
• T+09:58 Fourth stage ignition – The Taurus rocket's upper stage, an Orion 38 solid rocket motor to complete the powered flight for this launch, basically raising the perigee to achieve a circular orbit.
• T+11:10 Fourth stage burnout – The fourth stage completes its firing after consuming all of its solid-fuel propellant, injecting the stage and attached payloads into the desired orbit around Earth.
• T+13:05 Glory separation – NASA's Glory satellite is released into space from the rocket's upper stage to begin its climate-researching mission.
• T+13:15 CubeSat separation – The three tiny cubesats are ejected from the special deployer box attached to the rocket's upper stage, completing the ninth flight of Taurus.

"There is a history in all men's lives."

– William Shakespeare (1564-1616)

Chapter 5

Presenting the Evidence

Modus Operandi of a Debunker

The approach that so-called "debunkers" or skeptics take to disprove an alternative theory, discovery or evidence is very predictable and follows one of two methods.

1. One of the main reasons that new alternative evidence/theories suffer from credibility is that the original evidence instantly becomes the subject of "rip-off" and "copycat" re-productions. These people flood the public domain with reasons why this new evidence isn't legitimate – usually claiming to have re-created a close facsimile of the evidence in question, or pointing to a similar (earlier) discovery that was proven to be a fraud. As a result the original evidence becomes obscured and lost in a myriad of misleading, erroneous duplications.

These debunkers then take the position that just because they were able to closely duplicate the original evidence it must be false. The big problem with this position is, just because something can be closely duplicated, it doesn't disprove the original discovery. It only proves that the original discovery can be closely duplicated – nothing more! So effectively a cloud of confusion is created. A doubt and uncertainty is immediately cast upon the original discovery by introducing numerous conflicting information and data into the equation. The original evidence or discovery is then essentially lost in translation, and therefore ignored or dismissed as a hoax or fraud.

Whenever something cannot be explained the age-old "erosion", "natural rock formation", or "mutation" argument is hastily employed. This is also a common tactic used to dismiss the presence of pyramids and other anomalous structures on Mars and elsewhere in our Solar System. Scientists commonly use a term called "differential erosion" to explain their formation as nothing more than natural phenomenon.

And by the way, producing something similar that may have been caused or created through "natural" conditions doesn't disprove the original idea. You cannot infer or conclude something by comparing two distinctly different incidents, images or artifacts – regardless of how similar they appear. Such a comparison of evidence would never be admissible in a court of law. This is the typical modus operandi of mainstream science – producing a similar artifact or occurrence in a desperate attempt to explain the unexplainable. It is so transparent and childish. I would expect something a little more creative and calculated from such a group of pseudo-intellectuals.

I will draw the following analogy and compare this to the discovery of an unknown dog skeleton in North America and because little was known of its origins comparing it to a similar fully identified dog skeleton from Europe, and concluding that the skeleton from North America must have originated the same way. How ridiculous does that sound? What are the chances that the two skeletons are the same? I would think they would be very different in many ways. It is these kinds of wild assumptions and jumping to conclusions that get scientists in trouble and leaving them with the reputation of charlatans.

I will simply use the woeful and dismal track record of mainstream science, along with the countless frauds and deception it has perpetrated on the public over the years, against it. I describe hundreds of examples throughout my previous books. And what about the many ancient myths and legends which over the years have been proven to be factual? Don't they prove that mainstream science has been wrong time and time again? At one point I did try tracking this but it has gotten so out of control that I have stopped because it has become laughable and nothing more than a joke.

Much of what mainstream science says and presents is suspect, highly questionable, no longer believable and should be considered just as acceptable as anything alternative science and history proposes.

Mainstream science is held to a much higher standard therefore the expectation is that the quality of their information should be much more accurate.

Albert Einstein coined a couple of famous expressions. One was "education is what you have left when you have forgotten everything you learned in school". Another was "common sense is the collection of prejudices acquired by age 18". I believe this says it all. When we have broken free of the shackles and influence of mainstream academia and when our formal education stops is the time we start to think independently on our own. This is the time we really begin to learn as individuals and grow our intellect.

Taking Einstein's logic one step further it is probably prudent then for us to disregard or ignore what modern science and our educational institutions have taught us. Although I don't advocate such an extreme view, I do support seriously challenging and questioning everything they report. Their track record and reputation of having a hidden agenda is well known and documented. The property law doctrine *Caveat Emptor* encourages the "buyer to beware". In this case it should be the consumer, or general public, who should "beware" of the bill of goods they are being sold by the scientific community.

In light of recent archaeological and anthropological discoveries the credibility and relevance of modern science is steadily diminishing. It is grossly overrated as a source of reliable and impartial information and is rapidly becoming much like one subject it studies – a dinosaur.

The convenient "erosion", "natural rock formation", and "mutation" arguments are nothing more than blanket "escape clauses" for them because they have no other logical explanation. They are unwilling or unable to accept and grasp any new ideas outside of their exclusive little world which is based on tired, age-old paradigms and is not reflective of new emerging evidence from across the world. They are grossly out of touch with reality and falling further behind every day.

Unfortunately such is the mindset of conventional scientific thinking. Its arrogance prevents it from being open to new ideas and evidence especially if it doesn't come from them.

2. And then you have the pawns and followers who blindly insist on "jumping on the bandwagon" and obediently bowing their heads in approval just because they believe scientists are infallible and are the "last word". These stooges lack the backbone to stand up and challenge mainstream institutional doctrine, or to conduct their own objective research. Instead of judging the data or content, they choose to base their judgment on the source – the mainstream scientific community. How backward is that? Those who are not involved directly with concocting conflicting reproductions of the original evidence seize upon these "rip-off" and "copycat" ideas, theories or speculative research and use them as a rebuttal in their argument. Basically their claim is "because someone has come close to re-creating the original evidence it must therefore be false". I have never heard of more backward logic.

What you need to keep in mind is this: just because something can be closely duplicated doesn't necessarily disprove the original discovery. It only proves that the original discovery can be closely duplicated – nothing more! And just because something similar in the past has been disproven could also mean that it may have been subject to the same debunker methodology of disproving an idea or theory.

I am in no way implying that all alternative evidence is based in fact. What I am saying is be very cautious and keep an open mind and ask HOW something has been "disproved". Was it done through a sound reasoning process and the presentation of legitimate contradictory evidence? Was it subject to critical review? Or was it done using the debunker's methodology of disproving an idea or theory which I have described?

Seven Signs of Bogus Skepticism

The progress of science depends on a finely tuned balance between open-mindedness and skepticism. Be too open minded, and you'll accept wrong claims. Be too skeptical, and you'll reject genuine new discoveries. Proper skepticism must be careful not to throw the baby out with the bathwater.

Unfortunately, much of what comes out of the "skeptical" community these days is not proper skepticism, but all-out, fundamentalist disbelief. Such skepticism can be called pseudo-skepticism, pathological skepticism or bogus skepticism.

Here are seven major signs of bogus skepticism.

1. The skeptic has reached their opinion not after careful research and examination of the claim, but simply based on media reports and other forms of second-hand knowledge.

2. Making uncontrolled criticisms. A criticism is uncontrolled if the same criticism could equally be applied to accepted science.

3. The pseudoskeptical catch-22: "unconventional claims have to be proved before they can be investigated!" This way, of course, they will never be investigated or proved.

4. Evidence of refutal is anecdotal or otherwise scientifically worthless. Pseudoskeptics tend to accept conventional "explanations" for unconventional phenomena very easily, no matter how weak, contrived or far-fetched.

5. The skeptic rejects a discovery or invention merely because it has been believed for a long time that such a thing as the claimed discovery or invention is impossible.

6. The skeptic claims that the claimed effect contradicts the "laws of nature" (and therefore has to be wrong, since the skeptic and the scientific community he presumes to represent have of course already complete knowledge of the laws of nature).

7. The skeptic believes in scientific mob rule. "In Science, the Majority Consensus is Always Right".

Rebuttal to Challenges by Skeptics

Any theory that is proposed which is outside of the institutionally accepted, tired age-old paradigms is usually attacked by skeptics. Those engaging in these attacks are generally bigoted, uniformed people who have not conducted sufficient research or are too narrow-minded to consider or accept fresh new evidence. Their arguments fail to deal with the substance (details), but rather resort to petty name-calling rhetoric, accusing those who present alternative theories as practicing "pseudoscience", "pseudohistory" or worse. Typical arguments used by skeptics opposed to the idea of alternative historical and scientific theory include:

A particular theory or evidence hasn't been reported through the mainstream media or officially recognized and accepted by an established scientific institution therefore it cannot possibly be true.

They refuse to entertain any anomalous evidence not presented through conventional sources, regardless of how compelling or convincing it is, and generalize by labeling it "pseudo-science". In my first book *Evidence of Lost Ancient Civilizations: Case Closed* I make a legitimate case for media and scientific fraud and deception, and offer many examples. With such a lack of credibility why should we believe anything they say? Like politicians, both of these groups have a hidden and inspired agenda, as well as a notorious track record for delivering tainted and inaccurate representations of the truth.

Why would governments, archaeologists and scientists all lie about an advanced ancient civilization? What purpose would it serve?

The entire premise that this question is based on is wrong. There is no organized, hidden conspiracy or "master plan" contrived by scientists and governments. Rather it is a suppression bred through a false justification for national security, moral equivalence, personal greed, bigotry, ignorance, a feeling of moral superiority, a need to safeguard or protect an institution or ideology, or a desire to pacify a particular ethic group.

In most cases the participants are not even aware they are actively part of it. In their minds they are doing "the right thing", or in other words "the end justifies the means". In my books I explain four common forms of evidence suppression that lead to concealment of the truth. There is religious suppression, government/military suppression, institutional suppression, and nationalistic or ethnic suppression. In a way this forced suppression of evidence and discoveries could be called a "lie" or a "conspiracy". It all comes down to semantics. The bottom line is: there is a suppression of the truth, either intentional or not, that is taking place. The "purpose" it serves is self-explanatory. Each of the four forms of suppression must be looked at independently to determine its purpose, motivation and agenda as each one is different. There is no global single "purpose".

Where is all of the physical evidence and artifacts left over from an advanced ancient civilization?

The contention of skeptics is that physical archaeological evidence of buildings, structures, cities, settlements, technology, human remains or inhabitation dating back to 10,000 B.C. and earlier simply does not exist. Therefore the only other alternative is to cling to the conventional belief and wisdom concerning mankind's origins and evolutionary path put forth by mainstream academia.

Absence of evidence does not necessarily mean evidence absence. In actual fact it is much to the contrary. The amount of evidence is overwhelming. One does not have to dig very deep to find it if they are really and truthfully searching for it. It can be found all over the Earth. It is so plentiful, in fact, that it should be headline news.

We have come to accept institutionalized historical and scientific doctrine as gospel and not to question the research that has gone into its conclusions. Many of these conclusions are flawed, and have been arrived at through assumption or obtained through inaccurate data collection by so-called "professionals" in their respective fields.

It is much too easy to dismiss or ignore something that cannot be understood, explained or that doesn't fit a certain model that has been perpetuated for decades and even centuries. It is human nature for most of us to avoid the complicated when confronted with it. We are much more at ease dealing with the standard dogma that has been spoon-fed to us over the years because it is always easier to conform than to be an outsider and question the establishment.

The discovery, in October 2009, of a previously unknown ring around the planet Saturn is yet another example of how modern science is constantly learning new things and revising its model of our Solar System. This ring, which is made up of ice and dust particles, is so large that it would take one billion Earths to fill it, according to NASA's Jet Propulsion Laboratory. With the Hubble Space Telescope searching the heavens since 1990 how could something so massive, sitting right in our own backyard, evade scientists up until this time? We receive regular reports detailing discoveries of new planets (exoplanets) orbiting distant stars yet this Saturn ring has been undetected until now.

In much the same way ancient physical evidence has evaded scientists, and this evidence is nowhere near the size of one billion Earths. In fact it is just the opposite. It is fragmentary, scarce and scattered across the world, buried underground, submerged beneath oceans, or covered underneath dense jungle growth and vegetation. This also assumes that those who are conducting the search are doing so with an objective mindset. Many archaeologists, egyptologists, and anthropologists embark upon their search with a pre-conceived opinion. In other words they have already made up their minds, and any anomalous discovery outside of their established paradigm is rejected as impossible, a hoax or forgery, and goes unreported.

By embracing new science ideas a person is labeled a heretic, a rebel, a crackpot, or even a cultist. For professionals whose careers and livelihood depend on maintaining the status quo this is especially critical. It is important that they remain on the established, accepted side of the issue. After all, things such as project funding, government grants and subsidies are so much easier to acquire, and overall job security so much easier to achieve when you don't "rock the boat". New science ideas are often branded "pseudo-science", even if legitimate, accredited scientists conduct the research and analyze the data. The modus operandi employed by mainstream science is usually to attack the weakest part of such a proposal, creating the appearance that the entire theory must be flawed and rejected.

Most sciences have now developed beyond the point where physical evidence is required for corroboration. As an example, DNA testing can provide conclusive proof of genetic relationship. We don't need to bring back a person's relatives from the dead in order to prove a relationship. Geological testing can determine a great deal about our past thousands and even millions of years ago. We don't have to travel back to the past to know what went on at that time. Astronomy is now capable of not only determining how many planets orbit distant stars but whether those planets have the necessary conditions for sustaining life. We don't have to be living on a planet 30 light years from Earth to know information about it.

Certain laws of physics also can support theories where no physical evidence exists. Albert Einstein's theory of relativity made some incredible claims regarding the speed of light and time travel that have come to be accepted by mainstream science simply through mathematical calculations and minimal testing. There was no human or machine involved in the actual testing of his theory. One does not have to travel around the Earth in order to prove to a skeptic that it is round. We know it to be true. This much has been proven. If you find your house trashed and your television, stereo and other personal belongings missing, will you hesitate to call the police because nobody saw it happen? Would you want the judge to dismiss the case just because you only had forensic evidence, but no witnesses?

Such is the mindset of mainstream skeptics who refuse to even consider alternative possibilities. Their personal bias and prejudice toward new ideas prevents them from even entertaining alternative possibilities. They ask for evidence even though their own work is seriously flawed and questionable. This type of egocentric ignorance can be documented throughout history. It requires the work of visionaries such as Copernicus, Galileo and Magellan to prove what they believed, not current-day corporate sell-outs.

1. The lack of substantive proof or hard evidence does not mean that evidence does not exist – only that we have to examine and re-define what we consider true evidence to be: something that we can touch and feel or something abstract that can only be concluded through experimentation or calculation or quite possibly a combination of both. We must open our minds to new ideas and techniques available at our disposal and look at things in a different light.

For example, ask yourself the question: what is "technology"? Is it a piece of hardware such as a television, computer, cell phone, automobile or airplane? Or is the ability to travel sub consciously to different realms a "technology". Does telepathic communication constitute "technology"? Perhaps we are looking in all the wrong places or searching for hardware when we should be looking for a different kind of "technology".

There are some scholars who believe mankind's development is actually de-evolving or in a retarded state. Their position is essentially that with the evidence of advanced ancient artifacts (most of which are described in my earlier books) that have been discovered there is abundant proof that modern technology was mastered and in use by our ancient ancestors. Furthermore they maintain that the building of physical materialistic technology "outside of ourselves" was not necessary in ancient times. Those people possessed technology and skills that are beyond our comprehension – a spirituality and ability to function "within themselves," unlike our current reliance on physical technology and hardware.

2. The availability of hard physical evidence is limited to tangible objects such as buildings, skeletal remains, and ancient artifacts such as sculptures, pottery, etc. It does not apply to the abstract such as ideas, concepts, training, indoctrination, and genetically inherited skills acquired that were passed down through generations. It would be impossible to find proof of any engineering knowledge of how the Egyptian pyramids, or other global megalithic structures were built. It is unlikely that engineering drawings or mathematical calculations would remain. Much of this knowledge is intrinsic in certain individuals.

Master craftsmen would have passed their technical know-how (tricks of the trade) down to their children, or apprentices. A great deal of the "step-by-step how-to-do-it" instructions wouldn't have been written down – especially in a society where writing hadn't yet existed. Those specially endowed people who may have possessed knowledge of levitation techniques, for example, couldn't write this information down – it had to be acquired (taught) or genetically inherited. So we are left with "what you see is what you get".

The buildings and megalithic structures are there, standing in plain sight for all to see. However, the evidence (methodology) of how they were built eludes us. The abstract concepts, ideas, training, and skills employed are missing, will never be available and cannot be produced as "evidence". A civilization utilizing such intrinsic skills would leave very little in the form of evidence other than the finished product.

The Coral Castle, located 30 miles south of Miami, Florida is a prime example of what can be achieved through such ability. It was built by Edward Leedskalnin single handedly over a period of thirty years reportedly using magnetic currents. Leedskalnin, a 100-pound 5-foot tall man, appeared to have a gained a mastery of moving massive blocks through levitation. Ed frequently claimed to friends that he had discovered the secrets of the Egyptian pyramids. The site interestingly sits on a Ley Line, with Ed having to previously move the site as his original calculations were a little off.

He wrote a book about his theory and technologies called *Magnetic Currents*. There is a Ley Line running through the compound and visitors are free to play with it. The basic premise of the theory is that the Earth is a giant magnet. The north and south poles are both magnets which hold our planet together. He believed that gravity is not so much gravity as it is a magnetic force generated by the pull of the poles. So to move the stones you need to reverse that pull somehow, creating a field of energy between the stone and the ground.

Ed was apparently seen moving stones as if they were balloons, by levitating them. It is said that these Ley Lines harness energy, and one can exploit this energy in certain geographical locations. I explain this phenomenon in greater detail in my first book *Evidence of Lost Ancient Civilizations: Case Closed*. We also have the case of the acoustic levitation of stones in Tibet, where monks used instruments and mathematical calculations to levitate stones up through the air, up giant mountains. There is so much that can be accomplished with the power of nature. It was an ability given to us long ago. Sadly, however, humankind has decided instead to focus on technology that feeds its ego instead of working with a technology that is provided within the circle of creation.

As an example, when astronomers speak of extraterrestrial space travel to Earth the major problem is with the vast distances between the stars – at a minimum tens of light years to hundreds of light years distant. When you calculate this possibility using present-day propulsion systems it naturally appears an impossibility. On the most successful and powerful booster rocket, the Saturn V used on the Apollo missions, the propellant system basically consisted of burning liquid oxygen and liquid hydrogen contained within its storage tanks.

Final velocity after the three-stage burn to orbital ascent was 17,450 mph. On January 19, 2006 NASA launched the New Horizons probe to take humanity's first close-up look at Pluto and its moon Charon, scheduled for 2015. New Horizons attained an escape velocity of about 35,800 mph as it departed Earth orbit. This speed is so fast that the probe reached the distance of the Moon in only nine hours (compared to three days for the Apollo missions) and will reach Jupiter in just 13 months – the fastest speed man has ever achieved for a spacecraft departing the Earth. The Helios 2 probe launched on January 15, 1976 to study the Sun holds the all-time record for speed by a terrestrial spacecraft as it attained a maximum speed of around 150,000 mph at closest approach to the Sun in its highly elliptical orbit.

This type of technology is now 50 years old and is archaic. The most advanced propulsion systems that can be imagined currently such as nuclear, solar, electromagnetic and ion systems may be primitive compared with those of more advanced alien civilizations. Perhaps the most optimum method of space travel for extraterrestrials is through wormholes, somehow warping of space and time, the use of anti-gravity, matter/anti-matter or electromagnetic technology, psychokinesis or even teleportation in order to travel large distances quickly. Symbiosis has even been suggested as a potential form of space transportation. This involves the human/alien mind (most likely the pilot of a spaceship) interacting and functioning in tandem with a source engine or drive. The motion and action of the engine or drive is controlled directly through the thought processes of the pilot (controller).

The use of energy technology as a form of propulsion has been advanced recently. Without getting into the complex science of quantum physics, the structure of an atom, electron, proton, formulas such as $E = hf$, etc. I will provide a layperson's translation.

This form of propulsion involves quantum physics and the application of wave theory. According to this theory high frequency wave oscillation (hertz) created by a gravity generator can turn mass into light and reduce it to zero allowing travel well beyond the speed of light. Based on Einstein's theory of relativity ($E = mc^2$) mass has always been the largest obstacle to attaining the speed of light since resistance to mass increases, as you get closer to the speed of light. An infinite amount of energy would be required to move it.

John Hutchison, a Canadian inventor, has proven that mass can be reduced. In experiments, available on video, he has demonstrated that an object such as a 75-pound steel ball can have its mass reduced to such a point that it can be levitated. Since we currently lack the ability to produce such a gravity generator it is impossible to test this on a large scale and it currently remains only a theory.

If an extraterrestrial civilization has been able to put this theory into practice traveling twice, three, five or even ten times the speed of light is easily achievable. In fact the speed is unlimited. This theory is what the creation of galaxies and black holes is based on. Similar to a black hole as the vortex is reduced the speed increases. This is precisely why the center of a black hole appears to be the color black. The wave oscillation (speed) is so great that it appears to be a black color to the human eye. But because the speed (hertz oscillation) of the light waves inside of the event horizon is in a range outside of what the human eye is capable of viewing it appears to be a black color to us when in actual fact it is not.

What transpires at this level is essentially a micro universe. As an example, if an object is utilizing such a gravity generator and traveling at speeds greater than the speed of light it is totally invisible to us. As it slows it will suddenly appear into human sight. It will appear to the human eye as though it suddenly materialized out of thin air. The opposite is also true. We may see something and it instantly vanishes. This would mean the object suddenly accelerated to a greater-than-light speed using a form of quantum physics energy technology.

One reason (that is largely ignored) for the lack of abundant ancient evidence is because much of it was never (and currently is not) visible to the human eye. Only a small percentage of what transpires in our universe appears to the human eye available through the visible light spectrum. Objects appearing or events occurring in the high-end of the electromagnetic spectrum (Ultraviolet, X-rays. Gamma-rays) beyond the capability of human sight cannot be witnessed.

Ancient civilizations with the ability of such advanced technology would leave us little in the way of physical evidence. As explained earlier quantum theory has proven that speeds and events occurring outside the capability of human vision are definitely possible, and are even taking place at this time in our universe (formation of back holes, galaxies). Therefore, assuming that this technology was available in ancient times, the possibility of no remaining physical evidence being available is perfectly understandable.

Likewise the SETI Project (Search for Extra-Terrestrial Intelligence) has been searching space for evidence of extraterrestrial radio waves now for almost 40 years (on an unofficial basis). However, the entire premise with this program is flawed. There are those who even contend that it is simply a smokescreen program and that we have already been in contact with intelligent extraterrestrial life forms for many years.

Firstly, SETI blatantly disregards any possibility that intelligent alien life exists in our own backyard – within our very own solar system. There are five reasons why you cannot find something (i) there is nothing out there – we may be completely alone living in a ghostly silent universe, (ii) our low-tech, primitive radio signals have not yet reached other intelligent extra-terrestrial civilizations, (iii) those intelligent civilizations are not yet advanced enough and do not have the technological capability of being able to respond, (iv) those receiving our signals are ignoring our attempts at communication and choosing not to respond, or (v) that we have already been contacted and this information is intentionally being suppressed and withheld from the public.

Secondly, why must it be assumed that an alien intelligence uses radio waves in the gigahertz, kilohertz, or megahertz band to communicate? No doubt if they have developed the ability to travel tens or hundreds of light years in a short time then they must have developed a technology, totally foreign to us, to communicate with their home world. The use of primitive radio waves just would not be practical in their situation, therefore they would not employ them. SETI's search for radio wave signals is, just like the Saturn V propulsion system, based applying current views and technologies available to us, not what might be in actual use by intelligent, alien civilizations.

An advanced extraterrestrial civilization may very well have perfected the art of telepathy. We must stop using our current state and level of technology as a benchmark for extraterrestrial civilizations. This would solve the question of how to verbally communicate with different alien cultures and languages. The *Star Trek* television science fiction series had an easy solution to this – they simply called it a "universal translator". It allowed humans to be able to converse with any alien species and understand them. In reality this is much more complex and problematic.

Opening our minds and educating ourselves to new ideas and possibilities is essential if we wish to seek the truth. We cannot look for answers outside of our world, to the future, or to the past using present-day technologies or conditions as a measuring tool. We must consider that alien civilizations have highly advanced forms of propulsion, communication, etc.

3. The fact that we are dealing with extreme age – on the order of 5000 B.C. to 15,000 B.C. (or even older) presents a major problem in locating any evidence. Physical evidence is lost due to natural phenomena in many ways – through erosion, flooding (when sea levels were 330 feet lower than they are today), hurricanes, tornadoes, burial through glacial icing, earthquake, volcanic eruption, urban development, wars, and looting by treasure seekers.

Other factors contributing to the absence of physical evidence include the decomposition of man-made materials and structures by soil and atmospheric conditions, and the growth of plant life tearing buildings down in only a few hundred years. Witness the ancient structures in the South American jungle that have been overcome by the spreading of plant life. Most are barely visible from the ground and can only be detected through the thick overgrowth by the use of ground-penetrating radar from an airplane.

Chances of artifacts surviving in extreme environments such as the desert are a little better. A television program broadcast on the History Channel titled *Life After People* calculated that after 1,000 years you would have to look pretty hard to find evidence of human inhabitation. As proof simply look at the Chernobyl nuclear disaster site of April 26, 1986 in the Soviet Union. Only 20 years later Mother Earth had reclaimed herself. Twenty years after the explosion of one of the reactors at the Chernobyl Nuclear Power Plant trees were growing up through the streets, concrete buildings were crumbling and considerable wildlife was present despite the residual radiation. The economic resources required to excavate remote sites, including Antarctica, to dive the depths of our oceans are tremendous. This is where many of the answers now lie. Since mainstream institutions, which would rather ridicule new science ideas, hold the purse strings and usually operate through public funding for such massive undertakings the only hope of retrieving relics (physical evidence) from this time period seems to be through private funding.

4. The fact that the elusive ancient civilization we are searching for was a sparse population distributed across all continents – perhaps numbering only in the thousands – makes it that much more difficult to locate physical evidence. They were forced to re-settle with little more than the clothes on their backs and their rapid decline meant that there was very little time to build up elaborate metropolitan city structures leaving little for us to discover. The footprint left by such a small or scattered civilization would be elusive.

5. A small, isolated civilization wouldn't be that active in trade or commerce. As a result they would leave little physical evidence behind in the form of artifacts.

6. The fact that a good deal of the evidence already uncovered sits under lock, key and armed guard inside of the Smithsonian Institute, military facilities, or museums does not help in getting the information out to the public. Authorities (both government, military and academic) must be more forthcoming in releasing all of the evidence. This includes anomalous artifacts in their possession that cannot be explained.

The media must also bear some responsibility and take more of an initiative in aggressively pursuing the truth. They are reluctant to investigate or report on ancient anomalous findings, yet have no problem in digging into the private lives of celebrities, or destroying the personal lives of individuals in the public spotlight by reporting untruths. This is media hypocrisy at its finest.

They are supposedly "investigative journalists" trained to objectively report the facts. Yet, sadly, this is the furthest thing from reality. They position themselves as judge, jury and executioner. Today's breed of so-called "journalists" are only concerned with the entertainment and shock value of what they report, and not the substance, and put little if any effort into the investigative side of the story. This is precisely why ancient archaeological anomalies pose no interest to the media – because there is absolutely no entertainment value in reporting such stories.

The most naïve, uninformed, and uneducated group of skeptics make the instant (incorrect) assumption that the mere mention of advanced ancient civilizations automatically implies aliens.

Leaping to this erroneous conclusion means that since these so called "advanced ancient civilizations" are assumed to be aliens, then why didn't they simply provide all humans with the most up-to-date, state-of-the-art technology such as spaceships and not worry about inventing the wheel, the use of primitive modes of transportation such as trains, automobiles, airplanes and ships, or other landmark inventions over time.

Why only provide ancient humans with selective technological information, such as how to build pyramids and other megaliths using massive stones? Why not simply introduce Stone Age cavemen to 21st, 22nd or even 30th century technology right away, simply bypassing over all recorded history? If these ancient aliens were so intelligent why didn't they intervene in major world events and conflicts that occurred through the course of human history such as the many wars, diseases, famines, and natural disasters?

Let us assume for a moment that the theory of ancient astronauts (aliens) visiting Earth during ancient times is true. The first question to ask is why? What was their purpose? Since this assumption concedes that there is other, much more intelligent life in the universe, it would relegate our ancient ancestors to a minor, insignificant microcosm within the cosmos. Was their purpose simply to educate an insignificant primitive human race (us) and bring it "up to speed" as far as galactic technology was concerned – a traveling extraterrestrial tutor? Was their mission simply to dump some of their knowledge onto a backward civilization, then pack up their bags and move on to the next star system?

Stop and think how ridiculous that sounds. Think of the ramifications to the primitive world they would be leaving behind to suddenly have to deal with the complexity of the knowledge and wisdom taught to them. Remember one important fact: that any extraterrestrial civilization visiting us in ancient times would be thousands of years more advanced – and not only technologically.

An advanced alien civilization of such extreme age would no doubt have refined moral and ethical standards based on thousands (perhaps millions) of years of experience and practice. In fact, it is doubtful they would have survived that long otherwise. A malevolent, destructive alien culture would have either destroyed itself or have been destroyed by an even more advanced civilization had it not developed and adopted such high principles and standards.

Given this, most or all of the advanced civilizations in the universe would avoid harming fledgling civilizations. The guiding behavioral rule toward all other civilizations is probably this: avoid unnecessary harm and interference. Do not hurt any other civilization, nor hinder their development. If another civilization is clearly about to break this rule (through a powerful attack or through spreading a plague, for instance), and if this poses a definite and immediate threat to an advanced species, then it is permissible to intervene powerfully and even harmfully in order to prevent this. Under any other circumstances, however, an advanced civilization will probably not interfere harmfully in the development of another civilization.

There are several reasons for concluding that advanced beings would be helpful or at least benign, and are unlikely to harm fledgling civilizations such as ours. Here are the main reasons:

1. They still recall their own early history, including their primitive stages, their dark periods, and their mistakes; therefore, they may feel sympathetic toward our situation.

2. Any advanced alien civilization intent on capturing our planet would have done so long ago, before we desecrated it so much.

3. Any hostile civilization with advanced technology would have attempted to eliminate any developing civilization long before it reached the stage at which it could attack the more advanced one – that is, long before our present stage.

4. Advanced civilizations are probably letting us develop freely, without interference, in order to maximize the amount of information they gain; if they interfere and control us, they will learn less. Their greatest gain from us may be sociological and anthropological knowledge about our culture and civilization.

5. Intelligent life forms that are destructively aggressive and irresponsible will usually eliminate themselves or revert back to primitive conditions before they achieve interstellar communication or travel. If a ruthlessly hostile species manages to avoid these usual consequences, and then prepares for interstellar communication or travel, it may well be terminated by more advanced beings in the galaxy.

Having said all of this, selective intervention by a visiting alien civilization in ancient times would probably be the most logical approach for them and totally understandable. Their role would essentially be that of casual observers. They wouldn't become involved in drastically impacting human development and evolution, unless it meant preventing the extermination of the human species.

Those who suggest DNA manipulation was conducted by aliens on humanoid primates may have a valid point. However, consider that this may have been done to perpetuate mankind, and not for a malicious reason. Likewise, the exchange of technological information may also have been done strictly to assist mankind in its preservation and survival.

So if you consider the above argument, it is entirely possible that an extraterrestrial civilization could have visited Earth in our ancient past and passed along selective information, or become involved in mankind's evolutionary process in a discrete manner. This type of intervention would have been done to ensure mankind's continued existence. It would not have been their intention or necessary for them to have introduced space ships to primitive cavemen, or overhauled, reshaped and altered human history through a blanket introduction of technology.

In other words, E.T. may have been here but he certainly didn't reveal his full bag of tricks.

If extraterrestrials visited Earth in antiquity or are here currently why haven't they shown themselves? Where is the physical evidence such as spaceships and bodies?

In actual fact there is a significant amount of evidence in the form of photographs, videos, and eyewitness testimonies from scientific, military, and intelligence officials who have first-hand knowledge of ongoing top secret government programs.

One reason for the lack of physical evidence (spaceship, bodies) of an extraterrestrial visitation is because much of it sits guarded inside of protected military installations. Governments believe that releasing this evidence to the public would undermine their authority and could possibly lead to a de-stabilization of society, thus they have their own motives for wanting this evidence suppressed.

Another suggestion that has been put forward to explain the fact that we have so far found no evidence for advanced extraterrestrials is the Zoo Hypothesis. It was proposed by John A. Ball in 1973 in response to the Fermi Paradox, regarding the apparent absence of evidence in support of the existence of advanced extraterrestrial life. According to the Zoo Hypothesis aliens are intentionally avoiding making their presence known to humanity, or avoiding exerting an influence on human development. Our planet and our species are under close scrutiny, much like the animals in a zoo, without us being aware of it. We aren't able to see beyond the eyes which are looking into the microscope at us.

Consider that Earth and human activity are being secretly observed using equipment located on Earth or near Earth orbit in outer space (from Lagrange points) which transmits information back to the observers. It is also suggested that overt contact will eventually be made with humanity once humans reach a certain level of development.

The Dogon tribe of Africa had no idea about the existence of the star Sirius B until interaction with modern researchers.

This question casts doubt on the creational myth of the Dogon tribe of Mali, in West Africa that speaks of a race of reptilian aliens, Nommos, who came to Earth from Sirius, instilling the Dogon with ancient wisdom. This implies that modern day scientists or researchers somehow influenced the Dogon into fabricating such a story after meeting with them. What about stories passed down through the generations by the Shamans? They have been aware of such stories for thousands of years.

What about similar stories/legends recognized by other African tribes such as the Zulus or the Aborigines of Australia or Native Americans such as the Anasazi, Hopi, Inuit, Huron and Iroquois, who didn't interact with these scientists and researchers? What about similar stories from other countries such as ancient Sumeria, Babylon, China, Tibet and India? The Dogon were not the only tribe in Africa or culture in the world to adhere to this belief.

Unfortunately this type of question carries racist overtones. Most theories involving Africa come from a racist assumption that since Africa was more primitive and backward the people were less evolved and thus, were in no way capable of comprehending modern astronomy. This does a great disservice to the Dogon people and all native Africans.

Skeptics insist that extraterrestrial visitation stories from various ancient Earth civilizations, continents apart and having no prior knowledge of each other, were nothing more than an imaginary fabrication – the result of interaction with "outsiders" or visitors from the western world.

There is only one problem with this claim – the origin of these stories predates any interaction with western culture. Therefore they were formed and evolved without any outside influence and must have been based on some kind of tangible experience.

Why do we place so much credence in ancient mythology from global cultures?

Because there are no eyewitnesses from thousands of years ago stepping up to deliver testimony. The most significant aspect of this evidence is (a) the similarity and consistency of creation and extraterrestrial visitation stories from different cultures separated by continents who had absolutely no knowledge of each other, (b) the fact that these cultures had knowledge of specific astronomical facts such as star system/planetary alignments thousands of years ago that haven't been known until recently, or which can only be observed through a telescope and not observed by the naked eye, and (c) the incredible detail they possessed such as design of airships. There are curious and unexplainable parts of their histories which should not be so quickly dismissed – especially since they amazingly match with other global cultures. This is the reason why such weight is placed on their importance.

Many sunken ruins are nothing more than natural underwater formations.

While this may true in some cases it cannot be applied as a blanket statement. There have been sunken ruins and megaliths discovered around the world which upon initial examination appear to be natural formations, but after some investigation turn out to be artificial man-made structures. Many years of erosion and exposure to marine organisms often makes proper identification difficult.

The pyramids were built by humans. We know this because their graves litter the area. There are quarries where the blocks came from and saw marks on the blocks. From the Mastabas to the Djoser step pyramid to the Giza pyramids there is clear evolution in design. The dates have been described by the King Lists.

This is a typical "loaded" statement whereby the skeptic throws as much information into their challenge as possible, in a transparent attempt to confuse, overwhelm and demonstrate their "superior" knowledge of ancient history. There is an old expression that goes like this: "if you can't dazzle people with your brilliance then you can baffle them with your bullshit", which certainly applies in this case. Their intention is to intimidate the recipient into backing off any alternative theories and accede to the mainstream claim. However, after dissecting it one sentence at a time (and not as a whole) it becomes evident that such a claim is flawed and riddled with inaccuracies.

Just to assume that something is located in a country you cannot leap to the erroneous assumption that it was built in that place, and by the people who lived there at the time. One only has to look at the Statue of Liberty as an example of this. The statue was designed by French sculptor Frédéric Bartholdi and originally constructed in France, then shipped overseas in crates and assembled at its current location in 1886. The statue was a gift to the United States from the people of France. Most people aren't aware of this fact. A person not knowing this and witnessing it for the first time in 1886 would marvel at the ingenuity of the Americans for its construction.

Firstly, I actually happen to agree that the pyramids were likely built by humans – just not the ancient Egyptians. According to conventional history, precursors to Predynastic Egypt included several cultures ranging from hunter-gatherers to nomadic and farming cultures who settled throughout upper and lower Egypt (Delta region) along the Nile river. However, here is the problem. There is an unexplained, enormous leap in technological development from these cultures to the pyramid-building societies of dynastic Egypt.

If you accept mainstream doctrine – that these predynastic cultures were not advanced and simply nomads wandering the desert or farmers – then it is impossible to logically conclude that they were responsible for constructing some of the most impressive engineering marvels this world has seen to date. Where did they suddenly gain such knowledge? One day there were herding sheep and plowing their fields, and the next day they were shaping and maneuvering limestone blocks and granite stones weighing up to 80 tons with unparalleled precision – something not achievable to this day. Is such a scenario really believable? I ask you to consider this.

Secondly, one cannot leap to the erroneous assumption that just because human bodies/graves may exist near a particular object that it is automatically proof that those people were responsible for building that structure. History is ever-changing and the reasons for bodies littering any area are ever-changing as well.

Thirdly, as I exhaustively explain in all of my books, any work done to the pyramids at Giza by the Egyptians (humans) was nothing more than a restoration or refurbishment project – thus the reason for graves in the area. Any bodies found littering the area were those of people who participated in this nationalistic refurbishment project. We know this because the credit Khufu receives for the Great Pyramid is based strictly upon three very weak and circumstantial pieces of evidence.

- The legends told to and reported by Greek historian Herodotus who visited the pyramids in 443 B.C.

- The funerary complex near the Great Pyramid with inscriptions citing Cheops/Khufu as the reigning pharaoh.

• In the pyramid itself, on a granite slab above the ceiling of the main chamber, some small, red ochre paint marks that have a slight resemblance to a hieroglyphic symbol for the name of Khufu. It was later learned that this symbol was nothing more than a modern day forgery created by explorer Colonel Howard Vyse in 1837.

He was at the end of his seven-month expedition, running out of money and in a race with at least one other international team and was in desperate need of a sensational find. After an examination of the inscription, it should have been noted that the writing wasn't in the correct style used at the supposed time of its construction. In fact the style used wasn't adopted until centuries after it was supposedly written. The inscription also contains obvious grammatical errors.

Pharaoh Khufu himself left no indication whatsoever that he built the Great Pyramid. He did, however, claim to have done repair work on the structure. Furthermore the quarries and saw marks on the blocks represent a crude attempt by the Egyptians at restoring monuments which they inherited. There is no clear evolution in pyramid design. They basically took what was there, in a dilapidated condition from centuries of decay, and did a masterful job of restoring it. They even tried copying the design of the original pyramid(s).

However, these replicas were so poorly built that most of them today are nothing more than piles of rock and sand (Bent Pyramid, Red Pyramid, Step Pyramid). The only historical account of the Egyptians building the pyramids comes from the legends told to and reported by the Greek historian Herodotus who visited the pyramids in 443 B.C.

It is a matter of archaeological fact that none of the fourth Dynasty kings put their names on the pyramids supposedly constructed in their times, yet from the fifth Dynasty onwards the other pyramids had hundreds of official inscriptions leaving us no doubt about which kings built them.

In contrast to the older pyramids, third Dynasty pyramids were built with blocks manageably small enough to be moved by five or six men. Fifth and Sixth Dynasty pyramids, which were built later and are supposed to be more advanced, were so poorly built that most of them today amount to little more than large piles of rubble. How can this inconsistency be explained? What happened to the knowledge and expertise that allowed the building of fourth Dynasty pyramids, yet never saw this feat ever duplicated again?

Why do the inscriptions, decorations and glyphs that adorn other latter Pharaoh tombs (in the Valley of the Kings, etc.) not exist in Khufu's Pyramid? It is quiet obvious that the magic incantations that were required to spirit the pharaoh's soul away were highly important to the Egyptians – but why no interior inscriptions if the Great Pyramid was supposed to serve as Khufu's tomb? This is a major contradiction.

Why were those pyramids constructed after Menkaure's not built to the magnitude of Khufu's Pyramid? Why did the pyramids get smaller and smaller at Giza and throughout Egypt? The natural expectation is that a reigning pharaoh would want their pyramid larger and more lavish than that of their predecessor. Wouldn't Khafre want his bigger and better than Khufu's? Wouldn't Menkaure want his bigger and better than Khafre's? Debunkers will deny it, but it is an indisputable fact that there was de-evolution of technology over the course of Egyptian civilization.

Some skeptics will argue that the reason for reduction in pyramid size and quality was due to a decline in political power. They claim that pharaohs were no longer able to mobilize as much manpower or be able to pay for pyramids the size of the ones at Giza. But how does this help to explain the sudden emergence of advanced technology to be able to construct the Great Pyramid (Khufu's)?

How did this knowledge suddenly appear out of nowhere? The "declining political power" argument is nothing more than an assumption. The decline in the ability to construct pyramids is something that is tangible and obvious and it exists for all to see. We can observe and measure it with our naked eye. So bring forth the tangible proof that "declining political power" equals a decline in pyramid building ability.

Mankind has always demonstrated a positive progression in technology and architecture over time. It is a constant. Our buildings, bridges, airplanes, ships, automobiles, telephones, and computers are constantly becoming improved. This only makes sense. As we learn more and develop new technology we apply it and improve on the previous design/model. In ancient times there was no such thing as "earthquake-proof" structures. Today we have the ability to build such structures.

However, for some strange reason ancient Egypt defied this universal law of technological progression. Their ability to design and construct pyramids declined over the years and the remaining physical evidence speaks for itself. Their civilization was in fact regressive, not progressive. The original knowledge they had acquired was somehow lost through time.

And how do you explain the discovery of bones and remains in underground galleries of the earliest Egyptian pyramid – the 3rd Dynasty step pyramid of Djoser

2630 BC-2611 BC? They have been radiocarbon dated to generations before Djoser. This evidence certainly supports the theory that the pyramid was already there when the Egyptians settled and they simply re-used it. Of course, the predictable response by mainstream science and skeptics will be that these remains were moved there from a more contemporary location.

Because they are unable to bring anything substantive to the table they simply attempt to refute an argument by making outlandish claims, just like the "declining political power" argument mentioned earlier. These claims carry absolutely no supporting proof with them. This kind of statement is no different than responding to someone with an answer like "just because" or "that's the way it is" – a simply absurd response pulled out of the air.

In his book *Voyages of the Pyramid Builders* Boston University geology professor Dr. Robert Schoch details key anomalies in two radiocarbon studies; most notably that samples taken in 1984 from the upper courses of the Great Pyramid gave upper dates of 3809 B.C. (± 160 yrs), nearly 1,400 years before the time of Khufu, while the lower courses provided dates ranging from 3090 B.C - 2723 B.C (± 100-400 yrs) which correspond much more closely to the time Khufu is believed to have reigned.

Given that the data implies that the pyramid was built (impossibly) from the top down, Dr. Schoch argues that if the information provided by the study is correct, it makes sense if it is assumed the pyramid was built and rebuilt in several stages suggesting later Pharaohs such as Khufu were only inheritors of an existing monument, not the original builders, and merely rebuilt or repaired previously constructed sections.

Still further evidence that the dynastic Egyptians did not construct the Great Pyramid may be found in sediments surrounding the base of the structure, in legends regarding watermarks on the stones halfway up its sides, and in salt incrustations found within. Silt sediments rising to 14 feet around the base of the pyramid contain many seashells and fossils that have been radiocarbon-dated to be nearly 12,000 years old. These sediments could have been deposited in such great quantities only by major sea flooding – an event the dynastic Egyptians could never have recorded because they were not living in the area until 8,000 years after the flood. This evidence alone suggests that the three main Giza pyramids are around 12,000 thousand years old.

I dedicate a great deal of time in my previous books to discussion of this subject, so will direct anyone looking for further detail to examine them and form their own opinion based upon the evidence presented. Suffice it to say that, upon close scrutiny, the Egyptian pyramid construction theory (from start to finish) falls apart for the many reasons I explain.

The Sphinx was built by Khafre at the same time as the three Pyramids at Giza, around 2500 B.C.

The Sphinx pre-dates the 1st Dynasty of ancient Egypt. The evidence to support this is staggering and only a blind fool would deny this. I have long felt there is more to the Great Sphinx, its relationship to the Pyramids, and the time it was constructed. We have been looking in the wrong places all this time. Yes, there is prominent evidence that has come forth over the past 10-20 years.

Based on the work of Dr. Robert Schoch, we know the Sphinx has water damage and erosion that it is completely out of place. Dr. Schoch estimates the age back to an earlier period (at least 5000 B.C., and maybe as early as 7000 B.C or even 9000 B.C.), a time when the climate was very different and included more rain. Graham Hancock, John Anthony West, Robert Bauval, Egyptologist Mark Lehner and others have presented additional evidence that challenges the traditional thoughts about the Sphinx placing its origin at between 8000 B.C. and 10,000 B.C.

Firstly, the geological evidence that the Sphinx's erosion was due to water rather than wind/sand, makes it much older than previously believed, according to the book *Fingerprints of the Gods*. Secondly, astronomical alignments show that the Sphinx was clearly an astronomical marker facing east, which identifies the exact position on the horizon that the sun dawns on the spring equinox.

There is no written record of its construction by Khafre, only its repair. There is absolutely no documented evidence that the Sphinx was constructed during the time of any pharaoh and if so there is no trace of it. It is not widely believed that the Sphinx displays water damage and erosion which could not have occurred on or after the supposed date of construction.

In between the paws of the Sphinx is a stela, now called the "Dream Stela", which is inscribed with a story. The Dream Stela of Thutmosis IV was erected in the first year of his reign, 1401 B.C., and tells the story of the time that Thutmosis IV fell asleep under the Sphinx, which at the time was covered to the neck in sand. Thutmosis had a dream that the Sphinx spoke to him and promised that if he would free the Sphinx from the sand, Thutmosis would be destined to become king of Egypt. Based on this historical account the Sphinx had been at its present location for quite some time prior to the Thutmosis IV story.

Furthermore, common sense demonstrates the Sphinx's head to be completely out of proportion compared to the body, a curious fact when compared to the traditional style and detail of Egyptian construction in the supposed time it was built.

The Sphinx is an amazing piece of architecture. It was constructed facing east looking at the rising sun. Investigation of the Orion Belt positioning and alignment as seen in the Egyptian night sky has shown that the three pyramids of Giza are precisely aligned to the stars of the constellation Leo (the Lion) as it appeared in 10,500 B.C. By factoring in precession and turning back the computer clock it is possible to find the coincidental alignments among them, the Milky Way to the Nile and the Sphinx to the constellation Leo and thus dating the Sphinx to the Age of Leo (10,500 B.C.). And

12,000 years ago is well within the new highly controversial estimations for the age of the Sphinx.

If there was an advanced civilization on Mars why haven't we found evidence of this?

Before you can find something you must first be looking for it – and I mean seriously, not in the token casual manner that is being conducted today. If anything the major hotstop areas on Mars have been avoided for decades.

There is in actual fact overwhelming evidence to support the existence a former civilization on Mars – the glass-like tube tunnels, pyramid complexes, monoliths, trees, and the famous human "Face" – to name only a few. Just because we haven't found conclusive proof yet, it doesn't mean it doesn't exist.

In order to find things you must at least make a serious effort – something that NASA has not been making, for some strange reason, over the years. They have purposely been avoiding the more controversial regions that show the most promise.

There are many lost cities on the Earth and occasionally someone stumbles upon them. Some have been buried under the sand, underwater or under dense jungle growth and found with the aid of satellite photos. The evidence of any civilization that did reside on Mars would have long since been buried, and barely detectable to an orbiting spacecraft or surface roving vehicle.

Skeptics may argue that surviving human Martians re-settling on Earth would have no reason to engage in genetic manipulation using *Homo erectus* or any other primitive Earth hominid as a subject for experimentation purposes. The argument might be that those survivors would still be capable of breeding among themselves and of re-producing therefore there would be no need to play around with DNA testing. Their species would be capable of sustaining itself, and of growing, on its own here on Earth without having to create or manufacture a new human model such as *Homo sapiens*.

This argument fails to consider the following: (a) that conditions on Earth were not identical to that of Mars. Everything from climate to gravity was considerably different. Even the position of Mars in our Solar System was different, orbiting much closer to the Sun; (b) there may not have been any survivors who made it to Earth at all. Perhaps only their DNA was transported here by a third party and it was this third party which was responsible for the genetic engineering; (c) that there were no females among the surviving population which came to Earth. This assumes that the females of their species were exclusively responsible for child birth; and (d) for some medical or biological reason the survivors were no longer able to procreate. Their reproductive and immune system may have not operated here on Earth the same way as it did on Mars. Conditions on their new homeworld (Earth) may have rendered them impotent or sterile. By leaving their protective natural environment on Mars they may have suddenly become exposed to an entirely brand new set of threats.

Perhaps their Martian metabolism was susceptible to Earthborn viruses and diseases which rendered them incapable of reproduction here on Earth. Or maybe these viruses and diseases were killing off the remaining population at a faster pace than their birth rate. It further may be argued that if they were so advanced and capable of space travel to Earth then why wouldn't they be able to find a fix for their inability to reproduce? This question is more difficult to answer.

Firstly, as mentioned earlier, a third party may have been responsible for transporting the Martian survivors or their DNA to Earth. If this was the case then the technology belonging to the Martian civilization may not have been as advanced as believed, thus their inability to conduct space travel.

Secondly, I believe there is a limit to every level of technological development, regardless of the society – otherwise it would be called "magic". The Martian civilization probably lacked the time or knowledge to devise a way to combat the newly introduced and acquired viruses and diseases on Earth. The lack of reproductive capability created the need for them to combine their DNA with that of *Homo erectus* to create the modern *Homo sapiens* model and to further prolong their species and existence. The only other alternative was to see their Martian species slowly die out and become extinct on this new planet called Earth.

Skeptics insist that the astronomical alignment which has been incorporated into the design and layout of many ancient Earth megalithic sites is nothing more than a case of a culture's avid interest in astronomy. They dismiss any notion of potential contact or interaction with extraterrestrials as the reason for the influence.

So why was it so important for civilizations, continents apart, to replicate these constellations and star layouts using gigantic megaliths? Was it a mere coincidence? Was it nothing more than an obsession with astronomy?

Some skeptics have discounted an intentional construction alignment based on interaction with extraterrestrials in our remote past. Let us assume for one moment they are correct – that the reason for these worldwide monuments being astronomically aligned was due to a keen interest in astronomy – nothing more. This raises at least four problems.

Firstly, why go to all the trouble of constructing massive monuments, transporting and positioning stone blocks weighing several tons hundreds of miles in some cases, simply for astronomical purposes? Isn't this overkill of the highest degree? Wouldn't it have been much easier just to document these star and constellation alignments in their ancient texts or on the walls of their temples if they were simply being studied?

Secondly, if you take this position then it forces you to explain the technology that was used to build these megalithic structures. How did ancient people have access to precision cutting tools and lifting devices, some of which cannot even be duplicated in this day and age? Where did they learn of modern mathematical formulas which were calculated into their design?

Thirdly, how did these ancient people know of the existence of stars and planets thousands of years before the invention of the telescope? Where did they learn of precession of the Earth's axis?

Lastly, why was there such a similar global fascination with astronomy among cultures, continents apart? Did they collectively wake up one day and say to themselves "we think we will begin to study astronomy and the alignment of the stars and constellations. And furthermore, we will re-create these layouts by employing massive workforces for decades to build structures duplicating astronomical alignments here on Earth".

How ridiculous does that sound? All kidding aside it was either that or a common source (teacher) who traveled the world instructing them in astronomy, mathematics, construction and engineering principles and how to use giant stones to build massive megalithic monuments that would explain the related global pattern. This is a more likely possibility because of similarity in architecture such as pyramids appearing in all regions of the world.

So if we take the position that these ancient megalithic monuments were created simply due to an interest in astronomy, it creates a major quandary. However, if you take the position that ancient space explorers visited Earth and left their mark then it all suddenly makes total sense. After all, most explorers in Earth's history have left their mark, either purposely or by accident.

One has to keep an open mind to the possibility that these monuments could have been a tribute to our galactic ancestors – something resembling cargo cult worship that we see even in modern times. These ancient monuments/sites may have been created as a tribute to honor them.

As bizarre as it may sound we may indeed be dealing with what were repeated, ongoing visitations throughout human history to our planet by several different extraterrestrial races from multiple constellations or star systems. And yes, they would include Orion, Cygnus, Draco, Sirius in the constellation of Canis Major, and the Pleiades.

As explained, taking the other position leads to endless unanswered questions and makes no sense whatsoever. On the surface the skeptics challenge seems reasonable but collapses under scrutiny and closer analysis.

A certain anomalous artifact or discovery has been proven to be a hoax or declared so by its perpetrator, naturally implying that all such discoveries should be considered false as well.

Unfortunately, it must be recognized that there is fraud and deception in every profession. It is not exclusive to science or history. People applying for jobs embellish their résumé to make themselves appear more qualified. Trial lawyers commit a form of deception every day in our country by trying to sway jury members. Politicians and celebrities are masterful at lying and deceit. It shouldn't be so surprising. Most importantly, just because one piece of evidence is proven to be false it shouldn't force someone to abandon all objectivity and apply the same conclusion to all other evidence.

So does this also suggest that mainstream science is without its share of fraudulent claims? If you believe this then you obviously haven't read any of my books. They describe in explicit detail the relentless campaign of misinformation that has been waged on alternative science ideas. And why is this? It is because mainstream science doesn't have the answers and cannot debate the substance. Instead it would rather create a diversion by attacking the messenger or introducing a massive number of ideas to consider in a single question or statement in an attempt to generate confusion. This has been its modus operandi for many years.

There remain four major, undeniable, unexplainable mysteries that still linger. None of these enigmas have come close to having been reconciled by modern science – underwater ruins, cross cultural exchange, ancient technology, and massive megalithic construction.

Conventional science, much like the media, claim to be impartial observers and reporters of the truth. They base this assertion on the fact that they use the appropriate "scientific methodology" that alternative science does not. If this is the case then why have there been so many hoaxes and frauds committed by modern science? Did the scientists working on those projects follow proper "scientific methodology"? Why the need for so much misinformation? Why the suppression on the many anomalous discoveries I mention throughout my books – many made by scientists themselves? What is there to be afraid of?

The Peer Review process is mentioned as another way science audits itself. However, it is flawed as well. Those conducting the review can have a hidden agenda and therefore be critical of the work. They could be jealous of the work, or morally or philosophically in disagreement causing it not to be accepted or released. Whenever you are dealing with people you automatically introduce many variables into the equation.

It's important for people to realize that science is always wrong. Every scientific theory either already has or will in the future, be proven wrong and then replaced with a newer theory, which in turn eventually also gets proven wrong.

So now we know that "scientific methodology" and Peer Review don't work. What then distinguishes mainstream science from alternative science?

Many paintings in ancient caves depict animals which are not native to that region or creatures that simply don't exist such as a half-woman, half-bison. Skeptics insist that these artistic liberties can be attributed to the lack of carbon dioxide and other gases inside the cave. Their theory is that hallucinations in the cave were common.

If this is true then how was such incredible detail rendered into the paintings? They were not a one-off situation. They were carefully planned and orchestrated projects, and took several generations to complete. Artists suffering from hallucinations would exhibit erratic drawing techniques and not the high skill level that is demonstrated in these particular caves. And finally, what of their knowledge of animals that were not native to that region? Was this a hallucination as well?

The only reason people write about alternative history and lost ancient civilizations is strictly to sell books.

I can only speak for myself and not other authors. My motivation and first priority is to deliver the message, inform and educate, and to stimulate public awareness. In addition it is my hope to generate a constructive dialogue and national conversation through my work. It is not about being an armchair archaeologist. Human history is far different than what is being taught in our classrooms. It's truly disappointing how few people are aware of this. Unfortunately for reasons of politics, academics, and arrogance most people don't have a clue of some of the more amazing implications that these discoveries have.

Some people may be content in having their perception of life and human history shaped by an agenda-driven group of elitists. However, I am a firm believer that the search for truth is extremely important, and if it means that new discoveries force us to rewrite history and science textbooks and reconsider our views of the world, then we should not be afraid to do so.

Life is much too short. It is a journey about experiences (both good and bad) and continuous learning. How can you learn without objectivity and an open mind? Exposure and indoctrination to only one side of a subject does not constitute learning the real and total truth – only a distorted, manipulated and controlled truth.

How better to get the message out than a book? The internet is just one vehicle and I'll bet every author on the subject also has their own website – yet another vehicle. The fact that books and public speaking engagements happen to pay the author for their service is no reason to be critical. How is mainstream science with all of its checkered past and dismal track record any different? After all there is a considerable amount of time and effort devoted by authors in studying and researching this subject. Many dedicate their livelihood to it. Speaking from personal experience, it is very time consuming and not at all easy to compile reliable data on the subject of advanced ancient civilizations.

A certain commitment and passion is needed to write a book. It is not something that you simply conjure up out of the air for the sole purpose of earning a few dollars. Any such accusation by critics sounds more like envy or jealousy because they lack the objectivity, commitment, dedication and ability to write a book about such a subject. Instead, they prefer to hide in the comfort of a pack of followers rather than be leaders of a cause or idea.

How is it possible to research, investigate and write about ancient history and mankind's origins without actually traveling around the world, visiting and exploring the archaeological sites? What makes someone qualified to comment on or render a decision without being an archaeologist or scientist?

The entire premise which this question is based implies that traveling to remote locations to conduct investigation and research will automatically result in the uncovering of impartial evidence and facts. Is information/data acquired on site from eyewitnesses or second-hand sources really any better or more accurate than that obtained from independently verified sources through books or electronic media?

While having your picture taken standing beside the Great Pyramid or Sphinx in Egypt may be impressive, may result in ego gratification and enhance your career resume, it doesn't make your information any more reliable or legitimate than someone who has conducted an objective research project through the electronic media and other sources.

This is a common misconception. It is not necessary to be able to decipher or interpret cuneiform script and hieroglyphics. Traveling to the jungles of the Amazon, the deserts of Egypt, or the waters of the Caribbean for what are essentially photo opportunities does not make someone an "authority" or "expert". Such trips are nothing more than an attempt to promote a career or private agenda.

While formal training in sciences such as archaeology, anthropology, and paleontology is unquestionably a benefit, it becomes as much a liability and impairment as an asset. Remember that there is plenty of "baggage" that goes with the credentials. This includes pressure to conform to agenda-driven institutional policy, fear of project funding loss, avoiding the wrath of negative public and peer recognition and of becoming professionally ostracized. The credentials discourage independent and creative thinking and force you to become just another slave and voice of the "party line".

Make no mistake – a shovel, microscope or radio telescope aren't tools that are necessarily required in order to conduct a proper investigation. At one point in time this may have been true. However, in this electronic age where everything is driven by a "24-hour news cycle", where ratings, entertainment and the social media play such a prominent role (and also contribute to the confusion) it is much more important to be able to maneuver, steer and filter through the constant wave of misinformation and deception which is presented by academia, the scientific community and its willing accomplices in the mainstream media, and admittedly some well-intentioned laypeople voicing their opinions.

True students of ancient history and science are only concerned with seeking the truth, presenting it in an articulate manner, educating the public and not the publicity and media hype that surrounds it.

There is sufficient enough information available within the public domain to conduct thorough, responsible investigative research and to form a plausible theory or thesis. This includes an abundance of hard physical evidence and testimonies presented by many highly credible sources. And, as mentioned earlier, it is more a case of weeding through the trail of misinformation to separate the fact from fiction and testing for its validity.

We now live in a modern electronic age. Technology and communication are making the world a smaller place. There are many options for us to seek out information within the vast global media through the internet and television. There is no need to physically conduct exhaustive interviews with individuals or observe something first-hand. There is no need to travel to a distant archaeological site or location in order to scour the countryside looking for clues or artifacts or to listen to a story from a local resident or eyewitness.

Those people disagreeing with this position also probably believe that you should still go to the public library for books or to the local newspaper stand and ignore what the internet and eBooks have to offer. There is a good reason why newspapers and magazines are slowly becoming extinct – because people are looking elsewhere for information that is easily accessible and not outdated. It is time to crawl out of the Stone Age for those afraid to shake loose of tired old practices. It is time to accept the fact that proper research and investigation can be conducted without having to resort to age-old paradigms.

Technology is allowing more and more people to work from home. They don't need to be at their workplace in order to perform their job. Banking is being done online – there is no need to physically go to the bank. Movies can be seen or downloaded online – there is no need to go to your local video store or movie theater. Everything from shopping to dating can now be done online. We are an evolving, ever-changing global society, and rapidly becoming increasingly interdependent on one another. International borders are falling and information is now available which never was before.

The same holds true for research and investigation. The information is now available through non-traditional sources. It only makes sense to take full advantage of this tool.

But how do you go about separating the fact from the fiction?

A lot of it comes from simple common sense logic. Throughout my books I call this "common sense science" – a practice that any one of us laypeople is capable of. As impartial observers without any institutional affiliations or "baggage" we have a distinct advantage over the mainstream academic scholars and so-called intelligentsia. However, we must avoid speculation or becoming emotionally invested and attached to an idea or theory without first obtaining all of the facts.

Furthermore, the sources for your information are extremely critical. Do not rely on mainstream scientific opinions alone. By the same standards do not trust ridiculous far-fetched sources. Use a balanced cross section of opinion. Test the information that is provided by these sources by checking to see if it has been disproven. And, if so, was the argument against it valid and supported by legitimate evidence and data and not based on a false premise and assumptions. Most times opposing arguments are nothing more than bigoted attacks.

Following these steps will help to weed out the trustworthy sources and information which can withstand critical review – basically separating the contenders from the pretenders.

Some theories have absolutely no basis in fact and have little, if any, supporting evidence. They are so over-the-top that they can easily be dismissed as fraudulent without any investigation at all. The "9-11 conspiracy theory" is a good example of this. There are those who still believe that the U.S. government was responsible for the attack on the World Trade Center in New York City, and not terrorists. This idea is nothing short of absurd.

Some other theories may sound reasonable and appear to have a basis in fact. While they may appear enticing these are the ones that require considerable investigation. In some cases they may turn out to be only partially correct. It is important to research all aspects (both positive and negative) of these arguments.

The final type of theory is that which is indisputable and cannot be challenged. It remains totally unexplainable – a true unsolved mystery. It has corroborating physical evidence, photos, videos, expert and eyewitness testimonies, and documentation to support it and, most importantly, stands the critical review test. There may be skeptics who believe they can poke holes in it, and on the surface their arguments seem valid. But it usually turns out that they don't have all of the information or facts at their disposal and therefore are incorrect in their premise and assumptions. Don't ever presume that skeptics or debunkers themselves conduct any research of their own because that is definitely not the case.

You must avoid at all costs the pitfall that most researchers fall into – that is they normally have made up their minds beforehand. They have a pre-determined position in mind from the start, and simply collect evidence to support that conclusion. The proper methodology is to first gather conclusive evidence, and test it against arguments put forth by skeptics and contradictory evidence. If it passes this test then you can proceed to build a case in favor of a final conclusion. The end result shouldn't be known until after all of the empirical evidence is assembled.

And that my friends is how you go about separating the fact from the fiction, and conducting a thorough and complete investigation that ends in a result which is based on irrefutable facts. All this can be achieved without actually traveling around the world, visiting and exploring the archaeological sites by someone who is not an archaeologist or scientist.

Scientists are facing an uphill battle to warn the public about pressing issues due to dissenters in their ranks who intentionally sow uncertainty. They sap convictions by endlessly questioning data, dismissing experimental innovation, stressing uncertainties and clamoring for more research.

I must start by first rejecting the basic premise of this statement.

This statement implies there is a coordinated effort that exists to discredit the scientific and historical community. Nothing could be further from the truth. Such a claim is simply an overtly transparent attempt by them to divert the spotlight of attention from the woeful inaccuracy and incompetence of their results and theories to blaming someone else for the inaccuracy and incompetence of their results and theories. Their fingerprints are all over everything we have been taught in schools through the years – they created the theories and dogma and therefore they now "own them". It is too late to start pointing the finger of blame at someone else, just because certain inconvenient FACTS and TRUTHS start to emerge causing these age-old theories to start collapsing.

And what about the dismal track record of mainstream science? What about its purposeful and intentionally fabricated claims throughout the years? There are hundreds of examples and I describe several dozen of these in my books. Are we supposed to just forget about these and pretend they didn't happen? There exists a skepticism and well-deserved reputation of science which cannot be overlooked.

The ideas and credibility of mainstream science are not crumbling from the attack of "naysayers" and "Merchants of Doubt", but under the weight of decades of lies and deception it has been promoting as fact and truth. And what about the hundreds of examples I list in my books that overturn many long-held paradigms? Its theories and claims are nothing more than "works in progress" – not more credible or qualified than alternative theories and claims. In fact they are less credible because, given their scientific credentials, education and training, you would expect more accuracy and reliability.

Simply stated the real enemy of mainstream science is the TRUTH! This is what they fear the most. They fear the public learning the truth from another source.

Conventional science and history have been proven pathetically wrong time and time again. Their long-held paradigms are finally starting to lose traction and their true identity exposed for the world to behold. The most important part of their agenda has been to promote a half-truth and rely on their partners in crime from the mainstream media to support their claims by reporting them as "officially recognized and investigated" work. It is all about perception. This has been their modus operandi and they have been doing so with impunity for a very long time. They cannot really believe what they preach because their arguments and theories are so incomplete and riddled with flaws.

The few examples listed throughout my books clearly illustrate their hypocritical nature and that their view and model of ancient history is, at best, nothing better than guesswork. Why else would their old-school doctrines have to constantly be revised, updated and re-written? So, I ask, is this any different (or more credible) than an alternative source? Why must we limit our education to fraudulent misinformation presented by a group of charlatans?

There is an awakening taking place in our society. People are hungry for knowledge. They are challenging mainstream institutional doctrine and beginning to look outside of established dogmatic sources for their information in search of the truth.

Why would they bother sending conventional missions into outer space at all if they are concealing a secret space program? What is the point of maintaining a costly fake charade such as the NASA program? There are three answers to this.

1. Because a sudden lack of interest, or suddenly going from the intensely competitive Apollo program and space race of the 1960s and 1970s to no interest at all would arouse much suspicion.

2. Because some valuable research can still be done using the resources of a conventional program such as satellite and space probe missions. A "black budget" space program would have its own agenda (no doubt military related) and certain limitations. It would only be capable of conducting limited activities for fear of being detected and exposed. So some research and investigation would be required by an agency such as NASA who could operate freely in public view.

3. The third, and most important reason, is both political and economic. There is a long-held misconception that the NASA program is extremely costly and onerous to

the economy. This is a short sighted and uninformed position. In fact its operation, surprisingly, is a positive revenue source. Are you surprised? Allow me to enlighten you as to what NASA actually contributes to the economy.

The cost to maintain an illusionary space program (NASA) is relatively insignificant when compared to the overall federal budget. This includes such programs as the International Space Station, Space Shuttle, Hubble & James Webb Space Telescopes, and various probes sent throughout our Solar System. You may find this hard to believe but the official NASA budget which has always publicly been a topic of debate over the years is insignificant when compared to other government branches.

NASA's budget over the past 30 years has averaged $17.5 billion per year – about 2 percent that of the Department of Defense (Pentagon) budget of $700 billion and DARPA (Defense Advanced Research Projects Agency) budget of $50 billion. Much of this $750 billion DOD and DARPA budget is allocated to "black" or top secret projects and some is even out of the control and authority of Congress. With a "black budget" program the money just plain disappears off the books – by the billions without any oversight. The NASA 2011 budget was $18.724 billion, representing 0.48 percent of the total federal budget ($3.8 trillion submitted). The DOD 2011 budget was $851 billion.

You can see where the emphasis has been, where the money has been diverted to over the years – not the traditional mainstream NASA space program but elsewhere. New technologies, many of them military, are constantly being developed.

By dedicating just a small percentage of the federal budget to a conventional space program it creates jobs within NASA and supporting industries in both the public and private sectors. NASA spending benefits not just the employees working at Kennedy Space Center or in Houston it also benefits the companies supplying rocket engines and computers, all the way down to suppliers that provide individual bolts. By creating and maintaining employment it allows people to spend and also generates tax revenue (even from astronauts) for federal and state governments, ensuring vibrant economies.

As an example, NASA's Ames Research Center generated 5,300 jobs and $877 million in total annual economic activity in the nine-county San Francisco Bay Area in 2009. Looking at the state of Florida, as another example, in fiscal 2010 the total economic impact of NASA in Florida was $4.1 billion in output, $2.2 billion in household income and 33,049 jobs. The injections also generated $314 million of federal taxes and $134 million of state and local taxes.

In fiscal 2010 the KSC Visitor Center (Kennedy Space Center) along with KSC business visitors contributed to the overall economy in Central Florida with $47 million injected into the regional economy. In fiscal 2010 all KSC based activities injected $1.83 billion of outside money into Florida's economy. This total consisted of $1.1 billion in wage payments to households and $717 million in direct commodity purchases from contractors. The output multiplier shows that each dollar of direct total spending for commodity purchases and wage payments resulted in $2.16 in total statewide output.

How do you measure the NASA stimulus? How much return does NASA get for every dollar it spends? Economists may argue over the exact numbers, but it appears that the United States economy gets at least $2 dollars back for every $1 dollar spent by NASA. In some instances, the ratio is up to $14 back for every dollar spent. Various studies have been done to support these numbers.

The Gross Domestic Product (GDP) measures the total output of all production units in the economy. GDP aggregates the productive activity in a particular country during a certain period of time. GDP represents the best single answer to the question, "What did we produce in a particular country in a given year?"

Analyses of the macroeconomic effects of the NASA space program attempt to identify and measure that portion of economic growth attributable to technological progress. A 1971 Midwest Research Institute (MRI) study of the relationship between R&D expenditures and technology-induced increases in GDP indicated that each dollar spent on R&D returns an average of slightly over seven dollars in GDP over an eighteen-year period following the expenditure.

Assuming that NASA's R&D expenditures produce the same economic payoff as the average R&D expenditure, MRI concluded that the $25 billion (1958) spent on civilian space R&D during the 1959-69 period returned $52 billion through 1970 and will continue to stimulate benefits through 1987, for a total gain of $181 billion. The discounted rate of return for this investment will have been 33 percent.

Other statistics on NASA's economic impact may be found in the 1976 Chase Econometrics Associates, Inc. reports ("*The Economic Impact of NASA R&D Spending: Preliminary Executive Summary*", April 1975. Also: "*Relative Impact of NASA Expenditure on the Economy.*", March 18, 1975) and backed by the 1989 Chapman Research report, which examined 259 non-space applications of NASA technology during an eight year period (1976–1984) and found more than:

• $21.6 billion in sales and benefits
• 352,000 (mostly skilled) jobs created or saved
• $355 million in federal corporate income taxes

According to the *Nature* article, these 259 applications represent only one percent of an estimated 25,000 to 30,000 Space program spin-offs.

In 2002, the aerospace industry accounted for $95 billion of economic activity in the United States, including $23.5 billion in employee earnings dispersed among some 576,000 employees (source: *Federal Aviation Administration*, March 2004).

Since 1976, there were 1,400 NASA inventions that wound up as products or services, such as kidney dialysis machines, CAT scanners, and even freeze-dried food. NASA has published a 224-page booklet on its spin-off technology from 2011 alone.

Suddenly cutting off all funding to a conventional space program and shutting it down would place undue pressure on the economy. Looking at this from a business perspective by the time you factor in what the NASA space program and related industries have injected into the economy the federal government's investment not only pays for itself, but results in a net gain. Therefore there is little financial or economic risk for the government to abandon such a charade.

Another benefit for sustaining the image of a public space program like NASA is that it allows for collaboration and the free exchange of ideas, information and technology with other scientific agencies in other countries – a political implication. Such co-operation would be almost impossible to achieve otherwise.

So you can see the existence of a fake space program does have certain advantages, and there is absolutely no net cost or downside. In fact it becomes a revenue source and is an asset to the economy. The perception that the NASA program is a costly fake charade is grossly inaccurate.

What reason would NASA or a government have for starting up a secret space program?

1. Because of an ongoing series of disasters on Earth (Japan nuclear reactor, BP oil spill, earthquakes, volcanic disturbances), there is more of a sense of urgency to look for another home. Famed theoretical physicist Stephen Hawking estimates that humans have only 1,000 years left on planet Earth, growing ever-closer to extinction as a result of their actions on the planet. Somewhere nearby, perhaps the Moon or Mars would be suitable.

We are in the midst of a natural cataclysmic cycle. According to the U.S. Geological Survey earthquakes, volcanic eruptions, tsunamis and geological disturbances have been on a dramatic increase for the last several decades. Magnitude 6.0 earthquakes are now common. NASA data indicates planetary changes across our Solar System are part of a huge natural cycle that has to do with alignments. Planet Earth has limited resources, limited energy, limited environment, living space, etc.

Another reason for developing a secret space program is due to the threat of an asteroid impact. The possible approach of Hercolubus (Tyche) – a gas giant planet which lurks in the outer reaches of our Solar System is another reason. Tyche is located in the Solar System's Oort cloud, first proposed in 1999 by astrophysicists John Matese, Patrick Whitman and Daniel Whitmire of the University of Louisiana at Lafayette. It orbits our Sun in a far elliptical orbit, is four times the size of Jupiter, with a helium and hydrogen atmosphere and is most likely to have many moons.

On February 13, 2011 NASA officially confirmed that it was tracking Hercolubus, which scientists called Tyche. The NASA Wide-field Infrared Survey Explorer (WISE) telescope showed a giant planet next to our Solar System. This planet fits the exact description of Planet X or Nibiru of ancient Sumerian mythology. The realization that an inevitable global cataclysm is imminent could have lead to the creation of a fast-tracked space program to save a select few of an endangered species – *Homo sapiens*. Why not announce this intention to the public? The answer is simple: to avoid creating and inciting mass panic and hysteria. It could all be part of a long term plan to "cherry pick" people to privately colonize a new planet.

2. To further investigate anomalous evidence on the Moon and Mars such as buildings, structures and various other sites. Off-world civilization records may contain libraries, maybe even translatable libraries. This would provide access to incredible new and advanced technological and medical discoveries. The first government or organization to find this information would be sitting in a great bargaining position with the rest of the world.

3. Perhaps the intention is to even destroy some of this evidence before the public becomes aware of it.

4. What better way is there to investigate the presence of alien civilizations on another planet without alarming the general public? A clandestine military space program could conduct exploration with impunity and with very little accountability.

5. Probably the most important reason to develop a behind-the-scenes military presence in outer space is to counteract a growing alien threat. Mounting evidence indicates that an increased amount of extraterrestrial activity has been monitored within our Solar System. In 1984, U.S. President Reagan in a public address established the tone and seriousness of this endeavor when he deliberately, or inadvertently, let slip the remarks that the world may one day unite to fight a threat from outer space. This was followed by a series of subsequent remarks during the latter days of his term of office. The best way to refine and experiment with new, advanced technologies and/or weapons systems, which sometimes fail miserably and produce disastrous results, is to do it without anyone knowing. This eliminates political posturing, emotional public reaction and criticism, and media scrutiny.

Skeptics scoff at the idea of a secret space program. If there isn't a secret space program then how do you explain the hundreds of eyewitness reports and testimonies from such highly credible sources as veteran military, intelligence and scientific professionals, including astronauts? You can dismiss the work of alternative "New Age" science and history researchers if you wish. However, it is not so easy to ignore the work and opinions of these highly reliable sources.

"Those who fail to learn from history are doomed to repeat it."

– Socrates (469-399 B.C.)

Chapter 6

The Evidence

The Curious Dissolution of the Space Exploration Program

Proposed budget cuts are forcing NASA to suspend plans for ambitious, expensive missions to many destinations throughout the Solar System.

The White House's budget request for 2013 kept overall NASA funding flat allocating just $1.2 billion to the space agency's planetary science program. That was a 20 percent cut from the 2012 allotment of $1.5 billion, and further reductions are expected over the next several years.

NASA officials say this funding picture leaves no room for multibillion-dollar "flagship" planetary missions – a departure for the space agency, which has launched roughly one such effort per decade since the 1970s. Those missions include the Cassini spacecraft's study of the Saturn system and the so-called Grand Tour of the solar system by the twin Voyager spacecraft.

So for the moment, there are no plans to develop more planetary flagships beyond the $2.5 billion Mars Science Laboratory (MSL), which dropped the one-ton Curiosity rover onto the Martian surface in August 2012 to investigate the Red Planet's potential to host life as we know it. NASA launched MSL in November 2011 on a scheduled two year mission.

There is no room in the current budget proposal from the President for new flagship missions anywhere, according to John Grunsfeld, NASA's associate administrator for science.

NASA is continuing to work on an astrophysics flagship mission, the James Webb Space Telescope. This huge instrument, billed as the successor to the agency's Hubble Space Telescope, is slated to cost $8.8 billion and launch in 2018 at the earliest.

NASA divides its planetary exploration missions into three classes: Discovery, New Frontiers and Flagships. Flagships are the most ambitious and priciest of the three, with costs running into the billions of dollars.

NASA has developed roughly one planetary flagship per decade, beginning with the Voyager mission to the outer Solar System in the mid-1970s. The Galileo mission to study Jupiter and its moons followed in 1989, and in 1997, NASA launched Cassini toward the Saturn system.

The Curiosity rover is the most recent NASA planetary flagship and perhaps the last for a while. Because of the proposed budget cuts, plans for possible future flagships –

which include a Mars sample-return mission and a probe that would study Jupiter's ocean-hosting moon Europa – are on indefinite hold.

A flagship mission is not on the table, Grunsfeld commented.

This state of affairs is deeply unsettling to some scientists and space-exploration advocates.

"People know that Mars and Europa are the two most important places to search in our Solar System for evidence of other past or present life forms," Jim Bell, president of the nonprofit Planetary Society, said in a statement. "Why, then, are missions to do those searches being cut in this proposed budget? If enacted, this would represent a major backwards step in the exploration of our Solar System."

Bill Nye, CEO of the Planetary Society and host of the former TV show *Bill Nye the Science Guy*, voiced similar sentiments.

"We are on the verge of finding habitable environments on Mars and other worlds. These discoveries will change the world," Nye explained. "Curtailing this work now will lead to spacecraft that don't work right, missions that crash, and the dissipation of the remarkable aerospace workforce. It may well lead to other space agencies taking on the search for life, and finding it, albeit decades hence."

Doesn't Nye's statement "hit the nail on the head"? By constantly cutting back funding for space exploration isn't the U.S. government accomplishing exactly what it would like – delaying the discovery of extraterrestrial life as long as possible?

The 2013 proposed budget cut compels NASA to drop out of the European-led ExoMars missions, which aim to launch an orbiter and a drill-toting rover toward the Red Planet. These two missions are viewed as key steps toward an eventual Mars sample-return effort.

However, NASA officials stress that the agency is not giving up on planetary exploration in the near future. It's just scaling down, focusing on missions that may cost $500 million to $700 million instead of several billion.

The space agency is looking into sending such a "medium-class" mission to Mars in 2018 or 2020. The details of this pending effort have yet to be worked out, and won't be until NASA finishes overhauling its Mars exploration strategy – another move the agency is undertaking in response to the budget cut.

And NASA isn't abandoning flagships forever. Agency scientists and managers will keep laying the foundations necessary to enable ambitious missions, so they'll be ready to hit the ground running should the fiscal environment improve, according to Grunsfeld.

Grunsfeld said he hopes NASA can return Mars rocks to Earth for study by 2030 or so, and he also expressed optimism about potential flagships to destinations beyond the Red Planet.

It appears that NASA's long-term approach to space exploration is very limited and "safe". Manned spaceflight into low-Earth orbit (servicing space stations) and back along with development of a new space telescope appears to be their primary goal, at least for the near future.

Isn't it interesting how NASA continually finds creative ways to avoid conducting a proper and thorough exploration of Mars? What are they so afraid of? First it was because of the logistical problems caused due to the complexity of the mission. Travel, issues of food, water and oxygen, the harmful effects of microgravity, potential hazards such as fire and radiation and the fact that astronauts would be millions of miles away from help and confined together for years at a time were some of the reasons cited preventing NASA from embarking on such a mission. More recently budgetary cutbacks in funding are the reason.

While the financial excuse may be valid it is much too convenient and could be used for everything and anything at anytime. When was the money ever there? When wasn't there a domestic or international crisis that demanded the money? In the past we always found a way to find funding and maintain other social and economic programs. Are today's leaders less intelligent and imaginative? Are they less visionary or simply uninterested in the "bigger picture"? NASA would gain more respect and credibility if it simply admitted that the exploration of the Red Planet wasn't in their immediate plans.

Private investors who are developing space plane technology to carry paying customers into Earth orbit are not the answer. Even SpaceX's ambitious plan for a 2018 mission to Mars is not the answer because, being an arm of NASA, it will likely get caught up in red tape and suffer the same funding cutback fate – thus grounding any hope for serious interplanetary exploration.

The real answer is a commitment from global leaders to (a) agree that the continuance of the human species is the most important challenge currently facing our civilization and (b) rally to find the funding and resources to develop the technology required to send space missions in search of a potential new home for mankind. All of this is only true assuming one single major point – that the intention is sincere and not a charade.

Since the Apollo 11 Moon landing NASA and the United States government (and possibly Russia) have purposely stalled, delayed and retarded serious space exploration outside of basic Earth orbit. Just compare the progress in space exploration in a little more than a single decade from 1958-1969.

This period saw an incredible leap in technology and space exploration from the launch of the first satellite into Earth orbit (Vanguard – January 31, 1958) to the Moon landing on July 20, 1969. That is a simple, undeniable fact. But consider what has transpired since 1969: an international space station and telescope in Earth orbit; decades of countless Space Shuttle missions into Earth orbit; and the rare interplanetary probe launched as a token gesture to pacify public interest.

After 11 years of a sprint race, space exploration has slowed to a crawl. Even the Russians, who were primary competitors involved in the heated 1960s space race with the United States, have scaled back their exploration and are suspiciously much less ambitious.

But what is the reason for this new found apathy?

It is almost as if we are suddenly afraid to leave the friendly confines of our comfortable cocoon here on Earth. The appetite for space exploration and discovery has disappeared. The enthusiasm and sense of urgency that once existed is no longer there. The irony, however, is that mankind is in greater danger of extinction now than ever before.

But why have we suddenly become so complacent and content to remain here on Earth? What happened to our burning desire to reach for the stars and search for answers to our origins, to seek out a new home? Isn't this suspicious in the least?

This attitude can only lead one to conclude that (a) there is no concern among our leaders for the future of humanity's existence outside of Earth. They are too pre-occupied dealing with day-to-day issues, or (b) there is already a "master plan" actively in place to preserve humanity's continuance – an ongoing secret space program funded as a highly classified "black project".

On April 13, 2012 NASA put out a call for ideas for the next Mars mission in 2018. The fine print: The cost can't be astronomical and the idea has to move the country closer to landing humans on the red planet in the 2030s.

The race to redraw a new, cheaper road map comes two months after NASA pulled out of a partnership with the European Space Agency on two missions targeted for 2016 and 2018, a move that angered scientists. The 2018 mission represented the first step toward hauling Martian soil and rocks back to Earth for detailed study – something many researchers say is essential in determining whether microbial life once existed there.

Agency officials said returning samples is still a priority, but a reboot was necessary given the financial reality.

In the past decade, NASA has spent $6.1 billion exploring Earth's closest planetary neighbor. President Obama's latest proposed budget slashed spending for Solar System exploration by 21 percent, making the collaboration with the Europeans unaffordable.

Whatever mission flies in 2018, it will be vastly cheaper than the Mars Curiosity and will be capped at $700 million.

NASA is mainly seeking suggestions from scientists and engineers around the world, but you don't have to have a Ph.D. Anyone can submit a proposal online and go through a lengthy process.

Scientists welcomed the chance to offer input but worried about the budget uncertainty.

These constant budget cutbacks to Mars missions are nothing more than an obvious attempt to avoid stumbling onto tangible proof of intelligent life on Mars. And why would they need to do this? Firstly, to delay announcing for as long as possible that extraterrestrial life exists or has existed right in our own backyard and, secondly, with an active ongoing secret space program in operation for some time they have already known this for many years. There is no point in paying for duplicating the effort.

Budgetary concerns aside, the fact is that by purposely avoiding and delaying sending missions to Mars it becomes more and more apparent that there is something to hide. This is yet more evidence that a secret black budget space program currently exists.

The Other (Secret) Space Program

Throughout this book I have described the presence of many modern-day artifacts on Mars and elsewhere throughout our Solar System. But how could present-day human artifacts find their way to these distant locations when we have barely traveled to the Moon (total of only six official Apollo lunar landings from 1969-1972), and not returned there in 40 years?

The U.S. secret space program has been covered up by the ongoing fight over the trivial mainstream NASA budget in Congress, which is only $19 billion. Hard to believe isn't it? NASA's budget over the past 30 years has averaged $17.5 billion per year. From that small amount we got the International Space Station and flew the shuttle at least twice a year, if not three. Compared to the Department of Defense (Pentagon) budget of $700 billion and DARPA (Defense Advanced Research Projects Agency) budget of $50 billion, taxpayers got a lot for very little money (which probably gave the illusion of larger budgets). But the secret space program has a "black budget", which means the money just plain disappears off the books – by the trillions.

Rumors abound concerning a secret space program. Large spaceships in orbit, extraterrestrial "officers", secret Mars bases, secret alien cities on the Moon, ancient derelict spaceships in orbit around Mars, UFOs and the list goes on about connections to it.

Over time I have come to the opinion that there could very well be a secret space program. Many NASA and government officials associated with the conventional space program, boasting impressive scientific and intelligence credentials, have come forward to openly admit this. If there is covert interest in the anomalies on Mars, would there be a covert space program to investigate? Another component of this has to do with the Moon. Are there bases on the far side of the Moon? Based on expert testimonies I do not know for sure, but I cannot rule it out.

There is another reason to suppose the existence of an advanced, clandestine space program. An enormous amount of video from space missions has been downloaded and is available for anyone to see. This includes missions of NASA, the European Space Agency, Russia, and China. From this video evidence there can be no denying that there has been a great deal of activity in Earth's orbit. Much of what was recorded undoubtedly has conventional explanations. But, frankly, many events do not offer easy explanations. I firmly believe there is something highly unusual going on in Earth's orbit.

Look at it this way. If you believe there are anomalies on Mars, and if you acknowledge strange activity in Earth's orbit, you would have a very good reason to initiate a secret space program, would you not? You would want a way to investigate these things in a way that would not be seen by the prying eyes of the public. This way a thorough investigation could take place without alarming the public.

I've also come to the opinion that part of the classified world – the part that deals with the extraterrestrial reality – has essentially "broken away" from our own conventional civilization. That is, utilizing the jumpstart they received by studying exotic, alien technology, they have very likely achieved scientific breakthroughs that they have not shared with the rest of us. I think that these breakthroughs have enabled them to employ technologies substantially beyond what we are using, and that in all likelihood has contributed to their secret space program. Many of the UFOs we now see in our skies could be the result of such a secret space program.

It is important to emphasize that the above is primarily conjecture on my part. I consider it my working hypothesis. Proving it will require a great deal of effort and dedication. The quality of the evidence is directly related to the ease of acquiring it and the amount available. To find evidence presupposes that you have access or availability to it, which isn't the case in this situation. We must rely on a single source (NASA) for information and that source has their own agenda, is not co-operative and has no interest in revealing what they know. It also means not being sucked in by every new person who has claimed to have traveled to Mars. We need to remain clear-headed in our pursuit of the truth.

Is this an intentional attempt to acclimate the public to the idea of alien cultures and our interaction with them? Or is this just so much science fiction and wishful thinking?

If this secret space program (perhaps a joint USA-Russian effort) is proven to be true, then it is a conspiracy of the most epic proportions. Considering the available evidence from multiple sources, what is the degree of truth in these reports? A physicist who worked for Project Blue Book back in the 1960s out of Wright-Patterson Air Force Base described how, during that time, the United States Air Force had two UFOs that they would fly right out of Wright-Patterson AFB. He said they would open the hangar doors in the middle of the night and fly them right out of the hangars at full speed.

Researchers conclude that the U.S. military has its own UFOs indicating a decades-long military program of deep deceit and thorough lies about the true involvement of U.S. military agencies in secret UFO space technology and projects. It's highly likely that there are multiple, secret, classified, tightly compartmentalized UFO and space programs – not just a single space program but programs, plural, and that the U.S. military and NASA have been lying through their teeth to the public about all of this since at least the World War II era, if not longer.

There has been a very public NASA space program, which is always in various budget disputes and problems, but behind it there is another parallel space program that is quite real and more advanced than what we are seeing publicly. This program deals with unconventional technologies such as electro-gravitics and anti-gravity. Investigation has shown that there is a great deal more to the space program than NASA and the United States military have told the public. And in all likelihood, manned exploration started much earlier, has discovered much more and has more ancient roots by far than we have been told.

Testimony from a number of highly credible scientists (physicists) who have claimed that we have already been to Mars in a secret space program is absolutely shocking. Think this is fanciful science fiction? Well in fact there is good evidence that there was a follow-on secret space shuttle program run by the United States Air Force. In August 1989, The *New York Times* reported that the U.S. Air Force was disbanding a previously unknown secret operation of 32 secret military astronauts based in Los Angeles, who were associated with a parallel multi-billion dollar space shuttle program that the USAF was running out of Vandenberg AFB in California. This story reported that the USAF was abandoning a major space control center in Colorado and a $3.3 billion never-used spaceport at Vandenberg AFB, according to the Air Force.

Essentially, the thrust of the story was that the USAF spent billions of dollars on a secret 32-man astronaut corps and a secret spaceport and launch control center (LCC) and never used any of it. I simply do not believe this account as put forth by the USAF. I believe, in fact, that the opposite is likely to be true and that the U.S. military does have, and has had, not one but likely multiple secret space programs using both conventional aerospace technologies and also unconventional technologies. These unconventional technologies are the result of reverse-engineering from crashed alien spacecraft.

David Froning is an astronautical engineer who worked at McDonnell Douglas for over 30 years. He has worked on highly classified military defense programs and on leading edge aeronautical and aerospace technology during most of his flying, engineering, science and experimental time with the U.S. Air Force, McDonnell Douglas and his own aerospace consultancy – in research and preliminary design, and development of advanced aerospace vehicles, including their critical energy and propulsion technologies.

Froning has also worked on contract to NASA as well. Dr. Froning's credentials include: Associate Fellow of the American Institute of Aeronautics and Astronautics (AIAA); Fellow of the British Inter-planetary Society, Member of the AIAA Nuclear and Future Flight Committee and the AIAA Hypersonics Systems and Technologies Program Committee; and Past Scientific Committee Member of the International Academy of Astronautics (IAA).

In 1990 at a symposium at Tucson's University of Arizona Froning addressed an audience of astrophysicists, astronomers and engineers where he candidly admitted that rocket technology was ridiculously obsolete and new 'quantum-science' has developed "Modified Field" propulsion (anti-gravity), "Matter/Anti-matter conversion", "Exotic Field Tension" (time-travel) and "Trans-luminal" flight (faster than light travel). In other words, behind closed doors, *STAR TREK* technologies are absolutely real, yet the advantages of that reality remain deliberately withheld from the very people who are paying the bill.

I believe it is highly possible that the USAF has put up its own space shuttles, perhaps using X-20 Dyno-Soar style technology, and very likely using the facilities at Vandenberg AFB which they told us back in the late 1980s that they lavished billions of dollars on and never used.

Following is an excerpt from an email exchange between Dr. Richard Boylan and Col. Steve Wilson, USAF (ret.), former head of Project Pounce and Director-Skywatch International, Inc.

From: rich.boylan@xxxxxxxxx

To: Skywatch@xxxxxxxxx
Date: Tue, 19 Aug 97 08:37:56 -0700 Subject: Air Force Special Academy

RB: In the Star Wars City (SDI/01) organizational chart you posted, there is identified an "Air Force Special Academy" (AFSA), which takes its orders from Star Wars City in

Colorado Springs, CO. I take it that this is not the regular Air Force Academy, right?

SW: No it isn't the Regular Academy.

RB: Is it AFSA which trains the military astronauts who are quietly sent up from Vandenberg Air Force Base, CA, while the press keeps the public's attention on the Space Shuttle operating from Cape Canaveral, FL?

SW: Yes, Vandenberg and Beale AF bases are both involved.

How is it that for more than half a century since NASA was created it has made no fundamental scientific or technological progress in getting off this planet? Is it because this is just a cover for the actual (and more important) top secret space program where billions of dollars are being pumped into R&D through black projects? Or where have these billions gone – making paper airplanes?

There is even a photo of the secret astronaut corps named the "Magnificent Seven" that is available. They were the "Magnificent Seven" of the Manned Orbiting Laboratory (MOL) program, some of the best pilots the U.S. military had to offer. Two more crews would follow, including that of Bob Lawrence, the first African-American astronaut. The MOL program was part of the United States Air Force's manned spaceflight program, a successor to the X-20 Dyna-Soar project, which was cancelled on December 10, 1963. The program was supposedly intended to prove the utility of man in space for military missions. However, this was just a cover story for the Russians and the public.

These men, 17 in all, were set to make history in space as the first military astronauts, performing covert reconnaissance from Earth orbit. Yet while NASA's astronauts were gracing magazine covers and signing autographs, the MOL teams were sworn to secrecy. Most of the program's details remain classified even to this day.

According to the *New York Times*, the MOL was canceled in 1969. Well, that was from a news bulletin put out by the U.S. Air Force apparently as a cover for what actually was and is going on. A red herring that worked as everyone forgot about it.

A good way to put distance between the public and the media and the facts of the secret space program would be to generate a story covered by the *New York Times*, the newspaper of record, that yes, there was a secret program, but it has been entirely disbanded. This is the best way to cover-up a secret.

The trillion dollar question: where did all the money go and why are we in such debt globally? The short answer is: there is a separate space program, which we are all paying for, and we're not being told anything about it, and as a result, NASA appears to have become a bit of a joke. We have a special space program and it is apparently known as the United States Aerospace Command and it is a joint service agency. That means it includes Navy, Army, Air Force, Marine Corps, and it also includes the British Aerospace Command. It's basically where all the missing trillions of dollars have gone.

Robert Dean worked for NASA for over 30 years. In 2009 he thought it about time to reveal the origins of a NASA lost footage photographic library and evidence of a USSS fleet (detailing a transfer of admiralty from the USSS Curtis Lemay and USSS Roscoe Hillencotter) captured on film during the Apollo 13 Mission. NASA maintains they had lost 40 rolls of film with thousands of shots from the mission documenting this but a Japanese scientist, had a copy of everything from the Apollo missions due to their space agency's involvement and assistance in NASA's public space program missions.

This photograph (shown below) was taken by Apollo 13. You may remember Apollo 13. It was the one that never made it to the Moon. It had a small explosion on the way there, where an oxygen tank blew up and they were barely able to get to the Moon, orbit it, and return home to Earth. But they were not alone on that trip. While en route they took several pictures through the small windows in the command module. This is one picture that was held all these years by the Japanese Space Agency. You may notice the Japanese text at the bottom of the photo.

Objects 'B' and 'C' appear to be fairly large circular discs. Object 'A' is much larger and is seen moving into the picture from the right of the frame. Second photo from the top is a positive image of object 'A'. The bottom photo shows round discs entering or leaving the larger craft.

What is amazing about object 'A' is its incredible size – a staggering five miles in length! It is therefore perfectly understandable why NASA is keeping quiet about this – because they can't explain it. Apollo 13 encountered an object five miles long on their way to the Moon and nobody knows what it is. Now let us consider the magnitude of the size of this object and put it into perspective. The largest aircraft carrier in the U.S. Navy is staffed by a crew of around 5,000 personnel. How large a crew would a spacecraft five miles long require?

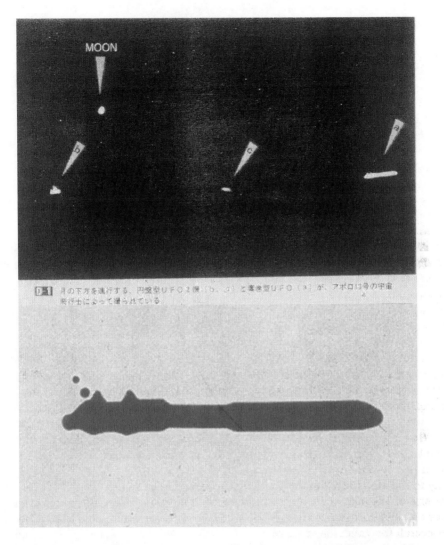

This secret space program launches satellites from several different positions on Earth. They maintain, apparently, an entire fleet of vessels in orbit. They have anti-gravity and zero-point energy, which the general public have a right to and won't see or know about for at least another ten years.

That's where the missing trillions have gone. In 1998, 1999, and 2000, $1.7 trillion dollars a year for three years disappeared off the books. Where is the outrage? Do you think there was a demand for answers? Who is accountable for this? Where did that money go?

The day before 9/11 Secretary of Defense Donald Rumsfeld announced that the government was missing $2.3 trillion dollars, which couldn't be accounted for. It disappeared off the books, somehow. He said that they were working on it, that it may be an accounting error.

Missing $2.3 trillion, after the already missing of $1.7 trillion a year for three years? There is where the funding is coming from for the Aerospace Command that United States Senator Daniel Inouye is talking about – a separate shadow government that you have no idea exists. And those guys have got the technology that is 100 years beyond establishment knowledge.

Cryptic comments by two Democrats on the Senate floor about a major program in the fiscal year 2005 intelligence authorization conference report point to a secret space effort of some kind that has been underway for years, but which has been unknown to the public.

Senators Jay Rockefeller IV (D-W.Va.), ranking Democrat on the Senate Intelligence Committee, and Ron Wyden (D-Ore.) both criticized the program without naming it on December 8th during debate on the fiscal year 2005 intelligence authorization bill. Rockefeller said it was "totally unjustified and very, very wasteful."

He said the Senate has voted for the past two years to kill it, "only to be overruled in the appropriations conference." While the new intelligence authorization conference report fully authorizes the effort, Rockefeller said, it is "unjustified and stunningly expensive." Wyden agreed, and said "numerous independent reviews have concluded that the program does not fulfill a major intelligence gap or shortfall, and the original justification for developing this technology has eroded in importance due to the changed practices and capabilities of our adversaries. There are a number of other programs in existence and in development whose capabilities can match those envisioned for this program at far less cost and technological risk."

Because they're talking about an expensive acquisition program, it's a logical inference to assume that we're talking about a satellite program, Steven Aftergood of the Washington-based Federation of American Scientists explained. He said Wyden's comments gave the most clues about what it may be, and the senator's statement that the program is not as important today as it was in the past suggests that it's something that might have made sense against the Soviet Union, but doesn't make sense against al Qaeda.

John Pike of GlobalSecurity.org in Alexandria, Va., said there are at least two possibilities – a stealthy reconnaissance satellite or Discoverer II comeback, a space-based JSTARS (Joint Surveillance Targeting Attack Radar System). Discoverer II, which was to have consisted of many small radar satellites, apparently was killed some years ago. Pike leans toward the stealthy spy satellite because there is more of an indication that there is actually something there, whereas he isn't sure what happened with Discoverer II. He doesn't know whether they really did drive a stake in its heart, or whether they took it so black (classified) that nobody could find it.

Gary McKinnon Prosecution

In 2002, amateur British computer hacker Gary McKinnon was arrested by the UK Hi Tech National Crimes Unit on the instruction of U.S. authorities. He is accused by the United States of perpetrating the biggest military computer breach of all time. It was alleged that McKinnon had penetrated secure networks belonging to NASA, The Pentagon and other government agencies.

As a result the U.S. Justice Department became intent on making him face trial and a possible 70-year jail term to be served in America. What contributed to the zealous determination of an embarrassed military establishment was what McKinnon found during his months browsing the networks. His testimony supported what many have suggested in recent years – that there exists a totally separate, highly advanced space program employing exotic energy systems and possibly reverse-engineered technology from extraterrestrial sources.

McKinnon, a systems administrator, hacked into 97 United States military and NASA computers in 2001 and 2002. The computer networks he is accused of hacking include networks operated by NASA, the U.S. Army, U.S. Navy, Department of Defense, and the U.S. Air Force. The United States estimates claim the costs of tracking and correcting the problems he allegedly caused were around $800,000.

McKinnon was originally tracked down and arrested under the Computer Misuse Act by the UK National Hi-Tech Crime Unit (NHTCU) in 2002 and informed him that he would face community service. The Crown Prosecution Service refused to charge him. Later that year the United States government indicted him. During the length of time between his indictment and beginning of extradition proceedings, with a growing media interest in his case, McKinnon had a number of opportunities to address the media.

He admitted in many public statements to unauthorized access of computer systems in the United States including those mentioned in the indictment. He claimed his motivation was to find evidence of UFOs, anti-gravity technology, and government suppression of "Free Energy", all of which he claimed was proven to exist through his actions.

One of his admissions involved hacking into the U.S. Space Command and NASA networks. There he explained he found a list of officer's names under the heading "Non-Terrestrial Officers". This didn't mean little green men. What he thought it meant was not Earth-based. He found a list of fleet-to-fleet transfers, and a list of ship names which didn't exist in any U.S. Navy, Air Force or government records. What he saw made him believe they have some kind of spaceship and program operating off-planet.

This clearly demonstrates that some type of conspiracy or cover-up is taking place at the highest level.

Could this reference to "Non-Terrestrial Officers" be those individuals involved in a secondary space program, outside of NASA, using alien spacecraft either obtained from various crash sites or through some type of joint Earth/extraterrestrial program?

Classified U.S. Government Documents

Apollo 18 was originally planned in July 1969 to land in the Moon's Schroter's Valley, a river-like channel-way. The original February 1972 landing date was extended when NASA cancelled the Apollo 20 mission in January 1970. Later in the planning process the most likely landing site was the crater Gassendi. Finally NASA cancelled Apollo 18 and 19 on September 2, 1970 because of congressional cuts in FY 1971 NASA appropriations. There was also a feeling after the Apollo 13 emergency that NASA risked having its entire manned space program cancelled if a crew was lost on another Apollo mission. Total savings of cancelling the two missions (since the hardware was already built and the NASA staff had to stay in place for the Skylab program) was only $42.1 million.

Before the cancellation, NASA was pressing for a more ambitious landing in Tycho or the lunar far side. It seems Copernicus, the final program goal as previously set for Apollo's 19 and 20, was also considered before the cancellation. Pressure from the scientific community resulted in geologist Harrison Schmitt flying on Apollo 17, the last lunar mission, bumping Joe Engle from the lunar module pilot slot.

The photo below shows a previously classified document which indicates a cancellation of Apollo 18, 19 and 20 missions. This is clearly explained in the first paragraph of the memorandum. However, the second paragraph mentions that "the Mission status has been altered. The revised status shifts from cancellation to postponement." Potential dates of reinstatement are also listed.

For some unknown reason the cancelled Apollo 18, 19 and 20 missions are suddenly officially reinstated. What urgent reason could there be for such a dramatic turnaround in policy? And more importantly where did the funding come from to finance these three highly expensive missions?

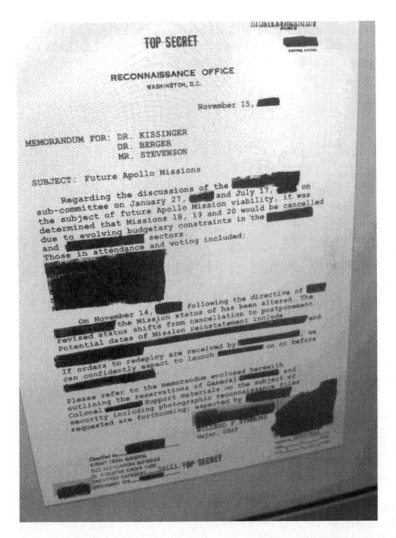

The photos below are taken from *Special Operations Manual, SOM1-01 Extraterrestrial Entities and Technology, Recovery and Disposal*, April 1954 Part 2. This manual explains how to respond to encounters with EBE's (extraterrestrial biological entities), handling, retrieval and preservation of UFOs and artifacts, the protocol for isolation and custody of EBEs, and a guide to the identification of various types of UFOs. This is only one page from the manual. There are many more leaked pages from this manual that are available.

While this is not direct proof of a secret space program it does indicate the U.S. government did have a secret Earth-based program dealing with extraterrestrial encounters. Therefore (a) the existence of aliens and their presence on Earth has to be assumed to be true, and (b) a special group within the military and Air Force must have been formed to conduct and oversee these encounters, crash retrievals, etc. So in actual fact this document establishes that, at a minimum, a program dealing with extraterrestrials was ongoing since 1954, and possibly led to an even greater level of participation through the development of space vehicles which used technology that was back-engineered from crashed ET ships. This is a logical progression in a program's evolution.

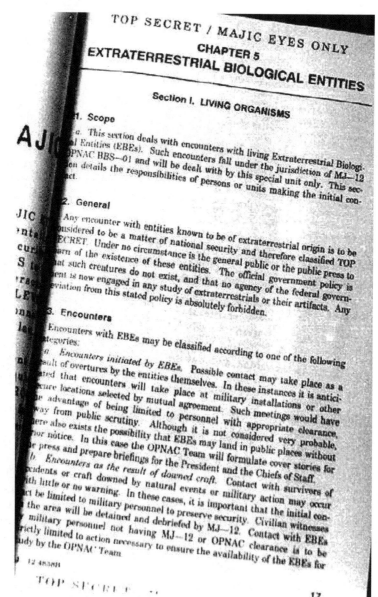

TOP SECRET / MAJIC EYES ONLY

CHAPTER 5

EXTRATERRESTRIAL BIOLOGICAL ENTITIES

Section I. LIVING ORGANISMS

1. Scope

a. This section deals with encounters with living Extraterrestrial Biological Entities (EBEs). Such encounters fall under the jurisdiction of MJ-12 OPNAC BBS-01 and will be dealt with by this special unit only. This section details the responsibilities of persons or units making the initial contact.

2. General

Any encounter with entities known to be of extraterrestrial origin is to be considered to be a matter of national security and therefore classified TOP SECRET. Under no circumstance is the general public or the public press to learn of the existence of these entities. The official government policy is that such creatures do not exist, and that no agency of the federal government is now engaged in any study of extraterrestrials or their artifacts. Any deviation from this stated policy is absolutely forbidden.

3. Encounters

Encounters with EBEs may be classified according to one of the following categories:

a. Encounters initiated by EBEs. Possible contact may take place as a result of overtures by the entities themselves. In these instances it is anticipated that encounters will take place at military installations or other secure locations selected by mutual agreement. Such meetings would have the advantage of being limited to personnel with appropriate clearance, away from public scrutiny. Although it is not considered very probable, there also exists the possibility that EBEs may land in public places without prior notice. In this case the OPNAC Team will formulate cover stories for the press and prepare briefings for the President and the Chiefs of Staff.

b. Encounters as the result of downed craft. Contact with survivors of accidents or craft downed by natural events or military action may occur with little or no warning. In these cases, it is important that the initial contact be limited to military personnel to preserve security. Civilian witnesses in the area will be detained and debriefed by MJ-12. Contact with EBEs by military personnel not having MJ-12 or OPNAC clearance is to be strictly limited to action necessary to ensure the availability of the EBEs for study by the OPNAC Team.

12 48308

TOP SECRET

17

Sun Cruiser Spacecraft

THE OTHER (SECRET) SPACE PROGRAM

The Solar and Heliospheric Observatory (SOHO) is a spacecraft that was launched on a Lockheed Martin Atlas IIAS launch vehicle on December 2, 1995 to study the Sun, and has discovered 2,000 comets. It began normal operations in May 1996. It is a joint project of international co-operation between the European Space Agency (ESA) and NASA.

Originally planned as a two-year mission, SOHO currently continues to operate after over ten years in space. In October 2009, a mission extension lasting until December 2012 was approved. In addition to its scientific mission, it is currently the main source of near-real time solar data for space weather prediction. The Large Angle and Spectrometric Coronagraph (LASCO) is one of a number of instruments aboard SOHO. LASCO consists of three solar coronagraphs with nested fields of view.

Photographs taken by SOHO/LASCO reveal incredible images of objects resembling gigantic spaceships orbiting our Sun (photos below). These objects have been nicknamed "Sun Cruisers" or "Star Cruisers". Are these objects simply orbiting rocks, asteroids, space junk, sunspots, the planets Mercury and Venus, or some other natural phenomenon?

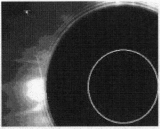
Notice the spacecraft in top left corner of this image.

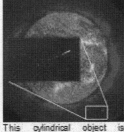
This cylindrical object is thousands of miles long and seems to be burning up close to the Sun.

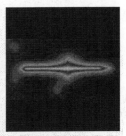
Another view of what looks to be some type of spacecraft.

NASA has offered explanations for these anomalies. According to them the most common sources of UFO claims occurring near the Sun are:

Planets: These always look very strange in LASCO images, because they're so bright that the image blooms, and the CCD pixels bleed along the readout rows. As a result some people claim that they're flying saucers, based on their appearance. There is another claim that they're previously unknown Saturn-like planets with rings around them.

Cosmic rays: High energy particles from the solar wind, and from the galaxy as a whole, whip around the SOHO spacecraft and interact with the detectors. These produce spots and streaks on the detector ranging from a single pixel, to large streaks that span a large fraction of the image. These are most evident during a solar storm, but are always present at some level. People have claimed that they've seen spacecraft-looking things that seem to be moving around, but which are actually cosmic rays when examined by an experienced observer.

Software glitches: Occasionally there will be problems with the software which produce the images for the web, and strange artifacts will appear in the data. These glitches are usually corrected within a few days.

Detector defects: There are defects which appear in the cameras from time to time, sometimes temporary and sometimes permanent. Those defects have been around forever, and were seen in the lab even before SOHO was launched.

Debris: Small pieces of aging insulation on the outside of the spacecraft, dust particles, micrometeorites etc., can show up in pictures.

A CCD (charge-coupled device) is an image sensor, consisting of an integrated circuit containing an array of linked or coupled capacitors which are sensitive to light. This is where NASA is claiming the so-called "glitches" are happening. I am amazed that NASA says that these images are CCD glitches. After a few years of examining these films how can a glitch be so constant? Shouldn't it be more random? How reliable a scientific tool is this device if it continually produces faulty readings and data? This means that NASA intentionally and knowingly launched a defective piece of equipment into space. But for what reason?

Debunkers claim that official NASA photographs are purposely manipulated by researchers through magnification and other image enhancing effects which distort the image, thus resulting in the appearance of spaceship-like objects. But what else can be done to arrive at a logical conclusion? Just leave the images as they are? In other words, should you be satisfied with "what you guess is what you see"? Shouldn't someone go a step further to try and get nearer the truth?

I'm not implying intentionally tampering with the photographs but doing something to get closer to solving the enigma. Is there any other way? Or should we just sit back and enjoy the SOHO pictures and blindly accept NASA/JPL's "explanations" for the anomalies?

NASA has conjured up a variety of so-called "explanations". However, none of them make any sense. Officially, most of these objects photographed near the Sun are explained away as the planet Saturn; a distant galaxy; a shining star; a comet; a CCD glitch; dust on the lens; overheated imaging circuits on SOHO; radiation; reflections, and so on. The only explanation remaining that hasn't been used is the Easter Bunny!

There are approximately 300 "natural" explanations for UFOs. But none mentions that they could be UFOs. Why is that?

Stellar matter is another explanation crafted by scientists. But remember some of these objects are supposedly a few thousand miles in length. So if they are stellar matter then why haven't they been mapped as asteroids or comets and cataloged as such? After all, some as small as a few hundred feet in size have already been given names.

So either they are CCD glitches or unidentified objects that NASA/ESA wants to hide.

There are countless anomalous images that researchers have downloaded from the SOHO/NASA website which mysteriously are removed after a short period of time. Why would this be necessary? NASA have never addressed why this happens.

As Ockham's razor states, sometimes the simplest answers are the correct ones. If it looks like a spacecraft, smells like a spacecraft, and moves like a spacecraft chances are it is a spacecraft. That is unless you would rather go with mysterious equipment glitches, ice particles that miraculously survived the heat of the Sun, or other rocks that didn't burn up from the heat of the Sun.

The SOHO/LASCO photo below shows two other anomalous objects. The image on the left appears to be an object breaking up near the Sun. It cannot be a comet for the simple reason that the direction of the tail is not what it should be.

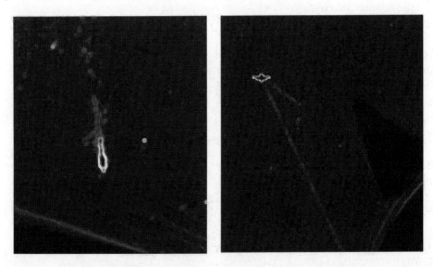

If these massive anomalies are spacecraft I highly doubt that they belong to us. I personally find it hard to believe that 21st century humans, even via a secret space program using reverse-engineered alien technology, would be capable of building spacecraft thousands of miles long. Not at our current stage of evolution.

Large Unidentified Spacecraft Observed in Low Earth Orbit

There have been a number of unidentified large objects (some form of spacecraft) seen and photographed in low Earth orbit. Some of these are easily explainable. The

International Space Station (ISS), NASA Space Shuttle, satellites, and even rocket boosters are possible explanations. However, the unidentified objects observed that I am referring to don't fall into any of these categories.

The image on the left below is of the International Space Station (ISS). Compare it to the unidentified object seen traveling in low Earth orbit on the right. The object on the right is absolutely massive and bears no resemblance whatsoever to the ISS.

 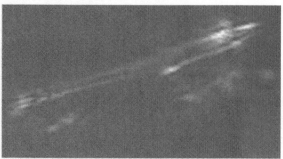

International Space Station in Earth orbit.   Unidentified spacecraft photographed in low Earth orbit.

If you are wondering what the NASA Space Shuttle looks like in orbit, here it is.

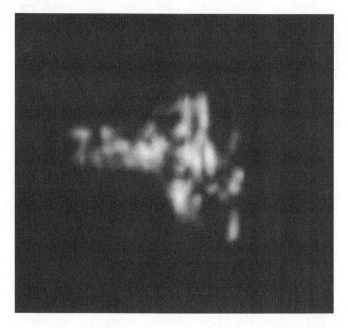

Keeping that image and its relative size appearance in mind, ask yourself what in the world could these two objects be?

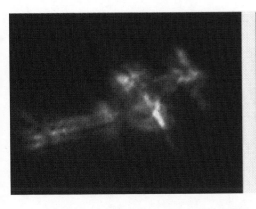
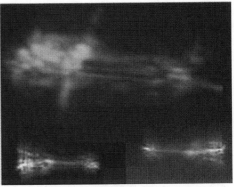

During Space Shuttle mission STS-88 the following unexplained objects appeared in low earth orbit near the Space Shuttle. The series of NASA images are STS-88-724-65.JPG to STS-88-724-70.JPG.

Are they extraterrestrial or classified black ops?

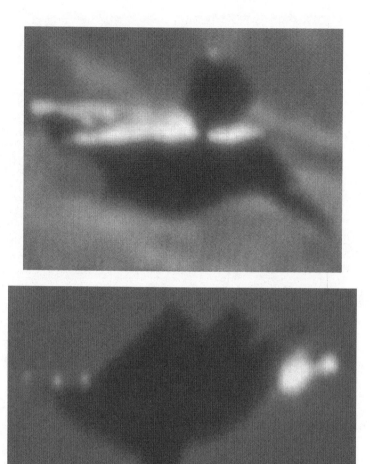

A man by the name of John Walson has discovered a new way to extend the capabilities of small telescopes and has been able to achieve optical resolutions not commonly achievable. Walson is an amateur astronomer and has taken images of the International Space Station, so is very familiar with that craft. With this new-found ability, he has proceeded to videotape, night and day, many strange and unseen objects in Earth orbit. The resulting astrophotographic video footage has revealed an abundance of machines, hardware, satellites, and spacecraft which otherwise appear as "stars" to the casual observer with the naked eye – if they appear at all.

What is most amazing about these spacecraft/machines is how they are able to expand and transform their shape and size in outer space.

There are hundreds of satellites in Earth orbit as you will read in the summary which follows. However, the images you will see are clearly of large and sizeable machines which have never been seen before.

So exactly how many known satellites are there In Earth orbit? How much 'space junk' is actually floating around up there?

According to the Union of Concerned Scientists there are more than 800 active satellites currently in Earth orbit. Amazingly, they represent four percent of the total number of objects currently cataloged by the U.S. space surveillance network. The rest includes abandoned satellites, spent rocket boosters, and other debris.

The United States owns more than 400 active satellites, just over 50 percent of all satellites. Russia and China have the second and third highest number of space assets, owning 89 and 35 satellites, respectively.

Civilian satellites, which perform tasks for the commercial, scientific, and government sectors, make up the majority of U.S. satellites. Russia's space assets are split nearly evenly between military and civil missions, though there are not separate military and civilian space programs. Only a very small percentage of other countries' satellites are military in nature.

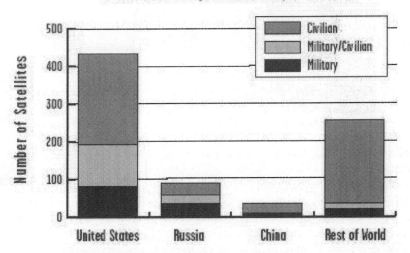

Approximately two-thirds of all active satellites are used for communications. Satellites for navigation, military surveillance, Earth observation and remote sensing, astrophysics and space physics, and Earth science and meteorology missions each comprise about five to seven percent of total satellites.

Satellite Missions

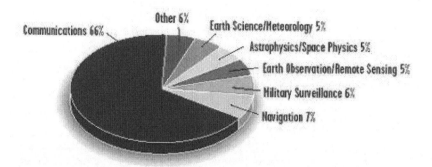

Satellites orbit Earth in several distinct regions of space:

• Low Earth orbits (LEO) – about 50 to 1,243 miles above Earth. This includes military intelligence satellites and weather satellites.

• Geosynchronous orbits (GEO) – 22,370 miles above Earth. This includes commercial and military communications satellites, satellites providing early warning of ballistic missile launch.

• Medium Earth orbits (MEO) – between LEO and GEO. This includes navigation satellites (Navstar, Glonass).

• Molniya orbit – a highly elliptical orbit with a 12-hour period. This includes communication satellites for regions near the North Pole.

• Orbital Debris – is any human-made object in orbit that no longer serves a useful purpose, including discarded equipment, abandoned satellites, bolts and other hardware released during satellite deployment, and particles from explosions or collisions.

The table below gives current estimates of orbital debris in three size categories. As the table shows, approximately 40 percent of all orbital debris larger than one millimeter in size is in LEO. Large numbers of naturally occurring particles (meteoroids) add to the total number of orbital objects less than one centimeter in size, but are not included in this table.

Estimates of Orbital Debris			
Average Size	1 mm - 1 cm	1 cm - 10 cm	> 10 cm
Pieces of LEO debris	140,000,000	180,000	9,700
Total pieces of debris	330,000,000	560,000	18,000
Source: Klinkrad, H. 2006. Space debris: Models and risk analysis. Berlin: Springer Praxis, 96.			

So, what is John Walson videotaping with his proprietary telescope videocam technique? Are these just satellites and space junk? Or are we seeing large and very advanced spacecraft for the first time that we aren't supposed to see?

Walson received the following comment about one of the videos. Does it answer all the questions? No, but perhaps some of them.

"Hello again. And, again, my congratulations on your superb astrophotography. MIT Lincoln Laboratory is the group which has built some of the things you are seeing. Much of what they do is what used to be the Star Wars project, which no doubt involves some of your objects."

Maybe some of Walson's images are of sensitive, secret U.S. military Star Wars machines and maybe even classified, secret weapons platforms in space, which the U.S. military has been rumored to have for at least 20 years.

Also remember the UK hacker Gary McKinnon, who got into the Pentagon database in 2001-02 and discovered a secret U.S. Navy file titled "Non-Terrestrial Officers". McKinnon now faces a life sentence in a U.S. prison for hacking into those Pentagon files.

Judging by the following photos taken by Walson at his home, it is clear that he has ventured into territory that is disconcerting to some government or military agencies who don't approve of him videotaping these large, mysterious orbiting machines. The result of Walson's investigation was the almost immediate startup of routine visits from numerous unmarked large helicopters which began regular day and night visits to his home. This included a twin-rotor Chinook passing directly over the roof of his home and a tree in his backyard (photo below). There are many other photos of helicopters flying over his home in addition to these. This demonstrates how serious these flights were and how clear the message was intended to be.

In addition to discovering and refining his optical telescope videotaping technique, Walson has also discovered how to actually hear and record the sounds in real time coming from the particular craft he is videotaping. By carefully aligning a satellite dish receiver with his telescope, he has been able to record some very unusual and intriguing sounds from the different spacecraft.

In summary, what you have seen are spacecraft parked or stationed in orbit above the Earth. It's clear the major space powers are far more heavily-invested in space than they will admit. As a reflection of that reality, there has been a lot of recent talk about anti-satellite weapons needed by competing countries to protect themselves. Most recently, China has been discussing its anti-satellite programs and even threatened to destroy or disable all GPS satellites which overfly Chinese territory.

It's anyone's guess how many billions the U.S. military and government have invested in black operations secret spying and surveillance programs, and military space weapons systems over the decades. John Walson's video images and sounds may well show some of these advanced machines. It is also within the realm of possibility some of these items might be products of non-human intelligence. Following are more examples of Walson's mysterious orbiting machines to consider.

This video freeze frame is of a sunlit spacecraft shown at the top of the picture. Below it is a second craft which happened to pass by at an extremely high rate of speed.

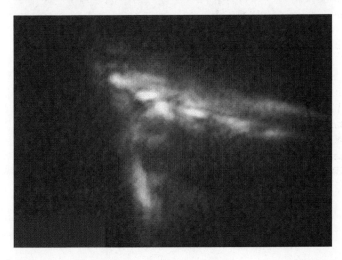

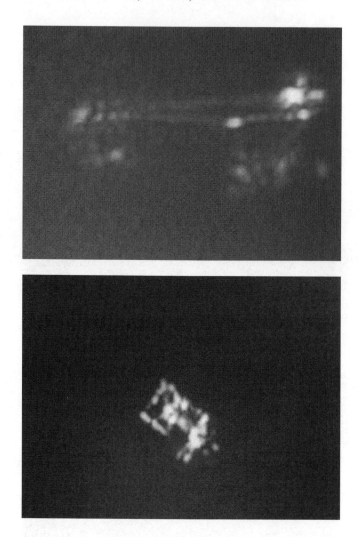

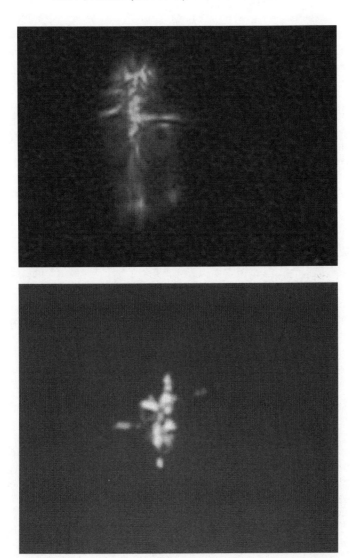

John Walson proceeded to post these images on a NASA spacecraft forum and simply asked if anyone could identify these spacecraft. Shortly thereafter NASA removed all traces of his images, and then deleted his posts. The reason given by NASA was that their forum does not tolerate anything to do with UFOs. However, there was no mention of UFOs in Walson's posting, he merely wanted them identified. So it can only be assumed that NASA themselves believed these objects to be UFOs and classified them as such.

The reason I believe that, at least, some the objects Walson videotaped in Earth orbit belonged to a top secret space program is because of the amount of attention given to his work by U.S. authorities.

Why such an avid interest by the U.S. military in the research by a relative "nobody"? What would be the reason for such a blatant act of intimidation? If Walson was simply making up this story then there would be nothing to fear – he would eventually be proven to be a liar and fraud.

Dispatching on ongoing barrage of military helicopters to his residence only lends credence to his story. It makes it more authentic, genuine and likely that he stumbled onto something that the U.S. government didn't want him or anyone else knowing about. If these videos were a hoax why care? If these objects in Earth orbit which he videotaped were alien in nature why care? On the other hand if they were of Earthly origin – top secret back projects whose technology was derived from reverse-engineered extraterrestrial spacecraft and hardware, then there would be a legitimate reason for such a concern by the military.

There are far too many examples and photographic evidence of unidentified spacecraft in low Earth orbit to list in this book. I have only included a select few accounts.

If the spacecraft and machines shown in this photographic evidence do not belong to us then why are they there? Where are they from?

After examining this evidence the only question that remains is: how many of these spacecraft are ours and how many are theirs?

NASA Mission Transmissions

Images taken from STS-48 (September 1991) from the Space Shuttle Discovery, revealed some kind of anomalous vehicles performing physics-defying anti-gravity maneuvers in Earth orbit. The NASA transmissions also show what appears to be use of ultra-high tech weapons against these same vehicles.

On September 15, 1991, between 20:30 and 20:45 GMT, the television camera located at the back of Space Shuttle Discovery's cargo bay was focused on the Earth's horizon while the astronauts were occupied with other tasks.

A glowing object suddenly appeared just below the horizon and slowly moved from right to left and slightly upward in the picture. Several other glowing objects had been visible before this, and had been moving in various directions. Then a flash of light appeared at the lower left of the screen and the main object, along with the others, changed direction and accelerated away sharply, as if in response to the flash. Shortly thereafter a streak of light moved through the region vacated by the main object, and then another streak moved through the right of the screen, where two of the other objects had been. Roughly 65 seconds after the main flash, the TV camera rotated down, showing a fuzzy picture of the side of the cargo bay. It then refocused, turned toward the front of the cargo bay, and stopped broadcasting.

A Columbia shuttle mission, half a decade later STS-80 (December 1996) revealed similar vehicles performing even more extraordinary orbital maneuvers before the Columbia's cameras climaxing at sunrise with an eerie image of an anomalous craft hanging directly against the constellation of Orion.

These two officially televised NASA shuttle transmissions were shown live to millions. They observed strange spacecraft performing unbelievable maneuvers in Earth orbit as the Space Shuttle crews amazingly looked on.

STS-82 had a similar close encounter with a strange spacecraft in February 1997. A strange conversation took place between STS-82 shuttle crew members. At one point during the mission a crew member remarked, "I wonder if they're taking pictures?" as the mysterious object/craft passes in front of them. Strangely enough there is a 20 minute gap in the NASA tapes from this mission where the astronaut's comments were supposed to appear. Hmmm!!! Am I the only one who senses that something isn't right here?

STS-82 was a Hubble Space Telescope servicing mission by Space Shuttle Discovery. The mission launched from Kennedy Space Center, Florida, on February 11, 1997 and returned to Earth on February 21, 1997.

Things were going well, in fact by early on the morning of February 18th. The fifth EVA (extravehicular activity) of the mission had been completed, astronauts Mark Lee and Steve Smith were climbing back into the airlock, securing the thermal cover and preparing to switch to orbiter back up systems while they waited to hear from MCC (Mission Control Center) if their job was completed, or another space-walk would be needed.

The time was 06-39 GMT. On screen was a view of the control room. Everyone seemed to be winding down for the evening (it was after midnight in the United States). The audio link to the two crew members had been left open.

Suddenly, one of the crew helmet microphones crackled into life and the tone of the voice caught the attention of listeners. This was the conversation:

Conversation starts at 06 hr 39 min 44s February 18th
"What was that flash?"
"I don't know"
"That light flashed possibly just here.....and again" (Laughs)
"...I see it"
"I just thought it was my imagination"
"I saw it too...so its not...there was two of 'em"
"There's another one...what are they?"
 (11 second silence)
"I just saw the lights flickering in here"
"I wonder if they're taking pictures?"
"What is that?"

"This thing passed (flashed?) in front of us"
"Where are the lights?" A third crew member.
"Which ones?"
"I dipped surveillance for a second, but I had that one the whole time"
"Yeah, I got that one too!"
Conversation ends at 06 hr 41 min 09s
NASA CUTS LINK

Astronauts Lee and Smith certainly seemed excited by what they had seen. At one stage, at least one other crew member, located on the flight deck, joins in. The video link from the satellite was cut, and the transmission closed down. However, according to one International News Agency the main link from NASA remained open for some time after the conversation, but no further reference made to the event.

In fact a few minutes later MCC started to go through normal "housekeeping" items. The sixth EVA never took place. NASA decided to bring the crew members back in.

By any standards, this was quite an unusual exchange.

When asked to comment NASA issued the following reply: "It could have been any number of devices or indicators on the Hubble or their suits. There were no reports of any kind related to UFOs on the STS-82 mission." This is a strange answer because in the original question there was no mention made of UFOs. The original question asked was if anyone could explain what the crew was referring to in their conversation.

An intensive investigation followed.

Space debris was one possibility. An investigation was conducted by an expert in the field to check out all known orbiting objects, since there was an exact time to work with. However, he came up with nothing passing closer than 45 miles, having checked over 8,000 possible targets tracked by NORAD.

Apart from listed items there are thousands of smaller pieces of space debris which are tracked by Space Command. Some hours before, the Shuttle was rumored to have adjusted its orbit to avoid debris from an earlier Pegasus launch.

Mission Control is in regular contact with Space Command Centre in order to provide early warning of any possible orbit conflicts.

It is possible that a cluster of unlisted, small particles, passed very close to Discovery. If they had been "tumbling" as they passed by, they would have reflected sunlight and possibly caused a flashing effect.

This of course raises the issue that such an incident could have been catastrophic had a collision occurred, and would highlight a weakness in the orbital warning system.

The incident has been investigated by a number of television companies, one of which actually interviewed one of the crew members involved. Unfortunately, he could not recall the event and was unable (or unwilling) to shed any light on the matter.

More recently, a well respected U.S. researcher with access to NASA archives has painstakingly went through all the video records, optimistic that he would find mention of the event. He spent many hours reviewing the mission schedules but was unable to come up with anything.

A (Freedom of Information Act) FOIA request for copies of telemetry data is being considered. That might tells us if any of the instruments on board Discovery failed, or showed any anomalies during the time period.

It seems that NASA's own records have a 20 minute gap around the time of the conversation. There's nothing sinister about this.

Regardless of who possesses this extraordinary technological capability (us or them), the power of this anti-gravity engineering staggers the imagination.

STS-75 was a Columbia Space Shuttle mission that launched in February 1996. The primary objective of the mission was to carry the Tethered Satellite System Reflight into orbit and to deploy it spaceward on a conducting tether. The tether system would be placed within the rarefied electrically charged layer of the atmosphere known as the ionosphere. The conducting tether is supposed to generate high voltage and electrical currents as it moves through the ionosphere across the magnetic field lines of the Earth. It was a breakthrough energy experiment.

In the middle of the project a problem occurred and the tether became overloaded with over ten times the anticipated amount of energy. The tether conductor cable broke separating it from the Space Shuttle. As the cable was floating out into space it was being filmed by the astronauts and was suddenly swarmed by dozens of unidentified flying objects. This video is widely considered the best proof of the existence of extraterrestrial life. It can't be explained by any scientist or video specialist.

Strange lights were also shown on a NASA live broadcast flying near STS-135 (ISS assembly flight ULF7) during the final mission of the American Space Shuttle aboard Atlantis. The mission launched on July 8, 2011.

On March, 13, 1989 the Space Shuttle Discovery was launched. Just 20 hours and 45 minutes into the mission at 0642 hrs EST, the following message was heard from a Discovery crew member.

"Houston, this is Discovery, we still have the alien spacecraft under observance."

The message was recorded by Donald Ratsch in Baltimore, Maryland. He is a member of the Goddard Amateur Radio Club, which monitors all NASA space flights.

Before this amazing message an amateur radio enthusiast in Ohio stated that the crew of the Shuttle told Houston Mission Control that there was something wrong, "We have a fire". It is thought that this was a code word for UFO and would alert NASA that the Shuttle had a problem.

Straight after the transmission it is alleged by another radio enthusiast, Mr. Oechsler, that NASA instructed the crew to switch frequencies to a secure mode.

The incident was reported by the media and the tape played on LBC (London Broadcasting Company).

For some time NASA denied that the actual message was transmitted from a Shuttle mission. However, NASA spokesman James Hatfield has since stated that the tape is genuine but the incident was a joke on the part of the astronaut.

What a ridiculous cover story. Are we now to believe that our trained scientists/astronauts are auditioning to become comedians? Is this where our taxpayer's money is going? When you listen to the tape you'll understand why no one felt there was any sense of humor in the astronaut's voice. It appeared quite a serious matter at the time. Furthermore, no American would use the phrase, "under observance". It is strange and highly unusual language for anyone to use, let alone an astronaut describing something. Did it really contain a report of an alien encounter? What did he really say?

In addition to the encounters described above, there have been numerous others documented by Apollo missions traveling to the Moon and even some Gemini missions which preceded the Apollo program. Some of these include Gemini IX, Apollo 11, 13, 15, and 16.

Astronauts aboard NASA space missions are unquestionably seeing some kind of non-conventional spacecraft. These craft are not behaving in a hostile manner. If fact, they have been of assistance in aiding some NASA missions which have developed problems. Either these spacecraft are extraterrestrial in nature or part of a secret space program being operated here on Earth. There can be no other explanation.

NASA Decline and Anti-gravity Space Fleet

Just one day after the successful landing of the final Space Shuttle mission on July 22, 2011 NASA announced that it was issuing layoff notices to about 3,200 contractors.

The shuttle program ended when the shuttle Atlantis and its crew of four astronauts landed at NASA's Kennedy Space Center on July 21, capping a 13-day delivery flight to the International Space Station (ISS). The mission was NASA's 135th shuttle flight and the last hurrah of the 30-year space plane program.

With the shuttles grounded and headed for museums, this big round of layoffs would significantly reduce the shuttle workforce, which was 6,700 personnel at the time.

In April 2011, the United Space Alliance, the contractor responsible for most of the work to maintain the space shuttles, announced that it would layoff nearly half of its 5,600 employees. At the time, United Space Alliance estimated that between 2,600 to 2,800 people would lose their jobs, due to the completion of tasks related to day-to-day operations of the shuttle fleet, according to a statement from the contractor.

Similarly, positions have been eliminated at companies like Lockheed Martin Space System and Boeing. Internally, NASA flight directors, who oversee ground teams in Mission Control, are also facing a time of transition.

Major decisions have been taken to lay off personnel and the Space Shuttle is now retired despite a Congressional request to consider ways to extend the Shuttle service life. Also, NASA managers have decided to trim the crew capsule of the Constellation Project – the Space Shuttle's replacement – from six to four. The Constellation aims to take astronauts to the Moon and Mars, and service the International Space Station (ISS).

There has been a steady decline in NASA's budget in real terms since the end of the Apollo missions in the early 1970s. NASA's decline is inevitable. If whistleblower reports are accurate, then NASA is little more than a cover for a highly classified anti-gravity space fleet that regularly takes hundreds of military astronauts into space. The alleged name of this secret project is "Solar Warden". Not everything is, as it seems.

President Ronald Reagan alluded to a highly classified space fleet in the June 11, 1985 entry in his diaries where he revealed that "our shuttle capacity is such that we could orbit 300 people." A succession of whistleblowers and aeronautical experts have come forward to reveal various details of advanced anti-gravity technologies that can, in the words of Ben Rich (former Lockheed Skunkworks CEO) "take ET home."

If Reagan's comments and whistleblower testimonies are correct, then the operational home of this secret anti-gravity space fleet is U.S. Strategic Command. The project name of the classified space fleet, according to several whistleblowers is "Solar Warden". The existence of Solar Warden, if true, proves that NASA is a cover program using antiquated rocket propulsion technologies. If so, the futuristic Constellation Program aimed to take astronauts to the Moon and Mars is a cover for an existing space program that regularly flies interplanetary missions using advanced anti-gravity propulsion technologies.

The first reference to Solar Warden occurred in March 2006. A reliable source revealed its existence and capacities and that all space programs are a cover that exists to deceive the people of this world. There were, as of 2005, eight ships, an equivalent to aircraft carriers and forty-three "protectors," which are space planes. One was lost recently to an accident in Mars orbit while it was attempting to re-supply the multinational colony located on Mars. This base was established in 1964 by joint American and Soviet teamwork. The technology to build these vessels came from back-engineering alien disc wreckages that have crashed on Earth, and at times with alien assistance. This reverse engineering is funded through a "black budget" allowing NASA be a cover for the general public.

Another source describing Solar Warden is an anonymous whistleblower known as Henry Deacon who works at Laurence Livermore laboratories as a physicist. Deacon confirmed the existence of a large manned base on Mars, supplied through an alternative space fleet (code named SOLAR WARDEN).

According to William Arkin's manual for military code names which designates specific two letter alphabetical sequences to distinct U.S. military projects, Solar Warden falls into a Joint Forces Command project. This suggests Solar Warden is operationally located within Strategic Command.

If Solar Warden has been successful in establishing a Mars colony using anti-gravity propulsion systems, then this might explain why anti-gravity research became highly classified in the mid-1950s. It also would explain why civilian researchers who successfully replicated anti-gravity technologies were ruthlessly suppressed as occurred to Otis Carr in 1961. This suppression was revealed for the first time in 2007 through the testimony of Carr's former protégé, Ralph Ring.

The fleet of spaceships in the Solar Warden program is alleged to have visited all the planets in our Solar System, except for Mercury. We have landed on Pluto and a few moons. These ships contain personnel from many countries and each person has sworn an oath.

Now a respected UFO researcher from the United Kingdom, Darren Perks, claims to have received the following email from the DOD (Department of Defense) under the freedom of information act on the matter:

> "About an hour ago I spoke to a NASA representative who confirmed this was their program and that it was terminated by the President. He also informed me that it was not a joint program with the DOD. The NASA representative informed me that you should be directed to the Johnson Space Center FOIA Manager. I have run your request through one of our space-related directorates and I'm waiting on one other division with the Command to respond back to me. I will contact you once I have a response from the other division. Did NASA refer you to us?"

With the reality of Solar Warden allegedly confirmed further credibility was given to the accounts of individuals by Laura Eisenhower, great-granddaughter of Ike, who admits to having knowledge of a colony on Mars and other secret NASA projects.

It is understandable why the U.S. so quickly was able to ramp up their conventional space program during the 1960s to meet President Kennedy's objective of "landing a man on the Moon during that decade". They no doubt borrowed or relied on technology drawn from the secret space program, which was under the control of the U.S. military.

A growing number of whistleblower and expert testimonies point to the existence of a highly classified anti-gravity space program that can place hundreds of military astronauts into space. NASA's steady decline since its Apollo heyday has nothing to do with the competence and expertise of NASA personnel.

The political reality is that highly compartmentalized military programs prevent advanced anti-gravity technologies into the public sector for commercial application. NASA's new futuristic Constellation Program, based as it is on antiquated rocket propulsion technologies from the 1940s, is a cover program and does not deserve to be funded. Instead, U.S. military and corporate projects involving advanced anti-gravity technologies and the means by which these were acquired need to be exposed to the public.

Now, as fantastic as this story is could it be credible? Indeed, what if our government found an alien craft? If so, certainly, you can't tell me that they wouldn't try to reverse engineer it. As a tax paying citizen I would be disappointed if they didn't try to do that. So, a crashed alien spacecraft, held by the government, and reverse-engineered is entirely within the realm of possibility.

Next is the idea that NASA's decline is also tied to all of this. Is that plausible or credible? It is certainly plausible. But, the best hoaxes and storytellers are plausible too. Truth has strange company. But, just imagine for a second that this is true.

If it is true then, the Moon missions were a deception (even if they occurred as promoted); every planetary mission and launch nothing more than a fraud; Skylab a fraud; the Space Telescope Hubble a fraud; the entire NASA budget a fraud; the entire government budget a fraud; every government official who knew of all this a fraud; truthfulness from the government a fraud; and last but certainly not least the deaths in the "official" space program totally needless.

If true, how much has all this cost? What benefits has it brought? What else is being funded through "black budgets"? Are we any safer from the aliens because of it? And do we really need protection from the aliens? Don't you think that they would have wiped us out with their superior technology by now, if they really wanted to?

Advanced Anti-gravity Aerospace Craft

Dr. Richard Boylan provides a well reasoned appraisal of the anti-gravity craft possessed by the U.S. military. Dr. Boylan cites a number of whistleblower sources to build an overview of the anti-gravity craft developed by various U.S. military contractors as a result of reverse-engineered recovered extraterrestrial vehicles.

It's worth keeping in mind that Boylan is certainly correct in his main thesis that military contractors have been working on advanced craft based on extraterrestrial technologies covertly supplied to them.

This should come as no surprise based on what Col. Philip Corso revealed in terms of his involvement in U.S. Army efforts to pass on extraterrestrial technologies to civilian industries from the Roswell wreckage available in his filing cabinet. Of course, the scraps of ET material in Corso's filing cabinet pales in comparison with the actual craft retrieved by elite UFO retrieval units on many occasions as whistleblowers such as Sgt. Clifford Stone claim.

While the details of each covert program cited by Boylan may be called into question due to the inherent problem in whistleblower testimonies that may be seeded with disinformation, his basic premise and overview appears well thought through. Boylan's research reveals that space-based weapons systems already exist and have been used for several decades.

This suggests that the Strategic Defense Initiative (SDI) is just a cover for a covert weapons program that has been underway for some time and has already been deployed. SDI therefore may be little more than an effort to take space-based weapons systems out of the "black world" of illicit black budget funding, into the "white world" of congressionally approved Special Access Programs that can be funded by federal appropriations. This allows the black budget funds raised through illicit sources that previously funded these covert programs to be earmarked for other "urgent" purposes.

This suggests that efforts to prevent the weaponization of space need to consider the covert programs already deployed and the need of military policy makers to get some of these into the 'white world' in order to gain Congressional funding for other 'black projects'. The proper focus should therefore be on making transparent the space weapons systems currently deployed, and to have some accountability process for the deployment and use of such weapons systems by Congressional committees. Turning back the covert deployment of space-based weapons is a much more difficult challenge than preventing their initial deployment which has already occurred.

Furthermore, the targeting of extraterrestrial vehicles by exotic weapons systems is certainly a major cause for concern as Boylan points out. However, as influential insiders such as Col. Philip Corso have indicated, there is genuine military concern over extraterrestrial violations of national sovereignty and human rights.

This has led to Corso and others supporting the deployment of such space based weapons systems. Consequently, there is great work to be done in bridging genuine military concerns over intrusive extraterrestrial activities, and military practices of targeting extraterrestrial vehicles with exotic weapons systems.

Mounting evidence has shown that it is apparent the American government is in possession of advanced extraterrestrial technology.

There are accounts from hundreds of individuals who have experienced encounters and gone public with the information they possess. This includes information about advanced U.S. craft, either by reason of being told such things by the extraterrestrial visitors, or by being abducted by rogue military-intelligence units and taken aboard one of these craft and taken to one of these installations, or viewed such craft once they arrived.

Inside sources and informants do not pretend to know everything that is in the American aerospace arsenal, nor everything about the operations and capabilities of the high-tech spacecraft that are about to be identified.

At this time there exists ten kinds of special-technology advanced aerospace platforms (military language for craft), all incorporating anti-gravity technology of some form.

These ten are:

• Northrop Grumman B-2 Spirit Stealth Bomber
• Aurora SR-33A
• Lockheed-Martin's X-33A
• Boeing and Airbus Industries' Nautilus
• TR-3A Pumpkinseed
• TR-3B Triangle
• Northrop's Great Pumpkin disc
• Teledyne Ryan Aeronautical's XH-75D
• Shark antigravity helicopter
• Lockheed-Martin and Northrop's jointly-developed TAW-50 hypersonic anti-gravity fighter-bomber

Before we examine these ten exotic aerospace craft, a brief overview of the different forms of generating anti-gravity fields is in order.

The most primitive antigravity technology is electrogravitic. This involves using voltages in the millions of volts to disrupt the ambient gravitational field. This results in an 89 percent reduction in gravity's hold on airframes in such vehicles as the B-2 Stealth Bomber and the TR-3B Astra triangular craft. And given the considerable ambient ionization field observed around the X-22A, it is reasonable to assume that extreme-voltage electrogravitics is also employed with these craft.

The next level up of sophistication is magnetogravitic. This involves generating high-energy toroidal fields spun at incredible rpm's, which also disrupts the ambient gravitational field to the extent that a counterforce to Earth's gravitational pull is generated. The early British aeronautical engineers called this dynamic "counterbary". This may have been used in some earlier American saucers and prototypes, but the secret Nautilus space-faring craft uses magnetic pulsing, which appears to utilize this technology.

The third level of sophistication that is used in the more modern American anti-gravity craft is direct generation and harnessing of the gravitational strong force. Such a strong force field extends slightly beyond the atomic nucleus of Element 115, an exotic element provided by extraterrestrial scientist-consultants to human scientists at S-4, a secret base south of Area 51. By amplifying that exposed gravitational strong force, and using antimatter reactor high energy, and then directing it, it is possible to lift a craft from the Earth and then change directions by vectoring the shaped anti-gravity force field thus generated.

Let us now examine these 10 advanced craft in more detail. The amount of information available for each varies. In some cases more is known, in other cases very little.

1) The B-2 Stealth bomber by Northrop-Grumman

The Air Force describes it as a low-observable, strategic, long-range heavy bomber capable of penetrating sophisticated and dense air-defense shields.

Retired Air Force Colonel Donald Ware passed on information from a three-star general he knows, who revealed to him that the B-2 Stealth bombers have electrogravitic systems on board. This explains why the 21 Northrop B-2s cost about a billion dollars each.

2) The Aurora SR-33A is a moderate-sized space-faring vehicle

The late National Security Council scientist Dr. Michael Wolf of NSC's unacknowledged Special Studies Group subcommittee, (formerly MJ-12), has stated that the Aurora can operate on both conventional fuel and anti-gravity field propulsion systems.

He further stated that the Aurora is capable of traveling to the Moon. Wolf had also disclosed that the U.S. has a small station on the Moon, and an observation post on Mars.

It is unlikely that Dr. Wolf would characterize the Aurora thus, unless it was a vessel already used in making such trips. He disclosed additionally that the Aurora operates out of Area 51, (Groom Dry Lake Air Force Station), at the northeast corner of the Nellis AFB Range, north of Las Vegas, Nevada.

3) The Lockheed-Martin X-33A military space plane

Is a prototype of Lockheed's other space plane, the single-stage-to-orbit reusable aerospace vehicle, the National Space Plane.

Lockheed-Martin does not say too much about its winged, delta-shape X-33 VentureStar, except to say that we are building it. To be at that stage of development for its public-program Space Plane, clearly Lockheed-Martin has already long since built prototypes, as well as an unacknowledged military version, which is dubbed the X-33A. The 'A' suffix stands for anti-gravity.

Colonel Donald Ware, USAF (ret.) revealed that he had learned from a three-star General that the VentureStar X-33 has an electrogravitics (anti-gravity) system on board. This virtually assures that the unacknowledged military anti-gravity version, the X-33 A, must surely also have electrogravitics on board. It is possible that what is called the X-33A is the Aurora craft which Dr. Wolf described.

4) The Lockheed X-22A is a two-man antigravity disc fighter

The late Colonel Steve Wilson, USAF (ret.), stated that military astronauts trained at a secret aerospace academy separate from the regular Air Force Academy at Colorado Springs, CO.

These military astronauts then operate out of Beale and Vandenberg Air Force Bases, in California. From those bases, these military astronauts regularly fly trans-atmospherically and out into space. One of the aerospace craft they use, Colonel Wilson reported, is the X-22A.

One informant, 'Z', aka "Jesse", who formerly worked at the National Security Agency (NSA), explained that the Lockheed X-22A antigravity fighter disc fleet is equipped with Neutral Particle Beam directed-energy weapons, that it is capable of effecting optical as well as radar invisibility, and that it is deployable for worldwide military operations from the new U.S. Space Warfare Headquarters, located in hardened underground facilities beneath 13,528-foot King's Peak in the Wasatch Mountains, 80 miles east of Salt Lake City, Utah.

An Army engineer, formerly associated with NASA, has confirmed that Lockheed had made the X-22A, the two-man anti-gravity fighter disc which has been seen test-flown in a canyon adjacent to the main Area 51 operations zone.

He explained why the X-22A is so nervously flown during test flights. He said that the original X-22A had a standard altimeter hard-wired into it, but that such an instrument would give faulty readings in the craft's anti-gravity field, which bends space-time. He had recommended that they instead use a gradiometer, which would function better.

Apparently his suggestion was finally taken up, since in more recent years the X-22As have been flying more smoothly and confidently at high altitudes over and near Area 51.

Another informant who wishes his identity kept private related operational details about military deployment of anti-gravity disc craft which sound like the X-22A. He reported that during Operation Desert Storm Iraq was pumped up and confident, since they had well over 50,000 troops ready to attack the Americans, and since the U.S. only had about 3,500 they knew that, because of the close proximity of troops the U.S. couldn't nuke them, so they were assuming an easy victory. Wrong.

Two photographs which this informant provided shows:

• a large disc-shaped craft slightly in front of American troops with a high intensity beam of light emitting out of it; then,
• where men, equipment, etc. had stood, there only remained dark charcoal-like spots on the desert floor. We have had this technology for quite a while.

The described disc was clearly an anti-gravity, levitating, aerial-weapons platform in the U.S. arsenal. Quite possibly it was the Lockheed X-22A two-man discoid craft, the real DarkStar, of which the unmanned drone X-22 DarkStar is but an aircraft "cover" program to disguise the existence of this manned anti-gravity fighter disc, the X-22A.

Further, as 'Z' noted, the real manned discs come equipped with the latest Neutral Particle Beam weapons, which take apart the target at the molecular level. Extraterrestrial craft do not incinerate humans. Only human military fighters are so deployed. So the above report does not deal with any extraterrestrial event.

5) The Nautilus is another space-faring craft

A secret military spacecraft which operates by magnetic pulsing.

It operates out of the unacknowledged new headquarters of the U.S. Space Command, deep under a mountain in Utah. It makes twice-a-week trips up to the secret military-intelligence space station, which has been in deep space for the past 30 years, and manned by U.S. and Russian military astronauts. The Nautilus also is used for superfast surveillance operations, utilizing its ability to penetrate target country airspace from above deep space, a direction not usually expected.

It is manufactured jointly by Boeing's Phantom Works near Seattle and EU's Airbus Industries Anglo-French consortium. A former Boeing executive who worked in their Phantom Works, Boeing's black projects division, (the equivalent of Lockheed's Skunkworks) confirmed that Boeing had teamed up with Europe's Airbus Industrie to manufacture the Nautilus.

6) The TR-3A "Pumpkinseed" is a super-fast air vehicle

The "Pumpkinseed" nickname is a reference to its thin oval airframe, whose contours resemble that seed.

It may be the craft identified as using pulse detonation technology for propulsion in a sub-hypersonic regime, and also uses anti-gravity technology for either mass-reduction or complementary field propulsion at higher speed levels.

As air breathers, these Pulse Detonation Wave Engines (PDWEs) could theoretically propel a hypersonic aircraft towards Mach-10 at an altitude in excess of 180,000 feet. Used to power a trans-atmospheric vehicle, the same PDWEs might be capable of lifting the craft to the edge of space when switched to rocket mode.

7) The TR-3B 'Astra'

A large triangular anti-gravity craft within the U.S. Space Fleet. Black projects defense industry insider Edgar Rothschild Fouche wrote about the existence of the TR-3B in his book, *Alien Rapture*.

Among the exotic space capable craft that may well be ferrying military personnel between the Earth and Lunar bases is the TR-3B (photo below). The designation is not the official military name, but one that has been assigned to the mystery craft by aerospace insiders that have been kept out of the need-to-know loop.

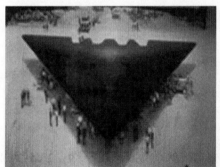

Alleged photo of TR-3B in staging hangar at Lockheed Skunkworks (left photo) and in flight (right photo).

The TR-3B has been seen by witnesses leaving or arriving at some USAF bases such as Scott Air Force base in Missouri and Wright-Patterson in Ohio.

The black, triangular shaped TR-3B was rarely mentioned – and then, only in hushed whispers – at the Groom Lake facility. The alien-looking craft has flown over the Groom Lake runway in complete silence and magically stopped above Area S-4. It hovered silently in the same position, for about 10 minutes, before gently settling vertically to the tarmac. At times a corona of silver blue light glowed around the circumference of the massive TR-3B. The operational model is 600 feet across.

The TR-3B is code named 'Astra'. The tactical reconnaissance TR-3B first operational flight was in the early 1990s. The triangular shaped nuclear powered aerospace platform was developed under the top secret, Aurora Program with SDI and black budget funds. At least three of the billion dollar plus TR-3Bs were flying by 1994. The Aurora is the most classified aerospace development program in existence.

The TR-3B is the most exotic vehicle created by the Aurora Program. It is funded and operationally tasked by the National Reconnaissance Office (NRO), the NSA, and the CIA. The TR-3B flying triangle is not fiction and was built with technology available in the mid 1980s. Not every UFO spotted in the skies belongs to them.

The TR-3B vehicles outer coating is reactive to electrical radar stimulation and can change reflectiveness, radar absorptiveness, and color. This polymer skin, when used in conjunction with the TR-3Bs Electronic Counter Measures and, ECCM, can make the vehicle look like a small aircraft, or a flying cylinder – or even trick radar receivers into falsely detecting a variety of aircraft, no aircraft, or several aircraft at various locations. A circular, plasma filled accelerator ring called the Magnetic Field Disrupter, surrounds the rotatable crew compartment and is far ahead of any imaginable technology.

Sandia and Livermore laboratories developed the reverse engineered MFD technology. The government will go to any lengths to protect this technology. The plasma, mercury based, is pressurized at 250,000 atmospheres at a temperature of 150 degrees Kelvin and accelerated to 50,000 rpm to create super-conductive plasma with the resulting gravity disruption. The MFD generates a magnetic vortex field, which disrupts or neutralizes the effects of gravity on mass within proximity, by 89 percent.

Do not misunderstand. This is not anti-gravity. Anti-gravity provides a repulsive force that can be used for propulsion. The MFD creates a disruption of the Earth's gravitational field upon the mass within the circular accelerator. The mass of the circular accelerator and all mass within the accelerator, such as the crew capsule, avionics, MFD systems, fuels, crew environmental systems, and the nuclear reactor, are reduced by 89 percent. This causes the effect of making the vehicle extremely light and able to outperform and outmaneuver any craft yet constructed –except, of course, those UFOs we did not build.

The TR-3B is a high altitude, stealth, reconnaissance platform with an indefinite loiter time. Once you get it up there at speed, it doesn't take much propulsion to maintain altitude. At Groom Lake there have been rumors of a new element that acts as a catalyst to the plasma. With the vehicle mass reduced by 89 percent, the craft can travel at Mach-9 (6,840 mph), vertically or horizontally. Insider sources claim the performance is limited only to the stresses that the human pilots can endure, which is a lot considering along with the 89 percent reduction in mass, the G forces are also reduced by 89 percent. The Lockheed SR-71 Blackbird holds the official Air Speed Record for a manned air-breathing jet aircraft with a speed of 2,194 mph.

The TR-3Bs propulsion is provided by 3 multimode thrusters mounted at each bottom corner of the triangular platform. The TR-3 is a sub Mach-9 vehicle until it reaches altitudes above 120,000 feet – then we really don't have any idea what it is capable of. The 3 multimode rocket engines mounted under each corner of the craft use hydrogen or methane and oxygen as a propellant. In a liquid oxygen/hydrogen rocket system, 85 percent of the propellant mass is oxygen.

The nuclear thermal rocket engine uses a hydrogen propellant, augmented with oxygen for additional thrust. The reactor heats the liquid hydrogen and injects liquid oxygen in the supersonic nozzle, so that the hydrogen burns concurrently in the liquid oxygen afterburner. The multimode propulsion system can operate in the atmosphere, with thrust provided by the nuclear reactor, in the upper atmosphere, with hydrogen propulsion, and in orbit, with the combined hydrogen/oxygen propulsion.

What you have to remember is that the three rocket engines only have to propel 11 percent of the mass of the top secret TR-3B. The engines are reportedly built by Rockwell. Many sightings of triangular UFOs are not alien vehicles but the top secret TR-3B. The NSA, NRO, CIA, and USAF have been playing a shell game with aircraft nomenclature – creating the TR-3, modified to the TR-3A, the TR-3B, and the Tier 2, 3, and 4, with suffixes like "plus" or "minus" added on to confuse further the fact that each of these designators is a different aircraft and not the same aerospace vehicle. A TR-3B is as different from a TR-3A as a banana is from a grape. Some of these vehicles are manned and others are unmanned.

Ex-NSA informant, 'Z', also confirmed that the TR-3B is operational. TR-3B is the code name for what everyone on Earth has seen. It is a very large triangular-shaped re-entry vehicle with anti-gravity technology. It is what the November 2000 issue of *Popular Mechanics* identified as the Lenticular Reentry Vehicle, a nuclear-powered flying saucer, the first version of which went operational in 1962 (the version which *Popular Mechanics*).

It was used in Gulf War's early hours with electromagnetic-pulse/laser cannons. It literally sat mid-air, firing long, medium, and short range to take out antennas, towers, communications, air traffic control towers, TV dishes and centers, etc. For three hours, three TR-3B triangles just sat there blowing up everything in sight.

Then the Stealth fighters had fun for the rest of the day into the early evening next night. Then carpet bombing followed from high altitude B-52 Strato-Fortresses. They dumped all the old, aged Vietnam-era crap munitions. The TR-3B has been in testing since the 1960s. But it has only been perfected since 1992.

It is a good remake of what President Truman first saw, the Roswell semi-circular craft. It is compartmentalized, built by the Skunkworks (Lockheed-Martin's classified plant at Palmdale, CA) and Boeing (Phantom Works, Seattle). It is housed in Utah.

'Z' was reminding of his earlier revelation that the U.S. Space Command has located its prime headquarters and anti-gravity space-launch fleet facility beneath King Mountain, the tallest mountain in the Wasatch Range east of Salt Lake City, Utah.

8) Northrop Aircraft Corporation has manufactured its Northrop anti-gravity disc

Nicknamed the "Great Pumpkin" from its brilliant golden-orange glow. These craft were first seen operationally test-flown in 1992 above the Groom Range ridge line at Area 51, Nevada. Later these intensely burning-bright orange-gold craft were seen being test-flown 60 miles north of Los Angeles, in the Tehachapi Mountains east of Edwards Air Force Base.

There the Northrop has its secret saucer manufacturing works buried deep within the mountains. When energized these discs emit their characteristic intense glow. It is reasonable to assume that this is due to strong ionization, and that electrogravitics is the methodology of their field propulsion.

9) The XH-75D or XH Shark anti-gravity helicopter

Is manufactured by Teledyne Ryan Aeronautical Corporation of San Diego. USAF Colonel Steve Wilson reported that many of these XH-75Ds were assigned to the Delta/National Reconnaissance Organization Division which retrieves downed UFOs.

That Division is also implicated in mutilating cattle as a psychological warfare program on the American public, to try to get citizens to fear and hate extraterrestrials through assuming that aliens are the ones cutting up the cattle.

Colonel Wilson also leaked a drawing of the XH-75D Shark (see below).

10) The TAW-50 is a hypersonic, anti-gravity space fighter-bomber

A defense contractor leaked details of this U.S. advanced TAW-50 war craft. Developed during the early 1990s, the capabilities of this war-bird are mind-boggling. And the technology shows that the Defense Department did not fail to utilize what it learned combing through the wreckage of various UFO crashes.

The TAW-50 was jointly developed by the Lockheed-Martin Skunkworks (Palmdale-Helendale, CA) and Northrop undoubtedly at their undeclared Anthill facility within the Tehachapi Mountains, northwest of Lancaster, CA. Both companies have a history of development of secret anti-gravity craft at these Mojave Desert facilities.

The TAW-50 has speed capabilities well in excess of Mach-50, a number the contractor calls "a very conservative estimate". Its actual speed is classified. Since Mach-1 is approximately 748 mph, this means that the TAW-50 is capable of moving considerably faster than 38,000 mph. In comparison, the velocity required to escape

Earth's gravity is 25,000 mph. Therefore the TAW-50 is capable of going into space, and frequently does.

The TAW-50 has a SCRAM (supersonic ramjet) propulsion system for passing through the outer atmosphere. The TAW-50 utilizes electrogravitics to maintain its own artificial gravity while in weightless space, as well as to nullify the vehicle's mass during operations. The TAW-50's power supply is provided by a small nuclear power generator that the contractor said is Normal-Inert.

The contractor said that the space plane uses electromagnetoferrometric power generation by the immersion of pellets in heavy water (deuterium) and specially-designed coil superconductive magnets, which yield enormous amounts of free electrons when placed in an immersion which has been triggered into an oscillating field-state flux.

The TAW-50 has a crew of four. Nevertheless, the TAW-50 flies so fast that it requires computers to fly it. These were developed by American Computer Company, who derived them from its Valkyrie XB/9000 AI (artificial intelligence) Guidance series. They utilize a RISC Milspec Superchip. There are 180 of them in the flight control system, and 64 more in the weapons guidance system, the contractor reported.

It can carry a combined payload of glide bombs and a package of MIRV (Multiple Independently-targeted Reentry Vehicles (military language for a group of intercontinental ballistic missiles), each of which can seek out and strike a different target. The MIRV pack also contains reentry-capable balloon countermeasures to make it very difficult for laser and other defensive weapons to track down where the real MIRVs are and intercept them.

The TAW-50 is armed with its own Kill Laser system, which can track and destroy SAM (Surface-to-Air missiles), STTA (Surface-To-Trans-Atmosphere missiles), ATA (Air-To-Air missiles), and ATTA (Air-To-Trans-Atmospheric missiles). The TAW-50's killer lasers can also knock down high-performance fighter interceptors. The TAW's Kill Laser is much smaller than the earlier 1980s-era SDI (Star Wars program) models, and has a miniaturized cooling core and 500 times the wattage. The contractor said it uses a spontaneous nucleonic burst to trigger the laser effect.

In addition, the TAW-50 is armed with microsuperexplosive HyperDart missiles. These are just a little larger than ordinary aircraft cannon ammunition, but travel at hypersonic speed for up to three minutes, and have enormous explosive capability. One HyperDart can blow apart a MiG fighter anywhere within 20 feet of the HyperDart. The TAW-50 carries several hundred HyperDarts.

Because the TAW-50 is designed to operate in space, it has on board a two-day air supply. This air supply can be extended by using its scoop system and traveling into the upper atmosphere to harvest more oxygen. The contractor did not reveal the size of the space fighter-bomber except to say "it's a pretty big thing."

The performance of the TAW-50 makes it virtually impossible to defend against. It can hide in orbit many hundreds of miles into space, orbiting at times at 22,000 mph. Then, without warning, it can dive straight down through the atmosphere at over 38,000 miles per hour on an 80-degree attack vector, reverse direction within 150 feet of the ground with very little loss of motion and without a glide turn, and almost instantly go vertically straight up at over 38,000 mph until long after it leaves the atmosphere and resumes orbiting in space.

The contractor noted that those electrogravitics allow it to change its mass to almost nothing in a moment, and reverse direction in a second, increase its acceleration to so many times G (Earth's gravity) it's not funny, yet they are able to nearly nullify the G-force on the pilots.

The electrogravitics are fourth-generation, with the ability to bring it to a complete standstill in under 2 milliseconds, if need be, without crushing the pilots, and keep it there for quite some time. The contractor notes that it is far too fast for tracking radars. And besides, what military aims its radar straight up?

The TAW-50 can be re-fueled and re-armed in orbit by docking with the secret undeclared Military Space Station that sits in orbit. The entire re-fueling and re-arming procedure takes under 10 minutes. Who mans the gas pumps? Military astronauts trained at the Secret Air Force Academy, located in the hills immediately west of the official Air Force Academy at Colorado Springs, CO. These military astronauts rotate duty by traveling to and from Vandenberg Air Force Base on other military anti-gravity vehicles.

The Cape Canaveral Space Shuttles have carried the arming platforms (classified as Defense Department payloads) up to the secret Military Space Station. The contractor reported that with a few extra tanks of LOX (liquid oxygen), the TAW-50 could fly to the Moon and back.

As of 2002, the United States has 20 TAW-50s in its arsenal. But, as the contractor commented, "You could take out an entire nation in under 10 days with only 10 of these, doing three attacks a day."

One can wipe out an entire city the size of suburban Cleveland in a single attack without having to use any nukes at all.

The electrogravitics for the TAW-50 was produced by GE Radionics. Pratt & Whitney designed the SCRAM atmospheric penetrator technology. American Computer Company created the artificial-intelligence supercomputers.

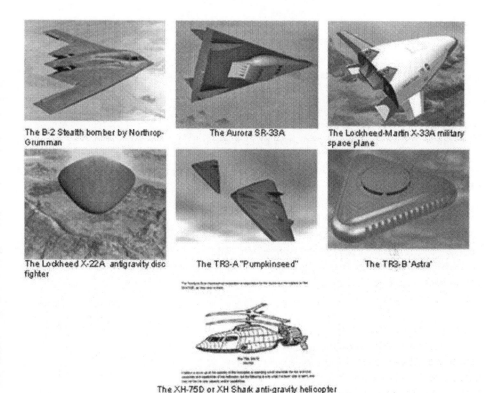

The B-2 Stealth bomber by Northrop-Grumman

The Aurora SR-33A

The Lockheed-Martin X-33A military space plane

The Lockheed X-22A antigravity disc fighter

The TR3-A "Pumpkinseed"

The TR3-B 'Astra'

The XH-75D or XH Shark anti-gravity helicopter

11) The Northrop Quantum Teleportation Disc?

Are the above the current state-of-the-art in advanced aerospace craft? No. There have been advances beyond mere anti-gravity field propulsion. Quantum particulate physics is now being used to update a variety of aerospace craft and their weapons systems.

In 1992, the Northrop disc slowly rose vertically from its flight pad and gradually reached flight altitude. But in 2005 these craft were able to depart from their flight pad and suddenly appear at flight altitude without any visible ascent. And it is not a matter of their ionization field having been turned off during ascent for stealth purposes.

The ionization field comes with electrogravitic field propulsion. If the ionization were turned off, the craft would have fallen from the sky. Rather what appears to be going on is that the Northrop engineers have incorporated quantum physics principles into the propulsion. Simply stated, Northrop appears to have harnessed quantum entanglement to achieve quantum teleportation. To the observer the craft simply ceases to exist on the flight pad and instantly begins to exist at, (in this case), an altitude of 1,000 feet.

If the interpretation of this observation is correct, then there exists an 11th entry in the U.S. anti-gravity arsenal, the Northrop Quantum Teleportation Disc.

If the black budget scientists keep advancing along these lines, we could foresee the day when a fleet of Air Force craft suddenly "cease to exist" on the air base runway and instantly appear at 35,000 feet altitude over a target city halfway around the globe.

The implications of the advanced anti-gravity craft back-engineered by humans are several. All of the anti-gravity technology is now in the control of the organization (satellite government) conducting the UFO cover-up.

According to Dr. Michael Wolf this breakaway organization has effective control of it. He should know. He was a high member of that Special Studies Group (formerly MJ-12), buried within the National Security Council.

As a result there remains a very high danger that they will use its growing anti-gravity fleet to try to repel the extraterrestrials and even conduct Space War. There are rumors that certain elements within the U.S. Air Force and the Naval Space Command are making preparations for such a Space War.

What can we do about this?

1. Develop a greater sense of self awareness and keep ourselves informed about the dangerous misuse of anti-gravity (and quantum) technology.

2. Contact our political representatives to express opposition to policies and weapons systems development that is oriented towards space warfare.

3. Encourage the release of this technology into the civilian sector, where it can revolutionize transportation, energy generation, large construction projects, and other peaceful uses.

4. Help to spread the word involving this worldwide cover-up and expose the perpetrators – those trying to monopolize the benefits of alien acquired technology.

Ultra-fast Military Vehicle Travels 13,000 mph

An experimental unmanned hypersonic glider was launched from Vandenberg Air Force Base 130 miles northwest of Los Angeles, according to the U.S. Defense Advanced Research Projects Agency (DARPA) who used Twitter to announce the launch Thursday, August 11, 2011.

The rocket-launched vehicle is part of an advanced weapons program, called Conventional Prompt Global Strike, which is working to develop systems of reaching an enemy target anywhere in the world within one hour.

A rocket carried the agency's Falcon Hypersonic Technology Vehicle-2 (HTV-2) to the edge of space, where it separated from the booster to maneuver through the atmosphere at 13,000 mph (Mach-20). Minutes into the flight, the agency said the mission was on track in its glide phase.

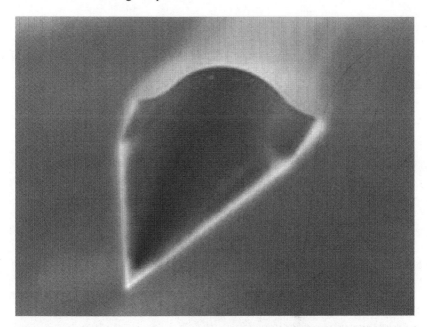

The Falcon hypersonic HTV-2 is an unmanned, rocket-launched, maneuverable aircraft that glides through the Earth's atmosphere at incredibly fast speeds.

HTV-2 crashed into the Pacific Ocean after a malfunction caused it to stop sending signals while flying at more than 20 times the speed of sound, military officials said. The vehicle plunged into the ocean after shifting into a mode that allows it to fly Mach-20, or about 13,000 mph. A similar vehicle was launched in 2010 and returned nine minutes of data before contact was prematurely lost.

The United States military is trying to develop technology to respond to threats around the globe at speeds of Mach-20 or greater (13,000 mph). At that speed a vehicle could fly from New York City to Los Angeles in 12 minutes.

Whenever you hear of such a story you should always approach it with guarded skepticism.

Firstly, ask yourself why the military would be releasing such information about classified projects. Could it be a scare tactic trying to intimidate the rest of the world into believing that the United States had highly advanced superior military technology? This might certainly act as a deterrent, if that was the intent. But isn't this releasing of classified information curious?

Secondly, you can guarantee that we are not being told the complete story. The HTV-2 mission may have been something completely different than what was publicly announced. Perhaps the vehicle was actually manned and not unmanned and the wreckage falling into the ocean was a piece of scrap junk planted and recovered by the military. Perhaps this mission involved a manned vehicle that was successfully launched into orbit. Perhaps the "crash into the ocean" was nothing more than a diversion to throw the media and those monitoring this project off the trail. For all we know this vehicle may not have crashed into the ocean at all. This misinformation press release may simply have been made to direct public interest/inquiry away from this project. Doesn't declaring this flight a failure take away much interest?

Black Budget Funding for Secret Space Program

Jane's Intelligence Briefing, 1997 – No. 1: The aero-diamond's aerospike engine and diamond platform could propel the craft to speeds of Mach-14.

The world knows about September 11, 2001, when the two World Trade towers melted down to New York City streets after terrorist-controlled airliners flew into them. The day before, on September 10, 2001, then Secretary of Defense, Donald Rumsfeld, declared his own war on the Pentagon bureaucracy for wasting so much unaccounted money. Rumsfeld said, "According to some estimates, we cannot track $2.3 trillion in transactions."

One of Rumsfeld's worried employees was Jim Minnery from the Defense Department's Finance and Accounting Service. He backed up Rumsfeld by saying, "We know the money is gone. But we don't know what they spent it on." Minnery, a former Marine turned whistleblower, risked his job by speaking out about millions of dollars missing from Department of Defense (DOD) balance sheets.

Twenty years earlier in the early 1980s, Department of Defense Analyst Franklin Spinney also made headlines exposing what he called "accounting games in which the books are cooked routinely year after year."

Trillions of dollars "cooked" – by whom, and for what reason? These questions have been on the mind of one researcher – Michael Schratt. Schratt has always had a passion for studying airplanes and even took some Parks College courses in aerospace engineering in St. Louis. He did not earn a degree, but he went on to become an autocad draftsman working on aerospace components. Today, he is an aerospace draftsman for Armstrong Aerospace based in Elmhurst Illinois.

Schratt's investigation has uncovered where all the black budget DOD trillions have been going over the past 60 years: to fund a top secret space program that no citizen in the United States knows about – including most of Congress.

If true, it means that NASA is nothing more than public window dressing for a much larger and more advanced American clandestine program intended to dominate and weaponize space. Schratt traces it all back to the 1940s when Presidents Roosevelt and Truman realized that non-human (ET), "celestial" and "interplanetary" technologies were interacting with our planet. By 1958 the public arm of a space program – NASA – was created in parallel with another secret space program.

Schratt believes that we're spending multiple billions of dollars on classified black budget programs with no congressional oversight whatsoever. One example is a document from the Library of Congress, in Washington, DC. There you can pick up a document called, *DOD Budget for Fiscal Year 1994* (photo below) or whatever year you like.

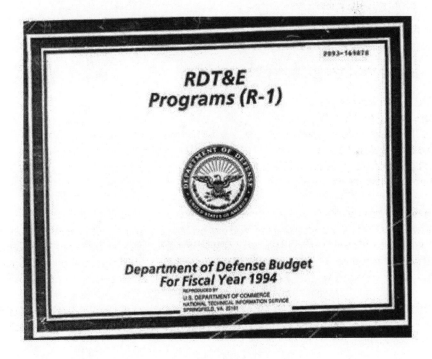

The new budget is handed out to Congress every January and the document has the subtitle: RD T&E Programs (R-1), which stands for Research Development Test & Evaluation Programs R-1. It's approximately 24 pages in length and when you go through this document, it describes a number of programs that the Air Force is involved in and the funding for particular programs and they are called "Program Elements" or "Line Item Numbers."

When you look through the budget document, it gives you specific details about a number of programs they are working on, such as Foreign Technology Division. And in the lists, it highlights programs called 'Senior Year' and 'Forest Green' (photo below).

Department of the U.S. Air Force Budget for Year 1994 RDT&E Program. Red dots highlight SENIOR YEAR and FOREST GREEN, for which there is no budget amounts given, in contrast to the budget amounts given in upper half of the page.

There are no details about what the program is and no details about how much was spent on the program. So we have no clue what is actually going on with these programs. It would lead one to believe that we are definitely running two space programs: one space program in the form of a public relations charade like we see in NASA. Then the other is a much more privatized defense contractor program that is exempt from congressional oversight.

A number of retired Skunkworks engineers who worked on those programs have said in interviews that these projects did reach the flying status, so a number of those programs became actual flying prototypes.

Wright-Patterson AFB Hangar #4, Bay E. Retired USAF pilot Warren Botz said that in 1966 he saw a large, 116-foot-diameter man-made flying saucer in this hangar during a 'Flying Tigers' reunion. The below diagrams of the MacDill discs near the WPAFB hangar. Just for reference, four sizes were seen at MacDill AFB by Jack D. Pickett (retired WWII combat veteran and publisher for USAF) during September of 1967, with only the large 116-foot-diameter craft seen by Warren Botz at WPAFB.

MacDill USAF classified 'flying disc,' Tampa, Florida (1967)

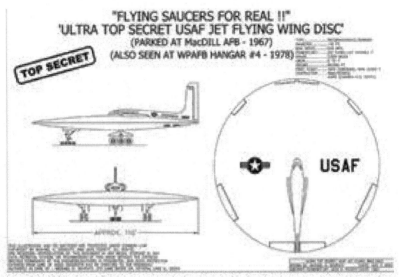

Drawing of 116-foot-diameter USAF 'flying disc' at MacDill AFB, Tampa, Florida (1967), and also seen at Wright-Patterson AFB in Hangar #4 in 1978.

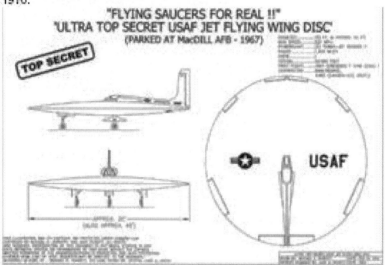

Drawing of 40-foot-diameter USAF 'flying disc' at MacDill AFB, Tampa, Florida (1967).

So what is the possibility that the ones that don't get developed – even those that get to the model stage and then are scrapped – could be a cover for a huge black program which could be related to the government's efforts to interact with a non-human (ET) presence?

It is entirely possible. Simply reference a document that was written by Ben Rich, former CEO of Lockheed Skunkworks. Rich took over the reins in 1975. Ben Rich was a very close friend of John Andrews, who was head of Special Projects at Testor's Model Corporation in San Diego, California.

Andrews would ask Ben Rich questions about classified aircraft and Ben never divulged any specific classified information, but he did provide John Andrews some interesting points.

One of these points was a question that John posed to Ben Rich. He was asking Ben if he was a believer in man-made UFOs and extraterrestrial UFOs. Ben's response was in a document dated July 21, 1986 hand written on official Lockheed letterhead. Both documents are shown below.

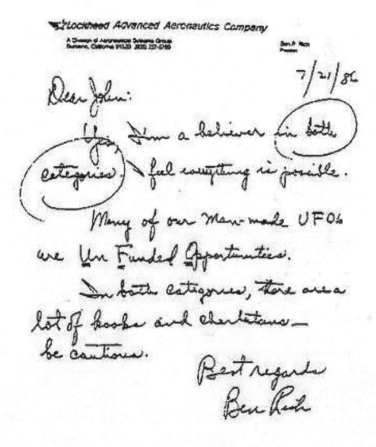

So, what exactly did Ben Rich mean when he talked about "unfunded opportunities?" Was he speaking of classified programs within Skunkworks that did not get proper funding? Or, was he speaking of hand-me-downs that we received from others?

Ben Rich passed away in 1995 but before he passed away, he dropped a number of bombshells. This occurred at Wright-Patterson AFB back in 1993. He gave a video slide presentation there and also at the UCLA School of Engineering Alumni speech – he gave on March 23, 1993. At the very end of his presentation, in both of these venues he completed his slides with the following quote: "The U.S. Air Force has just given us a contract to take ET back home."

He added that, "we also know how to travel to the stars." And he also mentioned at the UCLA speech, "It is time to end all secrecy on this as it no longer poses a national security threat and to make the technology available for use in the private sector."

He was telling us about a whole level of aircraft, of spacecraft, of advanced propulsion systems that are so far advanced. He even mentioned technologies that are 50 years beyond even what we could possibly dream of. Now, when you hear that coming from the Director of the Skunkworks, it is important to really consider it seriously. This gentleman knew a great deal and he was trying to tell us something important. It was about the space program that none of us have a clue about in the civilian world. This is what Ben Rich was trying to tell us about.

If you consider Ben Rich's testimony as credible then yes, there is a secret parallel space program to that of NASA.

We don't know for certain who the secret astronaut corps would be, but there is some indication of some of the craft they might fly.

There was an event that took place on November 12, 1988 – this is two days after the F-117A was declassified and put into the public domain. This was an exhibit to rally support for black budget aerospace programs. We know that California Congressman George Brown, Jr., was present. We also know that U.S. Senator Alan Cranston was present and a number of high-level military officials also attended this classified exhibit. This event was not open to the general public.

One aerospace engineer who was at this exhibit did come forward and provide details. He mentioned that there were a number of aircraft in this hangar. There were two semi-classified hovercraft that have now since gone into the commercial industry. He also described a flattened football, diamond-shaped aircraft.

The December 24, 1990 issue of *Aviation Week & Space Technology* showed a schematic drawing of what this particular aircraft looked like. It was 100 feet in length and approximately 65 feet wide – completely composed of heat-ablative thermo-resistance tiles – the same tiles that you would find on the Space Shuttle. Thermal Protection System (TPS) reinforced carbon can withstand up to 3,000 degrees Fahrenheit on re-entry into Earth's atmosphere.

On control surfaces along the leading and trailing edges of the aircraft; tricycle landing gear with wire mesh wheels; and this was a completely unmanned aircraft. This was one of the aircraft that was at the 1988 exhibit.

This was an unmanned aerial vehicle that had 121 launch tubes at the lower portion of the fuselage. It had the capability of launching a 1/10th megaton warhead at less than 1/10th of a second. There were 18 of these aircraft built during the Reagan Administration.

This means that nuclear missiles could be launched remotely from high in our atmosphere without having pilots inside those vehicles.

They could be to the Soviet Union in less than three hours and then return home and the Soviet Union would not even know what had happened because these things are extremely stealthy and could not be intercepted via missiles or aircraft.

Nobody knows where these aircraft are today. Some of them may be at a remote facility at Eglin AFB, Florida. They could also be at an underground facility called 'Dyson's Dock' at the remote test site in Nevada, also known as Area 51. The third option is Edwards North Base, Mohave, California.

According to the March 9, 1992 issue of *Aviation Week & Space Technology* 21 Northrop B-2 ATV stealth bombers have been built at the cost of $2.2 billion per aircraft. The Northrop engineers who worked on the program were getting really disgusted that the technologies associated with the B-2 were not being trickled down into the commercial airline industry.

What the engineers said is that a number of technologies that are actually in use on the B-2 were classified technologies. One of them referenced, T.T. Brown (Townsend Brown) Electrogravitic Patent No. 3,187, 206, specifically talking about how the B-2 electrically charges the leading edge of the wing to reduce the radar cross section. Then it negatively charges the exhaust gases to reduce the infrared signature. They also found out that a 1968 report from Northrop Grumman Corp. was that when you electrically charge the leading edge of the wing, there is a resulting drag coefficient reduction up to 60 percent. That could be retrofitted to the commercial airline industry, but it was not happening. And that's why the engineers were upset.

By reducing the drag on commercial airliners by 60 percent that would reduce fuel demand and consumption by a significant amount. The implications are staggering and this has so many applications, but is not being used and that was the reason Northrop engineers came forward.

In a day and age where we are fighting for every drop of oil and jet fuel we can get there is something almost criminal about the separation and suppression of advanced technologies from civilian applications.

It's our Constitutional obligation to question authority. An accounting should be made of these programs. They should be brought out into the light. Many of these programs represent absolutely no threat to the national security. That's why they should be exposed.

Unfortunately it is not that easy to get this secret opened up.

It would take a massive effort of engineers who have worked on the program willing to come forward with the hardware to back it up. We just can't have lights in the sky and we can't just have testimonies and documents. It's got to be a full frontal attack. We've got to have the actual hardware.

The U.S. Air Force, the industrial-military complex privatized sector, they all have archives, buildings, storage facilities with gun camera footage, with documentation, black and white glossy old time photos officially stamped "USAF Photographs" that used to be at MacDill AFB, Florida, Armed Guard facility. These facilities do exist. Some of the secrets are housed in those locations.

Some of the classified programs (spacecraft) did have stability problems and those photographs have never been seen. But they were man-made craft perhaps mimicking something that we have been trying to back-engineer (from an alien source).

That is exactly what Ben Rich might have been alluding to when he made that comment about "unfunded opportunities."

One startling revelation arising from this documentation concerns details about an aircraft at Norton AFB that looked like a flattened football, plus a group of other aircraft – and we can't even call them aircraft because they don't work on the principles of aerodynamic lift.

These were three craft measuring 24, 60 and 130 feet in diameter. They looked like a classic flying saucer, or almost like a Jell-O mold. There was an upper crew compartment that looked somewhat like a sphere with composite panels about a 35-degree angle from the centerline of the craft. The smallest craft had a crew of four that used off-the-shelf components. Now, that was very much stressed – off-the-shelf components.

This was a completely man-made craft according to the press release. An ejection system taken directly off the F4 Phantom was used on this particular Jell-O mold craft. There were six CCD cameras along the circumference of the upper crew compartment and one on top for a total of seven (cameras). They could all be used in conjunction with each other and produce an artificial image on the inside of the pilot's visor via the Apache display system.

Along the central column there was a nuclear containment device and an articulated arm on the lower portion of the craft and a number of copper capacitor plates that used the Biefeld-Brown effect. The Biefeld–Brown effect is an effect that was discovered by Thomas Townsend Brown and Dr. Paul Alfred Biefeld. The effect is more widely referred to as electrohydrodynamics (EHD), or sometimes electro-fluid-dynamics, a counterpart to the well-known magneto-hydrodynamics.

Extensive research was performed during the 1950s and 1960s on the use of this electric propulsion effect during the publicized era of gravity control propulsion research. During 1964, Major De Seversky published his related work in U.S. Patent 3,130,945, and with the aim to forestall any possible misunderstanding about these devices, had termed these flying machines "ionocrafts." Similar modern flying devices are now called EHD thrusters.

These craft were hovering off the floor and they were bobbing, just like you would see a large tanker at port, just bobbing on their own waves.

The U.S. military general who was giving the lecture at this exhibit stated that these craft could travel at light speed, or better. That demonstration coincided with a Norton AFB Air Show, which was public. But the exhibit (of Jell-O mold craft) inside the big hangar was not public.

This craft had two code names. It was called the 'Alien Reproduction Vehicle (ARV)' and it was also called the 'Fluxliner' because it was based on high voltage electricity. One official stressed that it contained off-the-shelf components. There was nothing alien specifically about the components of the aircraft. However, it might have been based on something that was alien and hence the name, 'Alien Reproduction Vehicle'.

They had a small VCR connected to a monitor showing this craft making hops, high speed hops – hopping and stopping and then moving and then making a hopping motion and they were showing this thing in motion. There was nobody in the cockpit when they had these on display. They were unmanned, but they did have the capability of being manned.

The implications are that if you look at the reference works and the literature from the vintage 1950s talking about atomic-powered spacecraft and nuclear-powered aircraft, it's clear that the nuclear energy for aircraft propulsion program in the 1950s, we were already working on ways to crack the gravity barrier. By 1960, we had the first working prototype. Now, that's nine years before astronaut Neil Armstrong landed at Tranquility Base on the Moon. That might be one reason why Neil Armstrong doesn't talk about Apollo 11 because he knows he **was not** the first man on the Moon.

Many conspiracy theorists have claimed that the Apollo 11 Moon landing was a hoax – staged in a remote Air Force Hangar somewhere in the southwest U.S. desert. While I believe this claim is unfounded it could be considered a fraud in so much as it mislead the world into believing that Neil Armstrong and Buzz Aldrin were the first humans to set foot on the lunar surface. However, mounting evidence indicates that an earlier classified "black budget" space program had already placed humans on the Moon prior to 1969.

Before the Apollo 11 Moon landing on July 20, 1969 there may have been both human and non-human craft already there. A secret space program may have traveled to the Moon some time before the official Apollo 11 NASA mission. Some researchers believe we have been traveling to the Moon since the early 1960s and established a lunar base.

Retired airline Captain and former CIA pilot John Lear has said that humans first landed on the moon in the early 1960s and on Mars shortly after that. In fact there is video circulating that shows us landing on Mars on May 22, 1962.

The literature in the aerospace industry starting in 1955 was full of references to atomic-powered spacecraft, nuclear engines, things that could be retrofitted to trans-atmospheric vehicles.

By 1960, all of that was completely removed from the literature. So, it's clear they made a breakthrough somewhere around 1960 where they started with these prototypes. It is very possible that we already had a flying prototype at that time that was probably capable of traveling to the Moon.

The implication of what that means to NASA while it is still using World War II German liquid rocket technology that's been obsolete for over 60 years is ridiculous. The Space Shuttles are being blasted up into the air, like firecrackers, using a primitive technology while a much more advanced form of spacecraft are available in a secret space program. The entire liquid rocket launch concept is flawed. There is a much more efficient way to reach outer space and government authorities know it.

The most amazing part of all this is that NASA employees, administrators, less than 5 percent of Congress and, in some cases, even our Presidents don't know either.

The probability is that the impetus for the secret space program was the growing ET presence and crash retrievals of their spacecraft technologies. Some researchers have even suggested that this program has been developed in conjunction with alien visitors to Earth. We do have in our possession a number of craft that certainly seem to mimic what we would classify as extraterrestrial vehicles.

In order to prove this we would have to speak to the engineers who worked directly on the program from Lockheed and also from SAIC (Science Applications International Corporation) in San Diego, California. They are aware of these craft also.

Ironically enough it could be catastrophic geological and environmental global events and the decline of fossil fuels which finally force the government to reveal what they have kept hidden for 60 years.

It is probably something they didn't consider when they started the secret space program. They didn't think about the implications of keeping this under wraps. And now that we are bogged down in so many global environmental issues we desperately need this technology. It's their decision whether they want to release the information or not, but it's clear that the time has come for this to be brought out into the open.

Classified Military and Intelligence Mission Launches

If you think that all rocket launches are strictly weather, communications and GPS satellites, Space Shuttle, or scientific missions you are sadly mistaken.

The United States has developed the most expensive and capable reconnaissance satellites the world has ever seen. American satellites can photograph terrorist bases, listen in on radio conversations, sniff out clandestine nuclear tests, and spot rocket launches anywhere in the world. The goal of these assets, simply put, is to prevent surprises.

Even with conventional NASA programs such as the Space Shuttle now over there have been a growing number of classified military spacecraft and payload launches in recent years.

Many of these were U.S. National Reconnaissance Office missions. The NRO is located in Chantilly, Virginia and is responsible for the design, construction and operation of the U.S. fleet of intelligence gathering reconnaissance satellites and services the satellite intelligence needs of the Central Intelligence Agency (CIA) and Defense Department (DOD). Their stated goal is achieving information superiority for the U.S. Government and Armed Forces.

Consider the following military and intelligence launches over the past 10 years:

DSP-22: The Lockheed Martin Titan 4B, known as B-39, launched the 22nd Defense Support Program missile-warning satellite with the Boeing Inertial Upper Stage-10. The launch was run by the U.S. Air Force. It launched from Cape Canaveral Air Force Station, Florida on February 14, 2004.

Gravity Probe-B: The Boeing Delta 2 rocket launched NASA's Gravity Probe-B to measure how space and time are warped by the presence of the Earth, and how the Earth's rotation drags space-time around with it. The spacecraft tested the predictions of Albert Einstein's general theory of relativity. It was launched from Vandenberg Air Force Base, California on April 20, 2004.

NRO: Lockheed Martin's Atlas rocket, AC-167, launched a classified payload for the U.S. National Reconnaissance Office (NRO). This was the final Atlas 2AS rocket and the last planned Atlas launch from pad 36A. It launched from Cape Canaveral Air Force Station, Florida on August 31, 2004.

NRO: Lockheed Martin's Atlas rocket, AC-206, launched a classified payload for the U.S. National Reconnaissance Office (NRO). This was the final flight for Atlas 3 and last Atlas use of Complex 36. It launched from Cape Canaveral Air Force Station, Florida on February 3, 2005.

NRO: The Lockheed Martin Titan 4B, known as B-30, launched a classified payload for the U.S. National Reconnaissance Office (NRO). The launch was run by the U.S. Air Force. It launched from Cape Canaveral Air Force Station, Florida on April 30, 2005.

STP-R1: The Orbital/Suborbital Program Space Launch Vehicle, nicknamed Minotaur, launched the STP-R1 experimental satellite into space for the Defense Advanced Research Projects Agency (DARPA). The four-stage rocket used U.S. government-supplied Minuteman 2 motors and Pegasus rocket stages. It was launched from Vandenberg Air Force Base, California on September 23, 2005.

NRO: The Air Force Titan 4B, known as B-26, launched a classified payload for the U.S. National Reconnaissance Office. This was the last Titan 4 flight, ending the program that began launches in 1989. It was launched from Vandenberg Air Force Base, California on October 19, 2005.

MITEX: The Boeing Delta 2 rocket launched the Microsatellite Technology Experiment (MITEX) for the Defense Advanced Research Projects Agency (DARPA). The experimental military mission features two small satellites and a Navy-developed fourth stage headed for geosynchronous orbit. The launch was run by the U.S. Air Force. It launched from Cape Canaveral Air Force Station, Florida on June 21, 2006.

NROL-22: Boeing Delta 4 Medium+ rocket launched a classified spy satellite cargo for the U.S. National Reconnaissance Office (NRO). The rocket flew in a configuration with two strap-on solid rocket boosters. This is the first Delta 4 mission from the West Coast. It was launched from Vandenberg Air Force Base, California on June 28, 2006.

NROL-21: The first United Launch Alliance Delta 2 rocket launched a classified payload for the U.S. National Reconnaissance Office (NRO). It was the first Atlas 5 launch from Vandenberg Air Force Base, California on December 14, 2006.

FALCON 1 (Demo Flight 2): The SpaceX Falcon 1 rocket performed a launch demonstration flight for the Defense Advanced Research Projects Agency (DARPA). This marked the second launch of the Falcon 1 vehicle. It was launched from Kwajalein Atoll, Marshall Islands on March 20, 2007.

NFIRE: The Orbital Sciences Minotaur rocket launched the Near Field Infrared Experiment (NFIRE) spacecraft for the Missile Defense Agency. It was launched from Mid-Atlantic Regional Spaceport, Wallops Island, Virginia on April 24, 2007.

NROL-30: The United Launch Alliance Atlas 5 rocket (AV-009) launched a classified spacecraft payload for the U.S. National Reconnaissance Office (NRO). It launched from Cape Canaveral Air Force Station, Florida on June 15, 2007.

DSP-23: The United Launch Alliance Delta 4-Heavy rocket launched the 23rd and final Defense Support Program missile-warning satellite. The largest of the Delta 4 family, the Heavy version features three Common Booster Cores mounted together to form a triple-body rocket. The vehicle delivered DSP-23 directly into geostationary orbit. It launched from Cape Canaveral Air Force Station, Florida on November 10, 2007.

NROL-24: The United Launch Alliance Atlas 5 rocket (AV-015) launched a classified spacecraft payload for the U.S. National Reconnaissance Office (NRO). It launched from Cape Canaveral Air Force Station, Florida on December 10, 2007.

NROL-28: The United Launch Alliance Atlas 5 rocket (AV-006) launched a classified spacecraft payload for the U.S. National Reconnaissance Office (NRO). It was the first Atlas 5 launch from Vandenberg Air Force Base, California on March 13, 2008.

C/NOFS: The air-launched Orbital Sciences Pegasus rocket deployed the Communication/Navigation Outage Forecasting System (C/NOFS) spacecraft for the U.S. military. It was launched from Kwajalein Atoll in Marshall Islands on April 16, 2008.

NROL-26: The United Launch Alliance Delta 4-Heavy rocket launched a classified spy satellite cargo for the U.S. National Reconnaissance Office (NRO). The largest of the Delta 4 family, the Heavy version features three Common Booster Cores mounted together to form a triple-body rocket. It launched from Cape Canaveral Air Force Station, Florida on January 17, 2009.

WGS-2: The United Launch Alliance Atlas 5 rocket (AV-016) deployed the second Wideband Global SATCOM spacecraft, formerly known as the Wideband Gapfiller Satellite. Built by Boeing, this geostationary communications spacecraft will serve U.S. military forces. It launched from Cape Canaveral Air Force Station, Florida on April 3, 2009.

STSS-ATRR: The United Launch Alliance Delta 2 rocket deployed the Space Tracking and Surveillance System Advanced Technology Risk Reduction (STSS-ATRR) research and development mission for the Missile Defense Agency. The mission was previously called Block 2010 Spacecraft Risk Reduction. NASA oversaw the launch. It was launched from Vandenberg Air Force Base, California on May 5, 2009.

PAN: The United Launch Alliance Atlas 5 rocket (AV-018) carried a classified satellite for the U.S. government known only as PAN. Details about the spacecraft mission and its operation were not released. It launched from Cape Canaveral Air Force Station, Florida on September 8, 2009.

STSS Demo: The United Launch Alliance Delta 2 rocket launched the Space Tracking and Surveillance System (STSS) technology demonstration mission for the Missile Defense Agency. It launched from Cape Canaveral Air Force Station, Florida on September 25, 2009.

WGS-3: The United Launch Alliance Delta 4 rocket launched the third Wideband Global SATCOM spacecraft, formerly known as the Wideband Gapfiller Satellite. Built by Boeing, this geostationary communications spacecraft will serve U.S. military forces. It launched from Cape Canaveral Air Force Station, Florida on December 5, 2009.

OTV-1: An April 23, 2010 article from *CNN* written by Barbara Starr, Senior Pentagon Correspondent titled "U.S. military launches mystery space plane on secret mission" described the mystery surrounding the highly classified U.S. military's Orbital Test Vehicle, the X-37B OTV (photo below), which launched into space Thursday, April 22, 2010 from the Cape Canaveral Air Station in Florida.

The X-37B OTV is a classified Air Force project that has never been fully explained by the Pentagon.

Was it an aircraft? Was it the next generation space shuttle? How much did it cost? And why is it such a secret?

The X-37B OTV is a classified Air Force project that has never been fully explained by the Pentagon. Some worry it may be the start of military operations in space – and that the plane might some day carry weapons to shoot down enemy satellites.

The sad part about this story is that there are probably spacecraft carrying weapons already deployed in space, as part of a black operations space program.

NROL-41: The United Launch Alliance Atlas 5 (AV-025) rocket launched a classified spacecraft payload for the U.S. National Reconnaissance Office (NRO), which oversees the nation's constellation of spy satellites. NROL-41 used a 193-foot rocket and was launched from Vandenberg Air Force Base on September 21, 2010. No details about the satellite's orbit or capabilities were released.

NROL-32: Information regarding the mission is evasive at best. The United Launch Alliance Delta 4-Heavy rocket launched a classified spy satellite cargo for the U.S. National Reconnaissance Office (NRO). The largest of the Delta 4 family, the Heavy version features three Common Booster Cores mounted together to form a triple-body rocket. The rocket blasted off from Cape Canaveral Air Force Station on Sunday, November 21, 2010. Brig. Gen. Ed Wilson, commander of the 45th Space Wing, had this to say: This mission helps to ensure that vital NRO resources will continue to bolster our national defense.

NROL-49: The United Launch Alliance Delta 4-Heavy rocket launched a classified spy satellite cargo for the U.S. National Reconnaissance Office (NRO). The largest of the Delta 4 family, the Heavy version features three Common Booster Cores mounted together to form a triple-body rocket. The launch was aboard the most massive rocket ever launched from the California coast.

The United States National Reconnaissance Office NROL-49 satellite is one of the largest payloads to be placed into a polar orbit around Earth, and will serve as both an early warning platform for incoming foreign threats and to observe known hostile regions. The launch took place on January 20, 2011 from Vandenberg AFB. Once the Delta rises into the midday skies, the launch will be visible around the Los Angeles region to the south as the vehicle darts south and out over the Pacific Ocean. The exact deployment time of the payload was not disclosed.

NROL-66: The Air Force Minotaur 1 rocket launched a classified satellite payload for the U.S. National Reconnaissance Office (NRO) on February 6, 2011, beginning a secret mission testing new ways to collect intelligence from space. The Minotaur launcher blasted off from Vandenberg Air Force Base, California.

OTV-2: The United Launch Alliance Atlas 5 rocket (AV-026) launched the U.S. military's X-37B, a prototype space plane also called the Orbital Test Vehicle. The rocket flew in the 501 vehicle configuration with a five-meter fairing, no solid rocket boosters and a single-engine Centaur upper stage. It launched from Cape Canaveral Air Force Station, Florida on March 5, 2011.

NROL-27: The United Launch Alliance Delta 4 rocket launched a classified spy satellite cargo for the U.S. National Reconnaissance Office (NRO) on March 11, 2011. The rocket blasted off from Cape Canaveral at Space Launch Complex-37 in Florida.

The NROL-27 payload supports the national defense_and all information about its mission and goals is a classified military secret. Some outside observers say NROL-27 may be a powerful military communications satellite for relay of vital national security data rather than a signals intelligence satellite.

NROL-34: The United Launch Alliance Atlas 5 rocket (AV-027) launched a classified spacecraft payload for the U.S. National Reconnaissance Office (NRO). The rocket flew in the 411 vehicle configuration with a four-meter fairing, one solid rocket booster and a single-engine Centaur upper stage. It was launched on April 14, 2011 from Vandenberg Air Force Base, California.

ORS-1: The Air Force Minotaur 1 rocket launched the Operationally Responsive Space 1, or ORS-1, satellite. ORS-1 will support the military's intelligence, surveillance and reconnaissance needs by hosting an innovative sensor system. It was launched on June 29, 2011 from Wallops Island, Virginia.

Following is a breakdown of total U.S. rocket launches per year over an 8-year period (2004-2011), and the number of those which were military or intelligence related. The extraordinarily high percentage of military/intelligence missions indicate the enormous emphasis that is being placed (as well as budgetary dollars allocated) on these types of missions.

YEAR	TOTAL U.S. LAUNCHES	NO. OF U.S. MILITARY AND INTELLIGENCE MISSIONS	OTHER COUNTRIES * ROCKET LAUNCHES
2011	13	6	25
2010	15	3	59
2009	26	6	47
2008	20	2	43
2007	20	5	39
2006	23	3	34
2005	16	4	34
2004	19	3	25

Data courtesy of Spaceflight Now

* Note that launches are also conducted by other nations such as the European Space Agency (ESA), Russia, China, Japan, India, Iran, Israel and South Korea.

All non military/intelligence related launches from 2004-2011 were either weather, communications or GPS satellites, Space Shuttle, scientific or other missions. Remember that the official mission description is only a press release and not necessarily the true mission objective.

These are just some examples of classified military/intelligence projects launched recently. The repeated launch of top secret payloads with such increased frequency is highly suspicious and indicates that the U.S. military is very actively engaged in some kind of space program. These payloads and missions could very well be intended to service or support such a program.

Eyewitness and Expert Testimony

Computer hacker Gary McKinnon broke into 97 Pentagon and NASA computers looking for evidence of free energy technology. He uncovered some interesting information. He says he found proof of artificial structures on the Moon that backed up Donna Hare's testimony.

Regardless of your moral opinion of what he did, McKinnon stumbled upon a secret space program which appears to be either an off-world alien fleet or a secret U.S. space program. He came up the names of some of our off-world U.S. space fleet (identified under the abbreviation: USSS), two specific space ships, (the USSS LeMay and the USSS Hillenkoetter), the names of the various "non-terrestrial officers" crews, their ranks, and transfer assignments between various "off-Earth" spaceships. In addition, McKinnon claimed to have found references to a top secret project named "Solar Warden" while snooping through NASA and Department of Defense (DOD) files. Rumors of a secret international space program called "Solar Warden" have been floating around for years.

Given the American DOD's desire for "total spectrum dominance," it shouldn't be too surprising that a secret U.S. Space Program exists. Indeed, there have been reports of secret shuttles making routine flights. And one can't help but be reminded, in the conspiratorial sectors of the unconscious, of Dr. Carol Rosin's information about fake alien invasions.

Dr. Rosin is an award-winning educator, author, leading aerospace executive and space and missile defense consultant. She is a former spokesperson for Wernher von Braun and has consulted to a number of companies, organizations, government departments and the intelligence community. She is the current President of the Institute for Security and Cooperation in Outer Space (ISCOS) which she founded.

According to Rosin, Wernher von Braun, the renowned German rocket scientist who was instrumental in the German V2 program and also the Saturn V rocket which landed men on the Moon, told her that there was a three stage program which would allow some form of totalitarian world government to take control. The first stage was a terrorist threat, followed by threats to Earth from asteroids and finally a fake alien invasion.

It may be that this concentration on alien invasion is a deep fear that the human race has within its subconscious. However, I do not discount the theory of a fake alien invasion. The world's governments have shown that virtually nothing is beyond them in their addiction to seize power and control. A fake alien invasion would be the ultimate threat to the human race and give them the excuse to introduce a totalitarian world government with the pretence that a draconian curtailment of civil liberties is necessary.

Dr. Rosin first met Wernher von Braun in February of 1974. It was at this time, shortly before his death in 1977, that von Braun confided to Rosin the details of this secret space agenda. Von Braun stunned Rosin by describing this plan, point for point, as well as describing in detail exactly where it was all leading: planetary control under an oppressive One World Government.

According to Dr. Rosin von Braun then gave her one supreme assignment to thwart this plan: to stop the weaponization of space. Failure to do so would lead to calamity for the human race as a secretive trans-national power, already in existence, would move to permanently take control of this planet through a hoaxed alien invasion from outer space.

According to von Braun, space based weapons, later known as the "Star Wars" program, were to be publicly promoted as our space "shield" against the evil Russians. Then they would be promoted as our defense against terrorists from Third World countries ("rogue" nations). Then their necessity would be justified as protection against asteroids and meteors, and the "last card," the final justification according to von Braun, would be their installation in orbit against an extraterrestrial threat from outer space.

Von Braun told Rosin that she would begin to notice a certain "spin" on the news, which would illustrate the need to build space-based weaponry because our enemies "might" have these weapons, so our intelligence community would proceed on the assumption that they do have these weapons. As we now know, this is exactly how the "Star Wars" program transpired.

Wernher von Braun maintained that all of these publicly announced threats were lies. He cited the reality of nuclear suitcase bombs being available even then, as well as chemical, viral, bacterial and biological terror weapons against which these space-based weapons would be useless.

More importantly, von Braun told Dr. Rosin in 1974 that we already had the technology to build anti-gravity vehicles and entire transportation systems which did not require so-called "fossil fuels" but instead used "beams" of energy, thereby eliminating all pollution from these sources permanently. Perhaps Dr. von Braun had seen anti-gravity vehicles with his own eyes in Germany before the end of World War II, as well as their continued development at other secret technology sites afterwards.

Von Braun further told Dr. Rosin that we had the ability to transform our war-based military/industrial complex into a space and energy industry for the benefit of all of humanity, and that we had the capability of building entirely nonpolluting transportation technologies using this same limitless energy, while ending the arms race without dislocating the jobs associated with it. Mankind could transition to a new industrial paradigm and usher in an era of peace and prosperity for everyone on Earth.

Of course, what is equally interesting is what Dr. von Braun left unsaid. If space-based weapons technologies are not really being developed to protect the U.S. and its allies against rogue nations and their weapons; if, indeed, such weapons are useless against suitcase nuclear bombs, as well as chemical, biological and viral weapons, then exactly why are they being developed? Could select populations of resistors, whether nation-states or isolated groups opposed to the coming of a New World Order, be singled out and eliminated?

That is certainly one possibility. Yet another possibility is that such space-based weapons will be part of the "smoke and mirrors" light show designed to terrify the population of the Earth when "Project Blue Beam" debuts, with its false, projected presentation of an alien invasion.

According to Dr. Steven Greer, the founder of *The Disclosure Project*, the prospect that a shadow, para-governmental entity exists that has kept UFOs secret and is planning a deception that will dwarf the events of 9/11 – a scenario that more people within the depths of our government have begun to reveal.

If Werhner von Braun already knew that anti-gravity technology existed in 1974, then we must also conclude that part of the coming alien "light show" and invasion scenario scheduled to frighten us into the arms of a One World Government, utilizing the technology described in Project Blue Beam, is based on anti-gravity alien craft under the planetary control of the unseen power which silently operates under the radar of the world's staged media.

Even Dr. Greer, who had brought Dr. Rosin to Washington DC to publicly testify about von Braun's warning and concern for the future of humanity based upon the nefarious plans he had uncovered, admits that he was at first skeptical of the reality behind this proposal.

Dr. Greer explains that since 1992 he has seen this script unfold by at least a dozen well-placed insiders. Initially he believed this just too absurd and far-fetched and yet others told him explicitly that things that looked like UFOs, but that are built and under the control of deeply secretive "black projects", were being used to simulate (hoax) ET-appearing events, including some abductions and cattle mutilations, to sow the early seeds of cultural fear regarding life in outer space. And that at some point after global terrorism, events would transpire that would utilize the now-revealed Alien Reproduction Vehicles (ARVs, or reversed-engineered UFOs made by humans by studying actual ET craft) to hoax an attack on Earth.

The goal of this hoaxed space alien invasion was simple: control thru fear, to drive governments of all nations to submit and unite under one central authority, a One World Government, and as Dr. Greer maintains to justify eventually spending trillions on space weapons thus uniting the world in fear, in militarism and war.

Of course, we have been purposely conditioned over the years to view any space aliens as threatening and predatory. Various films released by Hollywood studios have had their effect on the subconscious mind of the general public. This mental conditioning to fear extraterrestrials has been subtly reinforced for decades, in preparation for future deceptions.

The essence of the plan is simple: create an anonymous enemy "out there" in the limitless void of space by combining fact with fiction, and by hoaxing UFO events that can look terrifying. The plan is to eventually create a new, sustainable, off-planet enemy. Wernher von Braun warned of such a hoax, as a pretext for putting war in space.

Dr. Carol Rosin revealed this information before the national press in Washington, DC where she also said that she was willing to make the exact same statement under oath to Congress. Of course, the official mainstream media never saw fit to make mention of this startling pronouncement by her.

Wernher von Braun, his assistant Dr. Carol Rosin, and Dr. Steven Greer have done their best to warn the world at large of this coming deception based on secret energy technology, new visual projection technology and the continued demonization of space aliens by our media and our military/industrial complex.

Dr. Greer further reveals that space-based weapons are already in place – part of a secret parallel space program that has been operating since the 1960s. ARVs are built and ready to go. Space holographic deception technologies are in place, tested and ready to fire. And the mainstream media is an able and willing pawn.

The knowledge that technology may exist today which would end the need for mining, drilling, refinement and distribution of oil, gas, and coal, as well as traditional nuclear energy which could usher in a new age for the entire human race while eliminating the pretexts for the endless wars which have ravaged our planet for the last 200 years, must give us pause to ponder.

Donna Tietze (Hare) is a former photo technician at NASA's Johnson Space Center in Houston. She was interviewed on Washington DC radio station. The following is a partial transcript of a radio talk show that took place on May 6, 1995 on WOL-AM in Washington DC, and simulcast on WOLB-AM in Baltimore Maryland. The show is broadcast every Saturday night and is called *UFOs Saturday Night*.

Elaine Douglass: This is Elaine Douglass, WOL News-Talk Network, our show is *UFOs Saturday Night* and I'm here in the studio with Keith Morgan and our topic is the Face on Mars. We have a new guest on the air with us, Donna Tietze (Hare). Donna, you are also with three scientists who are on the air with us and that would be Stan McDaniels from California, Errol Toron from the east coast and Dan Drason who is in Colorado. The reason that I asked Donna to come on the show, Donna is in

Houston, Texas and kind enough to join us tonight to tell us some very interesting things she observed while working at NASA. Donna is an educator and she is working on her Masters in Education. In the past Donna, as I understand that you held a position for 15 years with a contractor at the NASA Johnson Space Center in Houston. You were a photo technician?

Donna Tietze: Correct!

E.D.: Donna welcome to *UFOs Saturday Night*. Tell me and tell everyone the incident that you recall as they say in the law court, did there come a time when you walked in a photo lab and someone told you something quite astounding? What happened that day?

D.T.: Yes Elaine, that's true. During the Apollo mission I worked at NASA throughout those Apollo missions and I did leave NASA at the time the space shuttles began. I worked in building eight in the photo lab. I had a secret clearance so I thought I could go anywhere in the building. And I did go into one area that was a restricted area. In this area they developed pictures taken from satellites and also all of the missions, the Apollo missions, flight missions, etc. I went in and I was talking to one of the photographers and developers and he was putting together a mosaic which is a lot of photos, smaller photos into a larger photo pattern. And while I was in there I was trying to learn new methods and new things about the whole organization and I was looking at the pictures and he directed my attention to one area, he said, look at that. I looked and there was a round oval shaped, well it was a very white circular shape of a dot and it was black & white photography, so I asked him if that was a spot on the emulsion and he replied, "Well I can't tell you, but spots on the emulsion do not leave round circles of shadows."

E.D.: So there was a shadow on the ground?

D.T.: Right, a round shadow. And I noticed that there were pine trees, now I don't know where this area was or what, you, pretty close to the ground what I saw but I didn't see outline of the continent. But I did notice that there was shadow under this white dot and I also noticed that the trees were casting the shadows in the same direction as this shadow of the circle of this aerial phenomena because it was higher than the trees but not too much higher than the trees but it was close to the ground and it was spherical but slightly elongated, not very much but slightly.

I then said, is it a UFO? And he said, "Well I can't tell you." And then I asked him, "What are you going to do with this piece of information?" And he said, "Well we have to airbrush these things out before we sell these photographs to the public." So I realized at that point that there is a procedure setup to take care of this type of information from the public.

E.D.: Isn't that remarkable gentlemen?

Stan McDaniels: Elaine, I was unable to really hear very much of that.

E.D.: Oh really?

S. McD: I did catch air brush it out.

E.D.: Alright, Stan can you hear this station break coming up?

S. McD: Uh, sure.

E.D.: So alright, we are going into that, we'll be back in just a couple of minutes

STATION BREAK

E.D.: Erol Toron, you are here?

E.T.: I'm still here

E.D.: Alright fine, Stan you said you could not hear the account that Donna gave?

S. McD: Not very well.

E.D.: Alright, Keith would you like to recapitulate what Donna said?

Keith Morgan: Stan, what she said was that she was in the photo lab at NASA and that she was looking at some photos and one showed an elliptical, white object that was casting a shadow on the ground above some trees and the technician in there, she asked him if it was a UFO? He said "I can't tell you." She said what are you going to do with this kind of information? He said "Well that is the kind of stuff that we airbrush out."

S. McD: Oh I see, thanks for that.

E.D.: So Donna that's approximately, essentially correct what you said, right?

D.T.: Right.

E.D.: Yes well I, Stan I think that's quite startling, don't you?

S. McD: It speaks for itself.

E.D.: Yes it certainly does, Now Donna there is another matter that you learned about when you were there at NASA. I believe this was through a third party, a person that you were spending some time with who was a fellow NASA employee?

D.T.: Right, in fact after we talked, I thought about another incident with a guard that I would like to convey too that's very important. This man that I had dated was in quarantine with the astronauts when they had come back from the Moon and I had talked to him about seeing this saucer (satellite photos) and asked him if he had heard anything about that and he told me that every astronaut, every Moon trip had been followed by craft, by saucers, that every one of them, every astronaut that went to the Moon, now I don't know about other sites but they all had seen it and all had been told to keep quite about it and they were threatened with jail and their whole retirement, everything taken away from them. He also told me that if I ever told that he said it, that he would deny it, that he would never admit that he told me all of that.

E.D.: Did you hear that Stan?

S.McD: No.

E.D.: Alright, ah, go ahead Keith, recapitulate. (Keith repeats everything of that part that Donna Tietze stated, to McDaniel).

S.McD: Oh yes I see.

E.D.: Yes and I believe that Donna you related to me, your friend came to believe that the UFOs were instrumental in getting Apollo 13 that was, our disabled mission to the Moon, was it 13?

D.T.: Right, well he said that it shouldn't have come back, I mean, there was no, ah, they had help. And that was all he would say.

E.D.: All he would say?

D.T.: He said it was impossible for that craft to have gotten back home.

E.D.: Donna you said that there was another matter that you wanted to relate to us.

D.T.: Yes, something that I didn't talk to you about earlier. I had an office, I was doing illustration work at another office, in another part of town. And a man that had been a guard at NASA during the time came into my office and he had a large gash scar on his forehead and he told me that he was a guard at NASA and that he was burning a lot of photographs of UFOs. That was his job.

E.D.: Really (surprised).

D.T.: And he said he stopped to look at one too long and one of the others, I gathered it was some type of military man, hit him in the head with a gun butt and knocked him out.

E.D.: What? (shocked).

D.T.: Because he had looked at one of the photographs too long, he did describe the photograph to me which I tend to believe was an accurate photograph.

E.D: Oh, my god!

D.T.: He explained that it was a craft on the ground and it looked like, it was like a regular saucer with like little bumps all over and he said it was like it was burnt. He said cows in the field all had their tails stuck straight up. At the time he said he didn't know when cattle were frightened, that their tails would stick straight up. And he described this to me and since then, I did describe it to someone that I thought might have looked at some of these photos, possibly and they did look kind of frightened that I should know about that one. The next several minutes later the conversation is more about UFOs following Apollo crafts to the Moon.

E.D.: The second part of her account had to do with the stalking of our space mission by UFOs of our space missions to the Moon and so on. She even said that they apparently helped in one case by bringing the Apollo 13 back. That was the impression that she got.

D.T.: Yes but they (aliens) also didn't want that craft to investigate the part of the Moon that they were going to, so they may have caused some of it too, but it was supposed, we were told not to go but we ignored it. Now that's what I've heard, that's some of the stuff he was telling me.

E.D.: Did he say that, your direct contact?

D.T.: Yes!

E.D.: That the United States was told not to go to the Moon?

D.T.: To that certain place on the back side of the Moon.

E.D.: And did he know why we weren't supposed to go there?

D.T.: I guess they didn't want us to see something back there, I don't know, I don't know that part. Interview then winds down a few minutes later and the show is out of time.

Clark McClelland is a retired Spacecraft Operator with NASA who, during a 34-year career, was responsible for ensuring the safety of numerous NASA missions including Mercury spaceflights, Apollo missions, the International Space Station and the Space Shuttle.

In a statement released on his website on July 29, 2008, McClelland revealed that he witnessed an eight to nine foot tall extraterrestrial in association with a Space Shuttle mission he was monitoring from the Kennedy Space Center.

He describes how as a former ScO (Spacecraft Operator), Space Shuttle Fleet, he personally observed an 8 to 9 foot tall extraterrestrial on his 27-inch video monitors while on duty in the Kennedy Space Center, Launch Control Center (LCC). Amazingly the extraterrestrial was standing upright in the Space Shuttle Payload Bay having a discussion with two tethered NASA astronauts.

He also observed on his monitors, the spacecraft of the extraterrestrial as it was in a stabilized, safe orbit to the rear of the Space Shuttle main engine pods. The incident lasted for about one minute and seven seconds – plenty of time for him to memorize all that he was observing.

It was a tall creature, about 8 to 9 feet tall. It had a humanoid body shape with two arms, two hands, two legs, two feet, a slim torso and a normal size head for its size. He wasn't able to distinguish the color of its skin. It appeared to have two eyes, but it was not detailed enough for any other comments.

He didn't know how it was able to communicate. It did move its arms a lot – almost like giving instructions. There were no voice communications. The space helmet was not as large as our two NASA astronauts, and had a viewport to look forward. It had a small, perhaps a communication device, attached only to the right side of the helmet.

There were no visible oxygen tank(s). It had a wide belt like wrapping around it. It did not appear to be tethered as the two astronauts were to the sides of the shuttle structure. McClelland observed nothing that appeared to be a weapon. The time of this amazing scene was one minute and seven seconds and he timed it on his astronaut chronograph watch.

It was an extraterrestrial and an alien spaceship!

Furthermore, McClelland wrote that he was not the only NASA official who witnessed the incident:

A friend of his later contacted him and said that he had also observed an 8 to 9 foot tall extraterrestrial inside the Space Shuttle crew compartment. Yes, inside our Shuttle! Both missions were DOD (Pentagon) top secret (TS) encounters.

McClelland's testimony is significant due to his impeccable credentials.

McCelland is a space program pioneer. He assisted in launching the Mercury, Gemini, Apollo, Apollo-Soyuz, Skylab, Space Shuttle, Deep Space Missions, and the International Space Station. He was involved in launching or witnessing 650 missions during his career. He was the Director of the NICAP Unit-3 actual X-Files at Cape Canaveral and the Kennedy Space Center, 1958 to 1992.

He has met with many NASA and other astronauts throughout the years and has been involved in the military and NASA space programs from 1958 to 1992. He recalls many experiences of extraterrestrials having been seen on the Moon, etc., by NASA astronauts and has related these and more.

According to McCelland NASA is not a civilian space agency – the Pentagon owns and controls NASA. Some of the DOD (Department of Defense) missions he participated in were top secret. Those missions carried top secret satellites and other space mission hardware into orbit where several crews met with extraterrestrials.

His website has a number of documents he has released to the public confirming some among the long list of achievements and testimonials arising out of his long NASA career. His claims of directly having witnessed events involving extraterrestrial life and technology while at NASA are a primary source of testimonial evidence.

McClelland's testimony can and should be used to initiate a Congressional investigation of extraterrestrial life. His statement is likely to lead to more serious attention by the scientific community to evidence of extraterrestrial life.

A number of conclusions can also be drawn from McClelland's statement given his credibility as a primary witness for events that have occurred at NASA. First, his statement helps confirm the reality of extraterrestrial life and technologies, and that NASA has been secretly suppressing this information on national security grounds due to the Pentagon's involvement.

This is consistent with recent analyses pointing to the Pentagon's role in getting NASA to suppress information on extraterrestrial artifacts discovered on the Moon, Mars, and elsewhere in the Solar System.

A second conclusion is that McClelland's testimony reveals that extraterrestrial vehicles and personnel are able to perform highly complex maneuvers in the vicinity of NASA spacecraft, and even perform docking maneuvers. This gives credence to whistleblower claims that NASA regularly sanitizes videos or photographs of any images involving extraterrestrial technologies or artifacts during space missions.

Finally, McClelland's testimony reveals that a parallel space program involving secret flights and missions does indeed exist. Furthermore, it suggests that there is a high level of cooperation between at least one extraterrestrial civilization and NASA/Pentagon. It appears that extraterrestrials may even be providing assistance in some space missions where difficulties arise as may have occurred with the tethered astronauts in his example.

McClelland's statement helps confirm other whistleblower testimonies of secret agreements concerning extraterrestrial life and technology.

In conclusion, McClelland's statement will be very helpful in exposing NASA's handling of whistleblower and eyewitness testimony of extraterrestrial life and technology associated with NASA missions.

Together with the recent disclosure by former astronaut, Dr. Edgar Mitchell over a government cover-up of extraterrestrial life, there is strong reason to begin a Congressional inquiry into NASA's and the Pentagon's roles in covering up evidence of extraterrestrial life.

Something occurred with the Soviet Cosmonauts in the Salyut 7 that orbited the Earth in 1985. This is a rather hushed secret that has been leaked to the west.

The six Soviet Cosmonauts in 1985 saw "celestial beings" on the 155th day aboard their orbiting space station. This was first reported by Cosmonaut Vladimir Solevev and Oleg Atkov as well as Leonid Kizim. This is what they said, "What we saw were seven giant figures in the form of humans, but with wings and mist-like halos as in the classic depiction of angels."

As the Cosmonauts were performing medical experiments in Salyut 7 high above the Earth, a brilliant orange cloud enveloped them, blinding them temporarily, and when their eyes cleared, they saw the angels with wings as big as jumbo jets.

The heavenly visitors, they said, followed them for about 10 minutes and vanished as suddenly as they had appeared. However, 12 days later, Cosmonauts Svetlana Savitskaya, Igor Volk, and Vladimir Dzhanibevok, who had just joined the others on the space station, also saw the beings. "They were glowing," they reported. "We were truly overwhelmed. There was a great orange light, and through it, we could see the figures of seven angels. They were smiling as though they shared a glorious secret, but within a few minutes, they were gone, and we never saw them again."

Now, let us deal with the Vatican connection.

As you know, the Hubble Telescope has been operating for a while. One of the things that certain officials or scientists connected to/or in your government are not telling you, and that the Vatican now knows, also, and has known longer than the United States Government, the Soviet Government, and the French Government, is that the Hubble Telescope in space has sent back the pictures of ethereal beings, bathed in this orange glow seen by the occupants of Salyut 7.

These "angels", according to scientists and astronomers, would cause a world panic and confusion because the Vatican knows that they – and here is the Vatican connection – are truly, "beings of light." But, these computer enhanced images have convinced scientists and astronomers alike that they are real, live angels. The Vatican's interest in the Hubble Space Telescope is that these beings are real, are being seen, but they are not the benign, friendly angels watching over us that the scientists think they are.

Scientists first thought they were a newly discovered star cluster because of the magnitude and brilliance of their colors. It became obvious, with the computer enhanced pictures, "that these were creatures we were seeing," according to one scientist at NASA. They were, "a group of seven angels flying together," in the NGC-3532, (CARINA) three-billion-year-old star cluster.

The scientists showed these pictures to the Vatican, and there were, "seven giant figures. All had wings and mist-like halos," reports one engineer. "They were about 80 feet tall and had wing-spans as large as airplanes. Their faces were round and peaceful, and they were all beaming. It seemed like they were overjoyed at being photographed by the Hubble Telescope. They seemed to be smiling at each other as if they were letting the rest of the universe in on a glorious secret."

NASA finally revealed to the Vatican that this was not the first time such a thing has occurred through the Hubble Telescope. In the Soyuz 8 mission a few years back, after 120 days into the mission, Soviet cosmonauts of that flight also encountered similar smiling angels.

The Vatican's interest, as they have told the three governments in secret meetings above, is that these "angels" are truly those that are assuming the guise of an "angel of light" as spoken of by the Apostle Paul.

Pope John Paul II was well apprised and advised of the above and had been for some time. He felt that we will see UFOs landing soon across the world. He further felt that these are not the benevolent beings they have been made out to be.

Setting aside the religious connection and implications this sighting of "angels" in outer space is truly incredible. Regardless of what the entities are – angels (evil or good), or extraterrestrial life forms – it is understandable why a secret space program was developed. It could investigate and perhaps even contact these entities without arousing suspicion of the general public on Earth.

A further glimpse into the military's secretive obsession with UFO technology was provided by Colonel Steve Wilson, U.S. Air Force (ret.), former head of Project Pounce – an elite Air Force/National Reconnaissance Organization Special Forces unit which retrieves downed UFOs.

Colonel Wilson reports that the first successful U.S. anti-gravity flight took place July 18, 1971 at S4/Dreamland (Area 51) where light-bending capabilities were also demonstrated to obtain total invisibilities. Present at this flight were notables such as

Admiral Bobbie Ray Inman (former National Security Agency director), who is now head of SAIC (Science Applications International, Incorporated) in San Diego, CA which makes the anti-gravity drives.

Colonel Wilson also revealed that the announcement by Lockheed about an unmanned, electric-propulsion reconnaissance unit with short wings named "Dark Star" was actually a "cover" project. The exotic technology being concealed is the real Dark Star designated the X-22A, and manufactured by the Lockheed Skunkworks at Helendale, CA. This Dark Star is an operational, 2-man, wingless anti-gravity craft.

The UFO-copycat anti-gravity craft was tested at Area 51 in 1992. Its metallic airframe in flight is obscured by an intense bluish-white light which pulsates off-and-on at about 2-second intervals. During the phase where the intense light is off, the craft frame disappears from optical view (and not just because its light was off), then reappears several hundred yards distant horizontally in the lit mode. Does that mean that this craft travels by small jumps through hyper-space? Gravity does bend space-time.

The U.S. also flies discs which glow an intense golden-orange during flight, made by Northrop Aerospace at their secret facility northeast of Lancaster, CA, which were also test flown in 1992. Colonel Wilson says the military began publicly flying their enormous Black Triangle antigravity craft (back-engineered from recovered extraterrestrial UFOs) on January 3, 1994.

Several sources state that the McDonnell-Douglas, Lockheed-Martin, and Northrop anti-gravity plants are connected underground by a super-fast tunnel shuttle system with Area 51 and other sensitive underground installations. Colonel Wilson says that the system – where magnetically levitated trains zip through almost vacuum tubes – is called TAUSS (Trans-America Underground Subway System). The tunnels are excavated by nuclear Subterrenes which can burn through rock and create six miles of tunnel per day.

The Colonel also provided the answer to the mystery "black helicopters" spotted around so-called cattle mutilation sites. These aren't your ordinary helicopters, but yet another U.S. anti-gravity craft designated the XH-75D or XH Shark made by Teledyne Ryan Aeronautical Corporation of San Diego. He says that many of these XH-75Ds were assigned to the Delta/National Reconnaissance Organization Division which retrieves downed UFOs. That Division is also implicated in mutilating cattle as psychological warfare on the American public – to try to get us to fear and hate extraterrestrials through assuming that ETs were responsible for cutting up the cattle.

Finally, Colonel Wilson stated that a super-secret mobile unit within Delta Force/the National Reconnaissance Organization is deployed with the "Equalizer" – an exotic-looking electromagnetic pulse six-feet-long, one-foot in diameter cannon mounted on a pedestal on the back of a military truck which is used to shoot down UFOs using low-frequency pulsed microwave energy. The Equalizer is built by LTV (Ling-Temco-Vought) in Anaheim, CA.

Anti-gravity technology is limitedly international. Russia is reported to have its own anti-gravity vehicles. And Paul Stonehill (a respected Russian UFO investigator) reports that the Russians in April 1988 started using space-time-bending anti-gravity technology to do time-travel. In June 1997, a reliable Washington, DC area intelligence source passed on information that China now has acquired anti-gravity technology.

A world-class UFO/ET research professional has additionally provided information that a renegade group in Japan also possesses anti-gravity technology. He reported that the possession of such extreme technology (which besides ultrafast deployment also involves radar and optical invisibility and potentially time-travel capabilities) by a sometimes-hostile Asian superpower such as China is seen by some Pentagon generals as destabilizing the West's military edge.

American scientist Dr. Michael Wolf claimed he was a member of the breakaway group (satellite government) for over 25 years. He attained a very high "Above Top Secret" clearance level and worked primarily on joint ET/human scientific projects. He died on September 18, 2000 from cancer after a long period of ill-health.

During his final years he spent time talking to various journalists about the UFO, ET, and secret space program cover-up. His bosses at the National Security Council (NSC) gave him permission to "generate a controlled leakage of secret information".

Dr. Wolf claimed to have worked in laboratories at Area 51, S4, Wright-Patterson Air Force Base (Foreign Technology Division), Indian Springs and Dulce, New Mexico. He served as a scientific consultant for the American President and NSC on ET related matters.

He was a member of the mysterious MJ-12 special studies group and appointed head of its leading agency – the Alphacom Team – which specializes in gathering information on the different ET races. His credentials included an MD in neurology; a PhD in theoretical physics; a BS in biogenetics; a JD in international law; and a DSc in computer sciences.

Dr. Wolf first came to public attention through his book *The Catchers of Heaven* released in July 1996 – a book primarily about his experiences while working for the satellite government.

It took 15 years of persuasion before his bosses finally allowed him to publish the book. But their conditions stated that this book must be fictionalized and contain three different denials at the beginning concerning its authenticity. They also reviewed *The Catchers of Heaven* before its publication.

Dr. Wolf is probably the highest ranking member of the satellite government to come forward so far – offering us an extraordinary insight into the UFO cover-up and the existence of a secret space program.

Some of Dr. Wolf's claims include:

• The first United States crash/retrieval of an extraterrestrial craft occurred during 1941 in the Pacific Ocean. Retrieved by the navy, dead Zeta Reticulans (alias the 'Greys') were found inside. Craft and bodies were taken to the Foreign Technology Section at Wright-Patterson Air Force base in Dayton, Ohio and studied by the Retfours Special Studies Group. After dismantling the craft, parts were sent to S4 and Indian Springs in Nevada. This craft crashed due to the recently invented pulse radar being tested on the nearby Tinian Island, located three miles south/south west of Saipan.

• Between that and the first publicly-announced Roswell UFO crash in 1947, there was another crash in 1946, as well as two other crashes in 1947. The Roswell Crash during July 1947 did happen and Colonel Phillip J. Corso's account of this event is accurate. Dr. Wolf had, in his possession, the official satellite government ET crash/retrieval list and while others occurred between 1941 and 1947 he was not willing to offer examples.

• Two UFOs did crash at Roswell in July 1947 after colliding with each other during an electrical storm. One contained 'Greys' the other 'Orange' ETs – both named due to the color of their skin. The 'Orange' types come from the Andromeda star system. The Santilli autopsy film is genuine – Dr. Wolf had seen other similar footage – and is an autopsy of an 'Orange' ET. There were two different autopsies being carried out on two different ET beings during the same period, hence the confusion.

• By 1954 the United States had four extraterrestrial corpses in the "Blue Room", Hangar 18 at Wright-Patterson Air Force Base, Dayton, Ohio. These bodies came from a series of retrievals of downed UFOs.

• His first major assignment was working alongside Dr. Carl Sagan and other top scientists. Their job was to understand the intricacies of a huge extraterrestrial beacon dubbed "The Monolith" first discovered floating out in space by Russian cosmonaut Yuri Gagarin and American Alan Shepard during 1961. It was eventually brought back for investigation in 1972.

The Monolith emits both light and tone signals along with a mathematical language. On closing your eyes, while tuned into these signals you see in your mind's eye a 3D film of the galaxy. But you are actually there as if part of this film. The images being seen today by the Hubble telescope are the same ones he saw 25 years earlier. According to Dr. Wolf said there are many Monoliths out in space and they were established by a group of extraterrestrial races long ago.

• Carl Sagan consistently denied the ET reality because his superiors threatened to cut off the funding to his department at Cornell University if he said otherwise.

• MJ-12 does exist and now has 36 members. He was reluctant to divulge names although confirmed that former American Secretary of State, Henry Kissinger and father of the hydrogen bomb, Edward Teller, were members. MJ12 regularly meet at various secret locations including the Batelle Memorial Institute in Columbus, Ohio.

• He briefed four different American presidents on the ET reality. Jimmy Carter was keen to end the UFO cover-up but when told of the religious implications he backed down. Carter had strong Christian beliefs. When told that religion is man-made and probably unique to this planet he broke down in tears.

• Both Ronald Reagan and George Bush were very knowledgeable on the ET reality – especially Bush, being former head of the CIA. Bill Clinton was the least aware. He knew of Area 51 but not S4. Clinton had 'Above Top Secret' and 'Need to Know' clearances but did not have the 'Umbra Ultra Top Secret Clearance' which gives access to upper level MJ12 secrets and 'Keystone Clearance' for information on ET research.

• Many people in MI5, MI6 and the SAS are aware of the ET reality. While reluctant to give names of those he briefed at Downing Street, when staying in London he became good friends with former Conservative cabinet and Defense Minister Sir Malcolm Rifkind. Rifkind was very knowledgeable on the UFO subject, especially the flying triangular craft. He believed the cover-up was justified – that people are not ready to be told yet.

• The Queen of England had been superficially told of the ET reality. Margaret Thatcher was also briefed but knew just a small part of the story.

• There has been a manned deep space platform in Earth orbit since 1968. It originally had three-man American crews as well as Russians. Since 1973, the space station received additional extremely-high technology, and has undergone many upgrades as well. The space station has been serviced by secret military spacecraft long before the first American Space Shuttle flew in 1981.

This disclosure makes it clear that the Cape Canaveral Space Shuttle launches, and the "first" American space station being assembled by NASA, are just government "cover" programs. Such programs have served to deflect the public from becoming aware before now of the existence of a black project military space station, and of classified military craft which can go well past orbit into deep space.

• In 1988 previous models of spacefaring military vehicles were superseded by the "Nautilus", a spacecraft with a rounded delta shape built jointly by special projects divisions of Europe's Airbus Industrie and Boeing Corporation. Nautilus has a propulsion system which utilizes magnetic pulsing. Nautilus-type craft made twice-weekly trips up into space and back, to service the secret international space station.

The Nautilus was based in a secret base (U.S. Space Warfare Headquarters), located in hardened underground facilities beneath King's Peak in the Wasatch Mountains, 80 miles east of Salt Lake City, Utah. It was positioned within a mountain so stealthfully that you could drive by and never know it was there. The principal headquarters of the U.S. Space Command has been relocated from Cheyenne Mountain, Colorado to this underground installation in Utah.

• Nautilus-class craft were also used at the beginning of the Gulf War, to penetrate Iraqi airspace from space. Soon thereafter, Stealth aircraft took over covert penetration operations.

• As far as the successor craft to the secret military Space Shuttle, it was replaced in 1985 with Aurora up to 1992, thus indicating that the often-rumored Aurora hyperfast aerospace vehicle not only was operational since 1985, but is already obsolete. Its successor was dubbed "Dark Star", an operational two-man, wingless anti-gravity craft. This is the Lockheed X-22A Dark Star, which uses technology perfected on Lockheed's "cover" program, a conventional unmanned reconnaissance drone, the X-22, also called DarkStar. In turn, the anti-gravity Dark Star became obsolete by another craft in 2001, yet another exotic space vehicle. So the Cape Canaveral Shuttle stuff you see is for Hollywood to direct.

• We unofficially landed on the Moon sometime before 1969. Our astronauts were observed then communicated with by extraterrestrials while on the Moon and warned off. That's why the last Apollo mission was cancelled at the last second. The astronauts have wanted to tell the truth but knew it could be interpreted as treason.

• NASA has played an integral role in the UFO cover-up. They have been designated as one of the primary organizations to eventually tell the world about the ET reality.

• Richard Hoagland is primarily correct concerning structures he has identified as artificial on Mars, and confirms that we have bases on both Mars and the Moon. The most recent "Face on Mars" photograph, which shows a very different image from the previous one, has been doctored by NASA in an effort to introduce misinformation and confuse the public. Authorities believe humanity is not ready for this knowledge.

• In a chamber at Giza, Egypt and another located between the paws of the Sphinx skeletons of 7-foot tall beings with large eyes have been discovered – their hands and legs chained together with silver. For some reason early extraterrestrial visitors could not break through silver.

• A Stargate has been discovered in a Giza pyramid. Investigating scientists believe it to be a lens which creates wormholes to various parts of the universe. It hasn't been activated yet. We need to know a lot more about this Galaxy and others before using it, such as where you want to go and how to prepare yourself. It's about what you dial in.

Co-ordinates have to be established. The problem is there are no traffic signs in outer space. Dr. Wolf felt this would be one of the last projects we'll learn about through our association with the ETs.

• There exists a group of xenophobic and paranoid generals, charged with the protection of American skies, who fear and hate the extraterrestrials and who are waging war against them. This breakaway group use Star Wars weaponry including a neutral particle beam to shoot down ET craft and imprison survivors while attempting to extract information by force. The very technology the ETs gave us is now being used against them. Despised by many within the satellite government this military group also uses aggressive methods against those who try to end the UFO cover-up. A concern being that this aggression will intensify as the big announcement draws ever closer.

• Proposals for the announcement have been postponed three times – partly due to an S4 incident in 1975 which halted negotiations with the 'Greys' and partly due to the huge religious and world economic implications. A "Life on Mars" admission is the foundation for future revelations.

• The Vatican is especially worried over such forthcoming announcements. They have asked the American government to hold back, especially on the religious question, so there is more time for them to prepare. Dr. Wolf said the Pope has changed the Roman Catholic view on God. Their future line will be "we are not in the image of God but our souls are".

• He had spoken at length to the extraterrestrials about God and death. Our bodies are merely containers for the soul. When people die their consciousness simply moves into another dimension. On the subject of God Dr. Wolf said some ETs call God "The Forever" – the creator behind everything in the universe. On Jesus Christ, he was of joint ET/human heritage – sent to Earth as an attempt to end human violence. Whether a Zeta, Pleiadian, Altaran, Human, etc., we share the same God – we are all family.

• Earth is one of the few planets which doesn't control its weather. One reason why ET ships crash during climatic extremes – especially those using gravity propulsion. Dr. Wolf says their craft are no different to boats in a violent storm – bobbing up and down on large rolling gravity waves. To counteract these difficulties some ETs surround their ships with plasma energy or fly inter-dimensionally through a storm.

Technology gained from the ET technology includes:
• LEDs
• superconductivity
• computer chips
• fiber optics
• lasers
• gene-splicing therapy
• cloning

- night-vision equipment
- super-tenacity fibers (such as Kevlar lightweight armor)
- stealth technology
- particle beam devices
- aerospace ceramics
- anti-gravity control flight

- During one afternoon in 1990 an ET craft, escorted by American F-16 fighters, landed in Puerto Rico, in a busy tourist area. The ETs stepped out and walked amongst the population. Dr. Wolf said it was an exercise to gauge the public reaction. The Mayor of this island wrote a letter to President Bush stating, "At first we were amused by all of the sightings but then people became distressed. What do I tell them?" The President passed this communication onto Dr. Wolf. It was stamped all over with the words T52-EXEMPT (E) which means this letter can never be declassified.

- While studying at MIT for his PhD in physics he discovered a new theory of wave particle duality which later developed into a neutral particle beam. Dr. Wolf had hoped and envisioned that this technology would be used for treating cancer. Instead it was used as a weapon as part of the SDI Program (Star Wars).

- The top secret space plane, The Aurora, runs on liquid methane and has anti-gravity on board. It carries an electromagnetic pulse weapons system which can knock out tracking radar. This plane is also capable of traveling to the Moon.

- Some military pilots are experimenting with mind control to guide advanced planes. Dr. Wolf explained some ET craft are living conveyances which are able to divide and reform. These craft are also responsive to thought commands.

- The underground base at Area 51 is a sprawling city, the size of Rhode Island, which continues to grow and has a sister base called S4, some 12 miles away, and another named Indian Springs. It employs hundreds of civilian and military and has at least eight different on-going black programs along with an annual $2 billion budget. There is intense security outside with martial law inside and is patrolled by elite guards. Some scientists live at the base for 6 months at a time. While their bedrooms are basic the ETs live in their own magnificently designed apartments. There are also shopping malls, military style shops and leisure areas including swimming pools, gymnasiums and basketball courts.

- Satellite government scientists have successfully created zero point energy and cold fusion. There needs to be a smooth transition into these new sciences otherwise the world economy could be devastated.

James T. Westwood, senior consultant, Military Science and Defense Analytics, Unionville, VA., Westwood spoke about the only real, secret flying saucer (UFO) hardware and operations program of the U.S. government. His discussion was in the context of UFOs reported in the international media over Iran's nuclear sites in December 2004.

By the early 1980s, U.S. joint operations organizations at national and regional levels were organized as "special technical" units to manage and control the black flying saucer program. In the hot wash-up of the Gulf War of 1990-1991, this group would make bold claims among those with top secret knowledge that it "won the Gulf War."

According to Westwood, there is a measure of truth to this claim because it really did "put the lights out" in Baghdad in early 1991. During that brief conflict, the joint special technical organization was known colloquially as "Starship Enterprise." Some boasting, said Westwood is a part of military morale, though this boast has preservation-of-security implications.

Other than the accounts described in this chapter there are countless other testimonies from expert eyewitnesses, corroborating the existence of a secret military space program that is operated by a satellite government outside of NASA.

Following is a list of many prominent experts and eyewitnesses. These individuals have contributed expert testimony supporting the presence of extraterrestrial life here on Earth and throughout our Solar System, as well as the existence of a top secret military space program, as described in this book. Much of their testimony is available in the public domain.

• Dr. J. Allen Hynek – astronomer, professor and scientific adviser to UFO studies undertaken by the United States Air Force.
• Col. Phillip J. Corso – staff member of President Eisenhower's National Security Council; Chief of the Pentagon's Foreign Technology in Army Research and Development, Intelligence Staff Officer.
• John Maynard – former DIA (Defense Intelligence Agency) and Military Intelligence analyst.
• Albert M. Chop – former deputy Public Relations Director at NASA; United States Air Force spokesman for Project Blue Book.
• Harland Bentley – former NASA Department of Energy official.
• Christopher C. Kraft – former Director of the NASA tracking base in Houston.
• Dr. Edgar Mitchell – Apollo 14 astronaut.
• Neil Armstrong – Apollo 11 astronaut.
• Buzz Aldrin – Apollo 11 astronaut.
• Scott Carpenter – Mercury 7 astronaut.
• Eugene Cernan – Apollo 17 astronaut.
• John Glenn – former Mercury astronaut; first American to orbit the Earth; third American in space; United States senator from Ohio.
• Gordon Cooper – Mercury 9 and Gemini 5 astronaut.
• James McDivitt – Gemini 4 and Apollo 9 astronaut.

- James Irwin – Apollo 15 astronaut.
- Alfred Worden – Apollo 15 astronaut.
- Dr. Jerry Linenger – STS-64, STS-81, STS-84, and MIR astronaut.
- James Lovell – Gemini 7, Gemini 12, Apollo 8, and Apollo 13 astronaut.
- Dr. Farouk El-Baz – scientist who taught geology to the Apollo astronauts.
- Victor Afanasyev – Solyut 6 cosmonaut.
- Yevegni Khrunov – Soyuz 5 cosmonaut.
- Major General Vladimir Kovalyonok – Salyut 6 cosmonaut.
- Dr. Brian O'Leary – former NASA astronaut.
- Maurice Chatelain – former NASA Director of Communications.
- Karl Wolfe – retired Sergeant with top secret crypto clearance for the U.S. Air Force at Langley AFB in Virginia; worked for the Director of Intelligence at Headquarters Tactical Air Command, Technical Group.
- Yevgeny Arsyukhin – Russian astronomer.
- Donna Tietze (Hare) – former photo technician at NASA's Johnson Space Center in Houston.
- Dr. Pierre Guerin – astronomer associated with the French GEPAN (Study Group into Unidentified Atmospheric Phenomenon).
- Victor Marchetti – former CIA official.
- General Douglas MacArthur – Chief of Staff of the United States Army during the 1930s who played a lead role in the Pacific theater during World War II.
- David Froning – astronautical engineer who worked at McDonnell Douglas for over 30 years.
- Richard Boylan, PhD., M.S. Ed, MSW, B.A. – an emeritus Professor of Psychology; star-cultures Anthropologist; Certified Clinical Hypnotherapist; Researcher/Investigator into the UFO cover-up.
- Col. Steve Wilson (USAF, ret.) – former head of Project Pounce and Director-Skywatch International, Inc.
- Command Sergeant Major Robert Dean – worked at NATO's Supreme Headquarters from 1963-1967, and during this time was stationed in the Operations Center with a Cosmic Top Secret clearance.
- Norman Bergrun – engineer and photographic expert who worked for NASA almost 30 years.
- Ben Rich – former Lockheed Skunkworks CEO.
- Henry Deacon – physicist with Laurence Livermore Laboratories.
- Dr. Carol Rosin – award-winning educator, author, leading aerospace executive and space and missile defense consultant; former spokesperson for Wernher von Braun; consultant to a number of companies, organizations, government departments and the intelligence community; current President of the Institute for Security and Cooperation in Outer Space (ISCOS).
- Dr. Steven Greer – American physician, ufologist, author, lecturer and founder of the Orion Project and The Disclosure Project.
- Clark McClelland – retired Spacecraft Operator with NASA who during a 34-year career was responsible for ensuring the safety of numerous NASA missions including Mercury spaceflights, Apollo missions, the International Space Station and the Space Shuttle.

• Dr. Tom Van Flandern – former Chief Astronomer for the United States Naval Observatory.

• Dr. Gilbert Levin – American engineer, founder of Spherix and famous for his experiments on Mars soil by the Viking program.

• Chandra Wickramasinghe – globally renowned astrobiologist and Professor of applied mathematics and astronomy at the University of Cardiff.

• Dr. Mark Carlotto – computer-optics scientist with the Analytic Sciences Corporation.

• Ronald R. Nicks and James Erjavee – two highly respected engineering geologists.

• Captain John Lear – retired airline Captain and former CIA pilot, as well as son of the famous inventor of the Lear Jet. He is a former Lockheed L-1011 Captain and is highly regarded in aviation circles.

• Robert M. Collins – former United States Air Force Captain.

• Dr. Michael Wolf – American scientist and former member of National Security Council's (NSC) unacknowledged Special Studies Group subcommittee.

• Sgt. Clifford Stone – spent 22 years in the U.S. Army as a part of an extremely elite and secret group that was rapidly dispatched to crash sites in order to recover UFO or ET craft, bodies, and artifacts.

• Dr. L. Parker Temple – has worked in the military space program since 1976; was a member of the Air Force Office of Space Plans and Policy in the 1980s; speech writer for Air Force Secretary Edward C. Pete Aldridge; holds PhD. in science and technology policy from George Washington University; currently program manager of orbital systems for BTG Inc.

• Dr. Michael E. Salla – an internationally recognized scholar in Exopolitics, conflict resolution and U.S. foreign policy.

• Farida Iskiovet – former UFO investigator for the President of the United Nations.

• Commander Mark Huber – formerly of Naval Intelligence who had access to top secret information.

• Sgt. Willard Wannal – served in Army Intelligence in the 1950s as he investigated UFOs.

• Major Wayne S. Aho – formerly Army Intelligence who submitted UFO research to Congress.

• Dr. James Hurrah – NASA space program.

• Franklin Spinney – Department of Defense Analyst.

• Warren Botz – retired United States Air Force pilot.

• Jack D. Pickett – retired WWII combat veteran and publisher for United States Air Force.

• William Cooper – served on the Naval Intelligence briefing team for the Commander of the Pacific Fleet between 1970-73, and had access to classified documents that he had to review in order to fulfill his briefing duties.

• Phil Schneider – former geological engineer who was employed by corporations contracted to build underground bases; worked extensively on black projects involving extraterrestrials.

• Don Phillips – former Air Force serviceman and employee on clandestine aviation projects.

• Ingo Swann – the first psychic employed in the CIA's remote viewing program that began in 1975: Project Star Gate, whose objective was to spy on extraterrestrials on the Moon who had bases located on the far side.
• Dan Sherman – trained by the US Air Force as an "Intuitive Communicator" – a high-tech telepath – and found himself in daily communication with two extraterrestrials as part of the U.S. military's preparation "for a future time in which all electronic communications would be rendered useless".
• Dr. Robert Wood – retired Deputy Director of McDonnell Douglas his company studied UFOs in the 1960s as part of an effort to understand future forms of space travel, before Lockheed.
• Major Kevin Randle – Vietnam and second Gulf War veteran and prominent UFO researcher. Randle served as public affairs officer, a general's aide, and an intelligence officer.
• Stanton Friedman – nuclear physicist, lecturer, and UFO researcher.
• Paul Hellyer – Former Canadian Defence Minister.

Surely such an impressive group of highly credible individuals cannot all be mistaken in their claims. You can dismiss the work of alternative "New Age" science and history researchers if you wish. However, it is not so easy to ignore the work and opinion of so many highly qualified professionals contained in this list. Many of these individuals do not intentionally seek public attention and have no financial motive to promote a fabricated lie.

The Majestic 12

Majestic Twelve, Majestic-12, MJ-12, Majic, are all forms of the code name for the control group authorized by President Truman on September 24, 1947 (see copy of letter below). The control group was formed to oversee a top secret Research and Development & Intelligence Operation and was responsible only to the President.

The need for this group was dictated by the discovery of a downed flying saucer scattered across two sites near the town of Roswell, New Mexico in July 1947. The bodies of four small aliens were found in the wreckage. Majestic Twelve is the most highly classified secret in the United States and its existence has never been divulged to Congress. The funds for MJ-12 are CIA confidential (non-appropriated).

TOP SECRET

EYES ONLY

THE WHITE HOUSE
WASHINGTON

September 24, 1947.

MEMORANDUM FOR THE SECRETARY OF DEFENSE

Dear Secretary Forrestal:

As per our recent conversation on this matter,
you are hereby authorized to proceed with all due
speed and caution upon your undertaking. Hereafter
this matter shall be referred to only as Operation
Majestic Twelve.

It continues to be my feeling that any future
considerations relative to the ultimate disposition
of this matter should rest solely with the Office
of the President following appropriate discussions
with yourself, Dr. Bush and the Director of Central
Intelligence.

The 1947 letter purported to be signed by Harry
Truman, authorizing "Operation Majestic Twelve".

All the alleged original members of MJ-12 were notable for their military, government, and/or scientific achievements and all were deceased when the classified documents first surfaced about its existence in 1984. The last to die was Jerome Hunsaker, only a few months before the MJ-12 papers first appeared.

The original composition was six civilians (mostly scientists), and six high-ranking military officers, two from each major military service. Three (Souers, Vandenberg, and Hillenkoetter) had been the first three heads of the Central Intelligence Agency. It was not clear who was the director of MJ-12, or if there was any organizational hierarchy.

The named original members of MJ-12 were:

• Rear Adm. Roscoe H. Hillenkoetter: first CIA director.

• Dr. Vannevar Bush: chaired wartime Office of Scientific Research and Development and predecessor National Defense Research Committee; set up and chaired postwar Joint Research and Development Board (JRDB) and then the Research and Development Board (RDB); chaired NACA; President of Carnegie Institute, Washington DC.

• James Forrestal: Secretary of the Navy; first Secretary of Defense (replaced after his death on MJ-12 by Gen. Walter Bedell Smith, second CIA director).

• Gen. Nathan Twining: headed Air Materiel Command at Wright-Patterson AFB; Air Force Chief of Staff (1953–1957); Chairman of Joint Chiefs of Staff (1957–1961).

• Gen. Hoyt Vandenberg: Directed Central Intelligence Group (1946–1947); Air Force Chief of Staff (1948–1953).

• Gen. Robert M. Montague: Guided missile expert; 1947 commander of Fort Bliss; headed nuclear Armed Forces Special Weapons Center, Sandia Base.

• Dr. Jerome Hunsaker: Aeronautical engineer, MIT; chaired NACA after Bush.

• Rear Adm. Sidney Souers: first director of Central Intelligence Group, first executive secretary of National Security Council (NSC).

• Gordon Gray: Secretary of the Army; intelligence and national security expert; CIA psychological strategy board (1951–1953); Chairman of NSC 5412 Committee (1954–1958); National Security Advisor (1958–1961).

• Dr. Donald Menzel: Astronomer, Harvard; cryptologist during war; security consultant to CIA and NSA.

• Dr. Detley Bronk: Medical physicist; aviation physiologist; chair, National Academy of Sciences, National Research Council; president Johns Hopkins & Rockefeller University.

• Dr. Lloyd Berkner: Physicist; radio expert; executive secretary of Bush's JRDB.

More recent alleged members have included Dr. Edward Teller, Dr. Henry Kissinger, Admiral Bobby Ray Inman, Admiral John Poindexter, Harold Brown, Richard Helms, Gen. Vernon Walters, and Theodore von Karman.

According to other sources and MJ-12 papers to emerge after 1984, famous scientists like Robert Oppenheimer, Albert Einstein, Karl Compton, John von Neumann, and Wernher von Braun were also allegedly involved with MJ-12.

Majestic Twelve documents can be identified by the following:

TOP SECRET/MAJIC/RESTRICTED DATA; EYES ONLY COPY___OF___ TOP; SECRET/MAJIC/RESTRICTED; EYES ONLY COPY___OF___ TOP SECRET/MAJIC; EYES ONLY COPY___OF___

One of the above will appear both at the top and bottom of each page. You will never see one version in a document along with any other version. Also on each page will appear; T52-Exempt (E) or just Exempt. T52 is the publication outlining procedures for automatic downgrade of all security classifications and the time period for declassification of each security level. This information is never to be declassified.

Each page of each document will be numbered consecutively and the number of pages will appear upon the cover sheet. Copies of Majestic Twelve beyond the original number are forbidden.

Top Secret Government Projects Related to Space Program

Some of the projects listed below are common public knowledge. Others are covert, funded through black budgets, with no congressional oversight whatsoever. In most cases these black projects are under operational command of Majestic Twelve.

Many of these clandestine projects directly or indirectly supported, or were in some way associated with the secret space program.

Intelligence Advanced Research Project (IARPA) – a United States research agency under the Director of National Intelligence's responsibility. In January 2008, Lisa Porter, an administrator at NASA with experience at DARPA, was appointed director of the activity formed in 2006 from the National Security Agency's Disruptive Technology Office (DTO), the National Geospatial-Intelligence Agency's National Technology Alliance and the Central Intelligence Agency's Intelligence Technology Innovation Center.

According to the Director of National Intelligence the goal of the agency is to "conduct research that generates revolutionary capabilities that will surprise our adversaries and help us avoid being surprised, and to counter new capabilities implemented by our adversaries that would threaten our ability to operate freely and effectively in a networked world."

Defense Advanced Research Projects Agency (DARPA) – an agency of the United States Department of Defense responsible for the development of new technology for use by the military. DARPA has been responsible for funding the development of many technologies which have had a major effect on the world. DARPA was established during 1958 (as ARPA) in response to the Soviet launching of Sputnik during 1957, with the mission of keeping U.S. military technology more sophisticated than that of it's potential enemies.

Today, DARPA's mission is still to prevent technological surprise to the U.S., but also to create technological surprise for its enemies. DARPA is independent from other more conventional military R&D and reports directly to senior Department of Defense management. DARPA directly manages a $3.2 billion budget.

Project Sign (1947-1948), **Project Grudge** (1948-1952), and **Project Blue Book** (1952 to 1969) – official United States government studies of unidentified flying objects (UFOs) undertaken by the United States Air Force. They were established to determine whether UFOs posed a threat to the security of the United States and to determine whether UFOs exhibit any unique scientific information or advanced technology which could contribute to scientific or technical research.

A report by Project Sign members was issued in 1948 and called *The Estimate of the Situation*. It concluded that flying saucers are probably real extraterrestrial spacecraft. However, Project Sign's final report directly contradicted their earlier report by stating that the existence of flying saucers could neither be confirmed nor denied. Project Blue Book was abandoned and its mission and information was consolidated under Project Aquarius in 1969.

Project Aquarius – established in 1953 by President Eisenhower under control of MJ-12 and Project Sign. The project contains all information collected by the United States since it began investigating UFOs (Unidentified Flying Objects) and IACs (Identified Alien Craft). At the time its information existed in approximately 15 or 16 volumes. This project became an independent project when Project Sign was eliminated in 1960. Project Aquarius referred to aliens as Alien Life Forms. The mission of Project Aquarius was to gather all scientific, technological, medical and intelligence information from UFO & IAC sightings and contacts with Alien Life Forms.

The information was to be used in the space program. In 1966, the project's name was changed from Project Gleem to Project Aquarius. The Project was funded by CIA confidential funds (non-appropriated). The project was originally classified SECRET but was upgraded to its present classification in December 1969 after Project Blue Book closed. This orderly file of collected information has been used to advance the United States Space Program.

Project Sigma – established in 1954 as part of Project Sign. The mission of Project Sigma was to establish communication with the aliens. First communication was established in 1959 through binary computer language. On April 25, 1964 a USAF (OSI) officer met with aliens at a prearranged desert location in New Mexico. Information was exchanged and a basic understanding was reached after several hours. It was learned through this effort that several species of alien life existed. Communication was eventually established with all of them.

Through communications it was determined that three categories existed. The project has been extremely successful. A fleet of UFOs flew over the White House, Capitol Building and the Department of Defense on July 19th, 1952 and, again, on July 25th, 1952. The world was electrified by large newspaper headlines and photos of squadrons of UFOs flying repeatedly over the nation's Capital in Washington, DC. President Truman in 1952 asked the CIA and later the NSA to broadcast a message to the extraterrestrials that we wanted to discuss a treaty. This went on to become known as Project Sigma.

Project Plato – established in 1960 after the United States established communications with the aliens. The mission of Project Plato was to establish diplomatic relations with the aliens. Project Plato made agreements in order to prevent hostilities between the United States and the aliens. An agreement was made with the malevolent aliens whereby they could abduct humans. The purpose of these abductions was to provide blood and other biological fluids as food for the aliens. The aliens agreed to furnish a list periodically to MJ-12 of the names of those abducted. Project Plato took whatever steps necessary to prevent public disclosure.

Project Pluto – established in 1947 after the Roswell incident. The mission of Project Pluto was to recover all crashed or downed alien craft, to recover all evidence of alien presence or technology, and to recover all alien bodies (alive or dead). Project Pluto developed cover stories to satisfy press and civilian curiosity. And was authorized use of deadly force and/or relocation to insure secrecy. Project Pluto was responsible for biological intelligence of the Alien Life Forms.

Project Pounce – its mission was to evaluate all UFO/IAC information pertaining to space technology. The goal was to duplicate the technology and/or improve upon it. Ultimate use of the technology would establish the United States as the dominate world power and close the gap in any confrontation with the aliens. An elite Air Force/National Reconnaissance Organization Special Forces unit was formed which retrieved downed UFOs. In 1953, the military formed "Alpha Teams" to find and retrieve crashed discs and any aliens found at the crash site.

Project Redlight – established in 1954. Its mission was to test a recovered alien craft. The mission was accomplished in part only. Project Redlight was terminated in 1963 after every (flyable) recovered craft exploded during test flights. There were no survivors among the human test pilots.

Project Snowbird – established in 1972. Its mission was to test fly a recovered alien craft. As far as we are aware this project is still on going.

Project ???????? – This project may or may not be ongoing. It cannot be determined if this project is still in existence. The mission of this project was to develop a low frequency pulse sound generator. The energy produced from this generator was to be concentrated so that it could be aimed and used as a weapon in order to destroy alien spacecraft and beam weapons.

The alien beam weapons were described as being able to incapacitate or destroy any weapons system known to date (1972). The aliens also possess a beam weapon which is described as being able to paralyze any human within range. Tests were described as having shown that the alien craft and weapons were extremely sensitive to low frequency pulse sound waves. This weapon was to be used to incapacitate the alien defenses in order to allow Project Excalibur to succeed in its mission. The initial technology used in this project was captured from the Germans during WWII.

The German sound generators were described as being able to knock down reinforced concrete buildings and shatter 4-inch thick armor from a great range. This technology is believed to further substantiate that Germany had recovered alien craft and had possibly had some dealings with the aliens prior to or during WWII.

Documents captured during and after WWII indicated that an alien craft had been recovered by Germany in 1939. A German built flying saucer was captured during the last few months of WWII.

Project Excalibur – established in 1972. Its mission was to develop a weapons system capable of destroying the alien underground base after the alien beam weapons have been incapacitated or destroyed. The alien underground base is located beneath an Indian reservation near the small town of Dulce, New Mexico. The device must be capable of penetrating 3,300 feet of tufa/hard pack soil and sustain no operational damage. This type is commonly found in New Mexico where the alien base is located. Missile apogee must not exceed 30,000 feet. Impact deviation will now exceed 165 feet. The device will carry a one-megaton warhead.

Operation UFO (NSA Operation in support of Project Pluto) – its mission was to form intelligence teams versed in all of the knowledge learned which would be the first on scene of any UFO crash site in order to secure the technology and prevent it from falling into foreign hands. Several teams existed throughout the world. The United States was specifically concerned that it did not fall into Soviet hands. This mission was to be accomplished no matter the country of occurrence. Many subsequent alien craft recoveries would occur in foreign countries as well as the United States. Operation UFO was also used to recover downed space hardware (especially used to recover nuclear weapons which became lost (usually by accident).

Operation Moondust – its mission was to provide a cover which would neutralize public curiosity while recovery of an alien craft was being conducted. The teams that made up the compliment of Moondust were the same teams that made up Operation UFO. Moondust was made public and its mission (to the public) was to identify and recover United States space hardware which might fall to Earth.

Operation Bluefly (supported Operation UFO and Moondust) – its mission was to provide quick reaction combat teams known as "Alpha teams" (fight for technology if necessary), mechanical and technological support in recovery, rapid and secure transport to secure storage and examination areas. There are several of these storage and examination areas in order to limit distance traveled and thus limit the possible chance of an accident that could expose cargo to public knowledge. Several teams existed throughout the world. Recovery and transport of both EBEs (dead or alive) and alien craft were accomplished. Bluefly was also utilized in event of recovery of space objects (of terrestrial origin), and event of recovery of lost nuclear weapons (usually due to accident).

Project Rainbow (also known as the **Philadelphia Experiment** later changed to **Project Phoenix**) – was allegedly an experiment conducted upon a small Navy destroyer escort ship (U.S.S. Eldridge) during World War II, both in the Philadelphia Naval Yard and at sea. The goal was to make that ship invisible to enemy detection. It has been claimed that the Philadelphia Experiment was partly an investigation into how

Albert Einstein's "Unified Field Theory for Gravitation and Electricity" might be used to advantage in the development of electronic camouflage for ships at sea.

Project Serpo – was allegedly an exchange program operated from 1965 to 1978 involving a 12-person joint-service U.S. military team and extraterrestrial visitors from a planet in the Zeta Reticuli star system. The true name is **Project Serponia**. The project was a disinformation cover story intended to fool anyone from discovering the truth and lead them on a wild goose chase. Under no circumstances was there any kind of exchange of our people for theirs.

X-20 Dyna-Soar Project – was cancelled on December 10, 1963. The program was supposedly intended to prove the utility of man in space for military missions. However, this was just a cover story for the Russians and the public.

Constellation Project – is the Space Shuttle's replacement with a capsule based system similar to Apollo. It aims to take astronauts to the Moon and Mars, and service the International Space Station (ISS).

Solar Warden – is a code name for a top secret fleet of anti-gravity space vehicles. It falls into a Joint Forces Command project. This suggests Solar Warden is operationally located within Strategic Command. NASA is little more than a public relations cover story for this highly classified anti-gravity space fleet that regularly takes military astronauts into space. As of 2005 the fleet consisted of 8 ships, an equivalent to aircraft carriers, and 43 "protectors," which are space planes.

Project Blue Beam – involves a false, projected presentation of an alien invasion by government authorities. This was revealed by Wernher von Braun, the renowned German rocket scientist who was instrumental in the German V2 program and also the Saturn V rocket which landed men on the Moon. According to von Braun there was a multi-stage program planned which would allow some form of totalitarian world government to take control. He made this startling disclosure shortly before his death in 1977.

Project Star Gate – a CIA-sponsored project researching the usefulness of remote viewing as a tool for intelligence gathering that began in 1975. Project Star Gate is the collective name for advanced psychic functioning or remote viewing experiments and programs that were undertaken for over 20 years to create a trainable, repeatable, operational and if at all possible, accurate method of psychic spying or information gathering for the U.S. military and intelligence agencies (CIA, NSA, DIA). Project Star Gate was allegedly used to spy on extraterrestrials on the Moon who had bases located on the far side.

President Eisenhower Meeting (Treaty) with Extraterrestrial Delegation

On the night and early hours of February 20-21, 1954, while on a supposed vacation to Palm Springs, California, President Eisenhower went missing and allegedly was taken to Muroc Field (now Edwards Air Force Base) for a secret meeting (photo below).

Leaked photo of an alleged meeting at Muroc Field (now Edwards Air Force Base) between one extraterrestrial group and American officials.

When he showed up the next morning at a church service in Los Angeles, reporters were told that he had to have emergency dental treatment the previous evening and had visited a local dentist.

A dentist later appeared at a function that evening and presented as the dentist who had treated Eisenhower. The missing night and morning has subsequently fueled rumors that Eisenhower was using the alleged dentist visit as a cover story for an extraordinary event.

The event is possibly the most significant that any American President could have conducted: an alleged First Contact meeting with extraterrestrials at Edwards Air Force base (previously Muroc Field), and the beginning of a series of meetings with different extraterrestrial races that led to a treaty that was eventually signed.

I will explore the evidence that the First Contact meeting had occurred with extraterrestrials having a distinctive Nordic appearance, the likelihood of an agreement having been spurned with this Nordic race, the start of a series of meetings that led to a treaty eventually being signed with a different extraterrestrial race dubbed the 'Greys', and the motivations of the different extraterrestrial races involved in these treaty discussions.

I will further examine why these events were kept secret for so long, and whether an official disclosure announcement is likely in the near future.

There is circumstantial and testimonial evidence supporting Eisenhower's meeting with extraterrestrials and the start of a series of meetings that culminated in the signing of a treaty with a different group of extraterrestrials.

The most intriguing are circumstances surrounding Eisenhower's alleged winter vacation to Palm Springs, California from February 17-24, 1954. Firstly, the "vacation for the President" which was announced came rather suddenly and came less than a week after Eisenhower's quail shooting vacation in Georgia. All this was quite unusual and suggested that there was more to the one week visit to Palm Springs than a simple holiday.

Secondly, on the Saturday night of February 20, President Eisenhower did go missing fueling press speculation that he had taken ill or even died. In a hastily convened press conference, Eisenhower's Press Secretary announced that Eisenhower had lost a tooth cap while eating fried chicken and had to be rushed to a local dentist. The local dentist was introduced at an official function on Sunday February 21, as the dentist who had treated the president.

Further investigation of the incident concluded that the dentist's visit was being used as a cover story for Eisenhower's true whereabouts.

Consequently, Eisenhower was missing for an entire evening and could easily have been taken from Palm Springs to the nearby Muroc Airfield, later renamed Edwards Air Force base. The unscheduled nature of the President's vacation, the missing President and the dentist cover story provide circumstantial evidence that the true purpose of his Palm Springs vacation was for him to attend an event whose importance was such that it could not be disclosed to the general public.

A meeting with extraterrestrials may well have been the true purpose of his visit.

The first public source alleging a meeting with extraterrestrials was Gerald Light who in a letter dated April 16, 1954 to Meade Layne, the then director of Borderland Sciences Research Associates (now Foundation), claimed he was part of a delegation of community leaders to an alleged meeting with extraterrestrials at Muroc Field (now Edwards Air Force Base).

In a subsequent article, Meade Layne described Light as a "gifted and highly educated writer and lecturer", who was skilled both in clairvoyance and the occult. Light was a well-known metaphysical community leader in the Southern

California area. The alleged purpose of him and others on the delegation was to test public reaction to the presence of extraterrestrials.

Light described the circumstances of the meeting as follows:

"My dear friends: I have just returned from Muroc Field (Edwards Air Force Base). The report is true – devastatingly true! I made the journey in company with Franklin Allen of the Hearst newspapers and Edwin Nourse of Brookings Institute (Truman's financial advisor) and Bishop McIntyre of Los Angeles.

When we were allowed to enter the restricted section (after about six hours in which we were checked on every possible item, event, incident and aspect of our personal and public lives), I had the distinct feeling that the world had come to an end with fantastic realism. For I have never seen so many human beings in a state of complete collapse and confusion, as they realized that their own world had indeed ended with such finality as to beggar description.

The reality of the "other plane" aeroforms is now and forever removed from the realms of speculation and made a rather painful part of the consciousness of every responsible scientific and political group.

During my two day visit I saw five separate and distinct types of aircraft being studied and handled by our Air Force officials – with the assistance and permission of the Etherians!

I have no words to express my reactions. It has finally happened. It is now a matter of history. President Eisenhower, as you may already know, was spirited over to Muroc one night during his visit to Palm Springs recently. And it is my conviction that he will ignore the terrific conflict between the various authorities and go directly to the people via radio and television – if the impasse continues much longer.

From what I could gather, an official statement to the country is being prepared for delivery about the middle of May.

Of course no such formal announcement was made, and Light's supposed meeting has either been the best-kept secret of the 20th century or the fabrication of an elderly mystic known for out of body experiences.

The events Light describes in his meeting in terms of the panic and confusion of many of those present, the emotional impact of the alleged landing, and the tremendous difference of opinion on what to do in terms of telling the public and responding to the extraterrestrial visitors, are plausible descriptions of what may have occurred.

Indeed, the psychological and emotional impact Light describes for senior national security leaders at the meeting is consistent with what could be expected for such a life-changing event.

A further way of determining Light's claim is to investigate the figures he named along with himself as part of the community delegation, and whether they could have been plausible candidates for such a meeting.

Dr. Edwin Nourse (1883-1974) was the first chairman of the Council of Economic Advisors to the President (1944-1953) and was President Truman's chief economic advisor. Nourse officially retired to private life in 1953 and would certainly have been a good choice of someone who could give confidential economic advice to the Eisenhower administration.

If Dr. Nourse was present at such a meeting, he did so in order to provide his expertise on the possible economic impact of First Contact with extraterrestrials. Another of the individuals mentioned by Light was Bishop McIntyre.

Cardinal James Francis McIntyre was the bishop and head of the Catholic Church in Los Angeles (1948-1970) and would have been an important gauge for the possible reaction from religious leaders generally, and in particular from the most influential and powerful religious institution on the planet – the Roman Catholic Church.

In particular, Cardinal McIntyre would have been a good choice as a representative for the Vatican since he was appointed the first Cardinal of the Western United States by Pope Pius XII in 1952. All Cardinal McIntyre's correspondence is closed to researchers thus making it impossible to confirm what impact the visit to Muroc had on him and what he communicated to other church leaders and the Vatican.

Cardinal McIntyre had sufficient rank and authority to represent the Catholic Church and the religious community in a delegation of community leaders.

The fourth member of the delegation of community leaders was Franklin Winthrop Allen, a former reporter with the Hearst Newspaper Group.

Allen was 80-years-old at the time, author of a book instructing reporters on how to deal with Congressional Committee Hearings, and would have been a good choice for a member of the press who could maintain confidentiality.

The four represented senior leaders of the religious, spiritual, economic and media communities and were well advanced in age and status.

They would certainly have been plausible choices for a community delegation that could provide confidential advice on a possible public response to a First Contact event involving extraterrestrial races. Such a selection would have constituted a "wise men" group that would have been entirely in character for the conservative nature of American society in 1954.

While Light may well have contrived such a list in a fabricated account or out-of-body experience there is nothing in Light's selection that eliminates the possibility that they were plausible members of such a delegation. At face value then, the selection of such a "wise men" group gives some credence to Light's claim.

It may be concluded then that following items all make up circumstantial evidence that a meeting with extraterrestrials occurred.

• The first is Eisenhower's missing night.
• The second is the weak cover story used for Eisenhower's absence.
• The third is Light's description of actual events at the meeting in terms of the psychological and emotional impact of the described meeting which is consistent with what could be anticipated.
• The final is Light's description of the composition of community leaders or "wise men" at the meeting.

These four items collectively provide circumstantial evidence that a meeting with extraterrestrials occurred and that Eisenhower was present.

There are a number of other sources alleging an extraterrestrial meeting at Muroc Field that corresponded to a formal First Contact event.

These sources are based on testimonies of whistleblowers that witnessed documents or learned from their insider contacts of such a meeting. These testimonies describe what appear to be two separate sets of meetings involving different extraterrestrial groups who met either with President Eisenhower and/or with Eisenhower administration officials over a short period of time.

The first of these meetings, the actual First Contact event, did not lead to an agreement and the extraterrestrials were effectively spurned. The second of these meetings did lead to an agreement, and this has been apparently become the basis of subsequent secret interactions with extraterrestrial races involved in the treaty that was signed.

There is some discrepancy in the sequence of meetings and where they were held, but all agree that a First Contact meeting involving President Eisenhower did occur, and that one of these meetings occurred with his February 1954 visit to Muroc Field.

The first version of Eisenhower's meeting is described by one of the most controversial whistleblowers to ever have come forward into the public arena to describe an extraterrestrial presence.

William Cooper served on the Naval Intelligence briefing team for the Commander of the Pacific Fleet between 1970-73, and had access to classified documents that he had to review in order to fulfill his briefing duties.

He describes the background and nature of the First contact with extraterrestrials as follows:

In 1953 Astronomers discovered large objects in space which were moving toward the Earth. It was first believed that they were asteroids. Later evidence proved that the objects could only be spaceships. Project Sigma intercepted alien radio communications. When the objects reached the Earth they took up a very high orbit around the equator.

There were several huge ships, and their actual intent was unknown. Project Sigma, and a new project, Plato, through radio communications using the computer binary language, was able to arrange a landing that resulted in face to face contact with alien beings from another planet. Project Plato was tasked with establishing diplomatic relations with this race of space aliens. In the meantime a race of human looking aliens contacted the U.S. Government.

This alien group warned us against the aliens that were orbiting the equator and offered to help us with our spiritual development. They demanded that we dismantle and destroy our nuclear weapons as the major condition. They refused to exchange technology citing that we were spiritually unable to handle the technology which we then possessed. They believed that we would use any new technology to destroy each other.

This race stated that,

• we were on a path of self destruction and we must stop killing each other,
• stop polluting the Earth,
• stop raping the Earth's natural resources,
• and learn to live in harmony.

These terms were met with extreme suspicion, especially the major condition of nuclear disarmament.

It was believed that meeting that condition would leave us helpless in the face of an obvious alien threat. We also had nothing in history to help with the decision. Nuclear disarmament was not considered to be within the best interest of the United States.

The overtures were rejected.

The significant point about Cooper's version is that the humanoid extraterrestrial race was not willing to enter into technology exchanges that might help weapons development, and instead was focused on spiritual development. Significantly, the overtures of these extraterrestrials were turned down.

Confirmation that the First Contact meeting involved extraterrestrials who were effectively spurned for taking what might be considered a principled stand on technology assistance and nuclear weapons comes from the son of a former Navy Commander who claimed that his father had been present at the First Contact event on February 20-21, 1954.

According to Charles L. Suggs, a retired Sgt from the U.S. Marine Corps, his father Charles L. Suggs, (1909-1987) was a former Commander with the U.S. Navy who attended the meeting at Edwards Air force base with Eisenhower.

Sgt. Suggs recounted his father's experiences from the meeting in a 1991 interview with a prominent UFO researcher:

> Charlie's father, Navy Commander Charles Suggs accompanied President Eisenhower along with others on February 20th. They met and spoke with two white-haired Nordics that had pale blue eyes and colorless lips. The spokesman stood a number of feet away from Eisenhower and would not let him approach any closer.
>
> A second Nordic stood on the extended ramp of a bi-convex saucer that stood on tripod landing gear on the landing strip. According to Charlie, there were B-58 Hustlers on the field even though the first one did not fly officially till 1956. These visitors said they came from another solar system.
>
> They posed detailed questions about our nuclear testing.

Another whistleblower who confirms that First Contact involved an extraterrestrial race being spurned for their principled stand on technology transfer is the son of the famous creator of the Lear Jet, William Lear.

John Lear is a former Lockheed L-1011 Captain who flew over 150 test aircraft and held 18 world speed records, and during the late 1960s, 1970s and early 1980s was a contract pilot for the CIA. Lear developed a close relationship with CIA Director (DCI) William Colby who was in charge of covert operations in Vietnam before becoming DCI.

According to Lear there had indeed been a warning from another race prior to an agreement being eventually signed, and he claimed they visited Muroc/Edwards and the following occurred:

In 1954, President Eisenhower met with a representative of another alien species at Muroc Test Center, which is now called Edwards Air Force Base. This alien suggested that they could help us get rid of the 'Greys' but Eisenhower turned down their offer because they offered no technology.

Cooper's and Lear's idea of more than one extraterrestrial race interacting with the Eisenhower administration is supported by other whistleblowers such as former Master Sergeant Robert Dean who like Cooper, had access to top secret documents while working in the intelligence division for the Supreme Commander of a major U.S. military command.

In Dean's 27-year distinguished military career, he served at the Supreme Headquarters Allied Powers Europe where he witnessed these documents while serving under the Supreme Allied Commander of Europe.

Dean claimed:

> The group at the time, there were just four that they knew of for certain and the 'Greys' were one of those groups. There was a group that looked exactly like we do.

> There was a human group that looked so much like us that that really drove the admirals and the generals crazy because they determined that these people, and they had seen them repeatedly, they had had contact with them, there had been abductions, there had been contacts.

> Two other groups, there was a very large group, I say large, they were 6-8 maybe sometimes 9 feet tall and they were humanoid, but they were very pale, very white, didn't have any hair on their bodies at all.

> And then there was another group that had sort of a reptilian quality to them. We had encountered them, military people and police officers all over the world have run into these guys. They had vertical pupils in their eyes and their skin seemed to have a quality very much like what you find on the stomach of a lizard.

> So those were the four they knew of in 1964.

There is some discrepancy in the testimonials as to which Air Force Base the spurned extraterrestrials met with President Eisenhower and/or Eisenhower administration officials. Cooper claims this occurred at Homestead Air Force Base in Florida, and not Edwards.

On the other hand Lear and Suggs suggest it occurred at Muroc (Edwards). In his letter, Gerald Light pointed to intense disagreement amongst Eisenhower officials in responding to the extraterrestrials at the Edwards AFB meeting. Such intense disagreement may predictably have occurred if national security officials were responding to an extraterrestrial request to abandon the pursuit of weapons technologies.

Given the intensity of the Cold War, the national security officials present may well have decided it was more prudent to seek better terms before agreeing to the extraterrestrials request. Light's testimony implies that the meeting at Edwards did not result in an agreement, but instead resulted in intense disagreement between Eisenhower officials.

Consequently, it appears that the Lear and Suggs version is more accurate, and that the First Contact meeting occurred at Edwards Air Force Base in February 20-21, 1954.

According to the testimonies examined so far, the February 20-21, 1954 meeting was not successful, and the extraterrestrials were spurned due to their refusal to enter into technology exchanges and insistence on nuclear disarmament by the U.S. and presumably other major world powers.

Cooper describes the circumstances of a subsequent agreement that was reached after the failure of the first meeting. While Cooper has a different version of dates and times for the 1954 meetings, he agrees that there were two sets of meetings involving different extraterrestrials meeting with President Eisenhower and/or Eisenhower administration officials.

Later in 1954 the race of large nosed 'Grey' Aliens which had been orbiting the Earth landed at Holloman Air Force Base in New Mexico.

A basic agreement was reached. This race identified themselves as originating from a Planet around a red star in the Constellation of Orion which we called Betelgeuse. They stated that their planet was dying and that at some unknown future time they would no longer be able to survive there.

The meeting at Holloman AFB has reportedly been the site of subsequent extraterrestrial meetings with the same extraterrestrials who it will be shown signed the 1954 treaty. In 1972-73, for example, the producers Robert Emenegger and Allan Sandler, had allegedly been offered and witnessed actual Air Force film footage of a meeting involving 'Grey' extraterrestrials that occurred at Holloman AFB in 1971.

Cooper explained the terms of the 1954 treaty reached with the 'Grey' extraterrestrials as follows:

> The treaty stated that the aliens would not interfere in our affairs and we would not interfere in theirs. We would keep their presence on Earth a

secret. They would furnish us with advanced technology and would help us in our technological development.

They would not make any treaty with any other Earth nation.

They could abduct humans on a limited and periodic basis for the purpose of medical examination and monitoring of our development, with the stipulation that the humans would not be harmed, would be returned to their point of abduction, would have no memory of the event, and that the alien nation would furnish Majesty Twelve (MJ-12) with a list of all human contacts and abductees on a regularly scheduled basis.

Another whistleblower source for a treaty having been signed is Phil Schneider, a former geological engineer that was employed by corporations contracted to build underground bases worked extensively on black projects involving extraterrestrials.

He revealed his own knowledge of the treaty in the following:

Back in 1954, under the Eisenhower administration, the federal government decided to circumvent the Constitution of the United States and form a treaty with alien entities. It was called the 1954 Grenada Treaty, which basically made the agreement that the aliens involved could take a few cows and test their implanting techniques on a few human beings, but that they had to give details about the people involved.

Schneider's knowledge of the treaty would have come from his familiarity with a range of compartmentalized black projects and interaction with other personnel working with extraterrestrials.

Yet another whistleblower source for an agreement being signed is Dr. Michael Wolf, who claims to have served on various policy-making committees responsible for extraterrestrial affairs for 25 years.

He claims that the Eisenhower administration entered into the treaty with an extraterrestrial race and that this treaty was never ratified as constitutionally required.

Significantly, a number of whistleblowers argue that the treaty that was signed involved some compulsion on the part of the extraterrestrials.

Don Phillips is a former Air Force serviceman and employee on clandestine aviation projects who testified having seen documents describing the meeting between President Eisenhower and extraterrestrials, and the background to a subsequent agreement:

We have records from 1954 that were meetings between our own leaders of this country and ETs here in California. And, as I understand it from the written documentation, we were asked if we would allow them to be here and do research.

I have read that our reply was well, how can we stop you? You are so advanced. And I will say by this camera and this sound, that it was President Eisenhower that had this meeting.

Col. Phillip Corso, a highly decorated officer that served in Eisenhower's National Security Council alluded to a treaty signed by the Eisenhower administration with extraterrestrials in his memoirs. He wrote:

We had negotiated a kind of surrender with them (extraterrestrials) as long as we couldn't fight them. They dictated the terms because they knew what we most feared was disclosure.

Corso's claim of a negotiated surrender suggests that some sort of agreement or treaty was reached which he was not happy with.

According to Cooper, the 'Grey' extraterrestrials signing the treaty were not trustworthy:

By 1955 it became obvious that the aliens had deceived Eisenhower and had broken the treaty. It was suspected that the aliens were not submitting a complete list of human contacts and abductees to the Majesty Twelve (MJ-12) and it was suspected that not all abductees had been returned.

Similarly, Lear argued that the 'Grey' extraterrestrials quickly broke the treaty and could not be trusted:

A deal was struck that in exchange for advanced technology from the aliens we would allow them to abduct a very small number of persons and we would periodically be given a list of those persons abducted. We got something less than the technology we bargained for and found the abductions exceeded by a million fold than what we had naively agreed to.

Other whistleblowers also suggested that the extraterrestrials who signed the treaty with Eisenhower couldn't be trusted. Schneider claimed that despite the treaty's provisions on the number of humans who would be abducted for experiments, the aliens altered the bargain until they decided they wouldn't abide by it at all.

As mentioned earlier, Col. Phillip Corso similarly believed that the extraterrestrials that the Eisenhower administration entered into agreements with couldn't be trusted.

Corso believed these forced a negotiated surrender suggesting an extraterrestrial agenda that was suspect.

While General Douglas Macarthur didn't directly mention any government treaty with extraterrestrials, he gave a famous warning in October 1955 suggesting that some extraterrestrial presence existed that threatened human sovereignty:

> You now face a new world, a world of change. We speak in strange terms, of harnessing the cosmic energy, of ultimate conflict between a united human race and the sinister forces of some other planetary galaxy.
>
> The nations of the world will have to unite, for the next war will be an interplanetary war. The nations of the Earth must someday make a common front against attack by people from other planets.

Macarthur may well have been alluding to the same extraterrestrials that Corso, Cooper and Lear believed had entered into an agreement with the Eisenhower administration.

Significantly, reports of contacts with extraterrestrials began to change once the alleged treaty began to be implemented.

The friendly "space brothers" reports involving contactees of the 1950s changed as reports of abductions began to emerge after the first recorded case in 1961 involving Barney and Betty Hill:

> Another apparent pattern that has occurred in Ufology is the dominance of the space brothers in the 1950s who were kind, interacted with people who became known as contactees, and took people for rides in their spacecraft. This pattern changed dramatically with the abduction of Betty and Barney Hill in the early 1960s.
>
> The space brother human types of the 1950s seemed to fade away, and they were replaced in the UFO literature with another type of alien. In the early sixties the first abduction of the Hills began a new pattern where the aliens were 'grey' evil aliens who would abduct people against their will, and perform medical procedures on them.
>
> Unlike the good space brothers of the 1950s these 'Grey' aliens were described by all, who were unfortunate enough to have met with them, as being distant and without emotions.

According to Wolf, the extraterrestrials were 'Greys' from the fourth planet of the star system Zeta Reticulum, while Cooper claims they were tall 'Greys' from Betelgeuse in Orion.

Wolf's and Cooper's differing versions likely reflect a close relationship between 'Greys' from Rigel and Betelguese, and that more than one species of extraterrestrials may have been covered in the treaty. Wolf has described the 'Greys' as having positive motivations in regard to their presence on Earth, but have been inhibited and targeted by rogue elements in the U.S. military. Similarly, Robert Dean believes that the extraterrestrials visiting Earth are friendly.

This contrasts with the testimonies of Cooper, Lear, Schneider, Corso and arguably even Macarthur over the true motivations of the 'Greys'. It is worth repeating Gerald Light's claim of a "terrific conflict between the various authorities" on whether to inform the general public or not.

It is likely that these differing perspectives on the motivations of the 'Greys' reflected an uncertainty that has continued to intensely divide policy makers up to the present on how to best respond to the extraterrestrial presence and what to tell the general public.

The uncertainty over the motivations and behavior of the 'Grey' extraterrestrials appears to have played a large role in the government decision not to disclose the extraterrestrial presence and the treaty Eisenhower signed with them.

The following passage from an alleged official document leaked to UFO researchers describes the official secrecy policy adopted in April 1954 – two months after Eisenhower had First Contact with extraterrestrials who were spurned by the Eisenhower administration:

> Any encounter with entities known to be of extraterrestrial origin is to be considered to be a matter of national security and therefore classified TOP SECRET.

> Under no circumstances is the general public or the public press to learn of the existence of these entities. The official government policy is that such creatures do not exist, and that no agency of the federal government is now engaged in any study of extraterrestrials or their artifacts. Any deviation from this stated policy is absolutely forbidden.

> Penalties for disclosing classified information concerning extraterrestrials are quite severe. In December 1953, the Joint Chiefs of Staff issued Army-Navy-Air Force publication 146 that made the unauthorized release of information concerning UFOs a crime under the Espionage Act, punishable by up to 10 years in prison and a $10,000 fine.

> According to Robert Dean, this draconian penalty is what prevents most former military servicemen from coming forward to disclose information.

The strategies for dealing with those former servicemen, corporate employees or witnesses brave or foolish enough to come forward to reveal classified information is to intimidate, silence, eliminate or discredit these individuals.

This policy involves such strategies as removing all public records of former military service men or corporate employees, forcing individuals to make retractions, deliberately distorting statements of individuals, or discrediting individuals. Bob Lazar, for example, claimed to be a former physicist employed with reverse engineering extraterrestrial craft. He described the disappearance of all his university and public records indicating how military/intelligence agencies actively discredit whistleblowers.

In the cases of the witnesses cited so far, Cooper, Schneider, Lear, Wolf, all have been subjected to some or all of these strategies thereby making it difficult to reach firm conclusions about their testimonies. Since the creation of controversy, uncertainty, and confusion is the modus operandi of military/intelligence agencies in maintaining secrecy of the extraterrestrial presence, then the testimonies of former officials/employees/witnesses need to be considered on their merits.

While issues of credibility, credentials, disinformation are important in the study of the extraterrestrial presence, a rigorous methodology for dealing with the efforts of military/intelligence agencies to discredit, intimidate or create controversy around particular witnesses, has yet to be developed.

For example, numerous efforts to discredit Cooper in particular by referring to inconsistencies in his statements, retractions, egregious behavior and stated positions, may be due in part or in whole to the policy of military/intelligence officials to discredit and/or intimidate Cooper from leaking classified information that he may very well have witnessed in his official capacities.

Since Cooper's military record does indicate he did serve in an official capacity on the briefing team of the Commander of the Pacific Fleet, it is most likely that much of his testimony is credible. Whatever inaccuracies exist in terms of his recollections of the timing of meetings between the Eisenhower administration and extraterrestrials may either have been due to memory lapses or perhaps deliberately introduced as a self-protective mechanism.

It has been pointed out by some whistleblowers that making retractions or sowing inaccuracies in testimonies is sometimes essential in disseminating information without being physically harmed.

The controversial Cooper had been subjected to undoubtedly the longest and most intense military- intelligence efforts to discredit or intimidate any whistleblower revealing classified information.

The non-disclosure policy developed for the extraterrestrial presence is most likely due to a profound policy dilemma on the part of responsible national security officials.

This dilemma comes from uncertainty over what the true benefits of the purported 1954 treaty were, and what the consequences of the treaty would be. While the signing of the treaty provided U.S. national security agencies an opportunity to study extraterrestrial technologies, and to observe the extraterrestrial biological program with abducted civilians, it appeared the treaty was not as beneficial as was first thought due to excessive abductions of U.S. civilians.

The subsequent behavior of the 'Greys' in their interactions with U.S. national security agencies was the most likely reason for deferring a decision to release news of the treaty and the extraterrestrial presence to the global public. According to Gerald Lights testimony, Eisenhower had indicated to those present on February 20-21, 1954, that an announcement would be made soon after the First Contact event.

Since this didn't occur, and a treaty was eventually signed with a different group of extraterrestrials, the 'Greys', this suggests that the national security agencies were deeply divided over the wisdom of disclosing this information, and alarmed by the possible public reaction to the 'Grey' activities.

At his farewell speech in 1961, President Eisenhower was possibly alluding to the growing power of national security agencies that dealt with the extraterrestrial presence and were gaining great power as a result of the dilemma over what to do with the extraterrestrial presence:

> In the councils of government, we must guard against the acquisition of unwarranted influence, whether sought or unsought, by the military industrial complex. The potential for the disastrous rise of misplaced power exists and will persist. We must never let the weight of this combination endanger our liberties or democratic processes. We should take nothing for granted. Only an alert and knowledgeable citizenry can compel the proper meshing of the huge industrial and military machinery of defense with our peaceful methods and goals, so that security and liberty may prosper together.

If the President was dissatisfied with the non-disclosure of the extraterrestrial presence, then his speech was indicating that the responsible national security agencies were both dominating public policy and taking a hard-line approach that was inconsistent with American democratic ideals.

In the subsequent decades, it appears that on a number of occasions, official disclosure was seriously contemplated. For example, Robert Emenegger and Allan Sandler claimed they were approached by the Pentagon in 1972 to produce an officially sanctioned video that would be used for official public disclosure of the extraterrestrial presence.

When the offer was later withdrawn, the reason given was that the time was no longer suitable due to the Watergate Scandal. While it is undoubtedly true that political factors would impact on making a formal disclosure announcement, it is more likely the case that non-disclosure was caused by lack of clarity over what the true motivations of the extraterrestrials were, and the impact an announcement would have on extraterrestrial activities.

Making any announcement of the extraterrestrial presence would naturally have lead to questions concerning the extraterrestrials' motivations and activities. If officials couldn't agree on appropriate answers, they most likely decided that it was better to defer disclosure rather than threaten national security by making inaccurate announcements.

The precise nature of the extraterrestrial abductions and the medical programs implemented by the 'Greys' has been extensively researched and discussed by a number of researchers. Their conclusions vary widely suggesting that the deep disagreement over the motivations and activities of the 'Greys', very likely mirrors that of official government sources.

As long as such uncertainty continues, it appears that disclosure may continue to be deferred until key global events no longer makes the non-disclosure policy viable.

An examination of the evidence presented in terms of whistleblower or eyewitness testimonies raises tremendous problems in terms of coming to a conclusive opinion over:

• first, the truth of the alleged First Contact meeting between Eisenhower and extraterrestrials.
• second, claims of more than one set of extraterrestrials meeting with the Eisenhower administration.
• third, the various policy issues that arise from the meetings and subsequent treaty that was allegedly signed.

Most perplexing is how to view the testimonies of whistleblowers who appear sincere, positively motivated and have plausible stories, yet are plagued by controversy, allegations of fraud, inconsistency and other irregularities.

Due to the official secrecy policy adopted towards the extraterrestrial presence, it may be concluded that some if not most of the controversy surrounding these individuals has been caused by military/intelligence agencies intent on discrediting whistleblower or witness testimonies.

While there continues to be uncertainty caused by the controversy surrounding whistleblower testimonies and the role of military/intelligence agencies in generating this controversy, the bulk of evidence points to a First Contact meeting having occurred during Eisenhower's Palm Spring vacation on February 20-21, 1954.

The testimonies suggest that the extraterrestrials in the First Contact event, a race of tall Nordic extraterrestrials were spurned due to their reluctance to provide advanced technology in an agreement. A subsequent meeting and treaty was then signed with a different set of extraterrestrials, commonly called 'Greys', who did not have the same reluctance in exchanging extraterrestrial technology as part of an agreement.

Most of the available evidence that has found its way into the public arena suggests that the extraterrestrial race with whom the treaty was signed, the 'Greys', are at best an enigma and at worst simply untrustworthy in their treatment of abducted civilians. The subsequent shift in witness reports from friendly extraterrestrial contacts to disturbing abductions, suggest that the Eisenhower administration had signed a treaty with extraterrestrials whose motivations and activities are an enigma as far as the general public interest is concerned.

The activities of the 'Grey' extraterrestrials apparently continues to raise uncertainty for U.S. national security agencies in terms of an appropriate strategic response.

On the contrary, the friendly Nordic space brothers faded from the scene since the Eisenhower administration saw them as not sufficiently motivated to serve the technological and strategic goals of U.S. national security agencies.

The question of when disclosure of the treaty signed by Eisenhower and of the extraterrestrial presence might occur is one that has long been anticipated. A recent economic event might be a signal that some form of disclosure is possible in the near future.

According to Craig Copetas, *Bloomberg News* correspondent in Paris, the World Economic Forum at Davos Switzerland from January 21-25, 2004, discussed extraterrestrials at one or more closed sessions. In a story published on January 21, Copetas claimed that forum officials maintain their five-day program on Partnering for Security and Prosperity requires an unambiguous examination of extraterrestrial presence on Earth.

The Davos Forum is a gauge for trends in the global economy and discusses various topics that have a long term effect on business. The inclusion of conspiracy theories of an extraterrestrial presence and technologies on the formal agenda has significance well beyond the hypothetical nature of the discussion.

Various world governments may well be tactfully letting the word out to their "friends in the business community", that they had better start exploring how a future disclosure of an extraterrestrial presence and technologies will influence the business world. Given the discussion at Davos on January 21, 2004, of a possible extraterrestrial presence, it might be speculated that a disclosure announcement may soon be made.

All of this information causes one to pause and truly consider the awesome nature of this occasion. At the same time, we must do whatever is necessary to make public the full details of the meeting, and the apparent spurning of what appears to be a principled extraterrestrial race that rejected technology transfers while dangerous weapons programs were in place in the U.S. and elsewhere on the planet.

The subsequent signing of a treaty at a later date with an extraterrestrial race willing to trade technology in exchange for limited medical experiments with civilians will surely go down in history as a deeply significant event whose effects continues to reverberate through human society. Finally, we must be alert to the mounting evidence that while a treaty was signed after the 1954 First Contact event, it may well have been with the wrong extraterrestrials, and that this might adversely impact on humanity if not dealt with in an open, transparent and truthful manner.

We live on the verge of a bold new future with many uncertainties over the secrecy surrounding the extraterrestrial presence. What best prepares us as this information enters into the public arena is our faith, democratic values, and dedication to truth.

While this meeting does not definitively prove the existence of a secret space program it does provide a clear motive for embarking on the development of such a program – especially if you have the ability to back-engineer spacecraft. What country or civilization would pass on such an opportunity if its survival depended on it?

The Power and Influence of a Shadow Government

The existence of a parallel governmental system using military personnel for its own purposes has been suspected for some time as illustrated in comments by Senator Daniel Inouye at the 1987 Iran-Contra Senate hearings:

> "There exists a shadowy Government with its own Air Force, its own Navy, its own fundraising mechanism, and the ability to pursue its own ideas of the national interest, free from all checks and balances, and free from the law itself."

To illustrate the amount of influence and power exercised by this breakaway group or shadow government let us look at a couple of examples.

The first piece of information comes from Dr. Michael Wolf. He was a high member of the Special Studies Group (formerly MJ-12), buried within the National Security Council. According to Dr. Wolf a satellite government has successfully back-engineered alien spacecraft. All of the anti-gravity and other technology is now in the control of this organization, which is responsible for the UFO cover-up.

Dr. Wolf explains that when President John F. Kennedy came into office, he was anything but shocked. He knew about the alien presence and the discs we had in our possession. He forced our military to release pieces of the alien technology to companies around the U.S. to back-engineer. The companies were told the technology was from the Soviets or Chinese.

He later threatened to disband the CIA if they did not stop the drug trafficking and warned he was going to announce to the American people that aliens were real and felt they were ready for the information to be released. As we all know he was murdered. Wolf claims that Oswald was not the shooter, nor did he fire a single shot. It was members of the Secret Service and CIA, under orders from this shadow government. Kennedy became the second martyr following the murder of James Forrestal.

Now let us look at the case of James V. Forrestal, former Secretary of Defense and Navy who served under President Truman from 1947 to 1949.

Forrestal was one of the few with early knowledge of the U.S. recovery of extraterrestrial spacecraft, and that aliens had been interacting with Earth for some time. Of the original group that were the first to learn the truth, several allegedly committed suicide, the most prominent of which was James Forrestal who allegedly jumped to his death from a 16th story hospital window at Bethesda Naval Hospital.

William Cooper, a former member of a Navy Intelligence briefing team from 1970-73, insists that Forrestal was in fact murdered by CIA agents who made his death look like a suicide. Based on classified documents Cooper claims to have read, two CIA agents entered the hospital room, tied a bedsheet around Forrestal's neck and to a light fixture, and threw him out the window to hang. The bedsheets broke and he fell to his death, screaming on his way down according to some witnesses "We're being invaded!" Secretary Forrestal's medical records are sealed to this day.

President Truman then slammed a lid on the secret and turned the screws so tight that the general public still believes that flying saucers are a joke.

Is it safe to have such a powerful organization in control and slowly maneuvering itself into a position of global dominance and deciding for the rest of humanity what is right for it? Yes, they may be abiding by an agreement made with extraterrestrials by President Eisenhower in 1954 but this right? If the President of the United States is not safe then who is? Are we all expendable?

The Nazi Connection

The Nazis provided a huge jumpstart to the secret space program through their research and development of alien technology beginning in the late 1930s.

It started after World War II. The Allied forces recovered some alien technology from Germany. It wasn't all that they had – some of it had disappeared. It appears that some time around 1939 Germany recovered a flying saucer disc. What happened to it isn't known. But what we did obtain was some kind of "ray gun" weapon. In fact United States General James H. Doolittle went to Norway in 1946 to inspect a flying saucer that had crashed there in Spitzbergen. Could this have been the mystery alien craft recovered by the Germans from 1939?

Bulgarian Physicist Vladimir Terziski wrote the following:

> "According to Renato Vesco, Germany was sharing a great deal of the advances in weaponry with their allies, the Italians, during the war. At the Fiat experimental facility at Lake Garda, a facility that fittingly bore the name of Air Marshall Hermann Goering, the Italians were experimenting with numerous advanced weapons, rockets and airplanes, created in Germany. In a similar fashion, the Germans kept a close contact with the Japanese military establishment and were supplying it with many advanced weapons."

Renato Vesco was a fully licensed aircraft engineer and a specialist in aerospace and ramjet developments. He attended the University of Rome and, before WWII, studied at the German Institute for Aerial Development. During the war Vesco worked with the Germans at the Fiat Lake Garda secret installation in Italy. In the 1960s, he worked for the Italian Air Ministry of Defense as an undercover technical agent, investigating the UFO mystery.

One Japanese source who worked as technician in an aircraft research bureau in Japan during the war related the following story: In July of 1945, two and a half months after the war ended in Germany, a huge German transport submarine brought to Japan the latest of German inventions – two spherical wingless flying devices.

The Japanese R&D team assembled the machines following the German instructions and there was something very bizarre and alien standing in front of them – a ball shaped flying device without any wings or propellers that nobody knew how to fly. Fuel was added, the start button of this unmanned machine was pressed and it disappeared with a roar and flames without a sign into the sky. The team never saw it again. The engineers were so frightened by the unexpected and unknown capabilities of the machine that they promptly destroyed the second prototype and choose to forget the whole incident.

The RFZ-5, also known as Haunebu I (photo below), was test flown on August 8, 1939. It had a diameter of 83 feet and a photograph exists, said to have been taken over Prague. With a crew of eight, it reportedly reached 2,500 mph and the upper atmosphere. It was also claimed to have been equipped with two "laser guns".

Flugkreisel-Erprobung, Stand / Anzahl Erprobungsflüge:

HAUNEBU I   (vorhanden 2 Stück)   52   E-IV
HAUNEBU II   (vorhanden 7 Stück)   106   E-IV
HAUNEBU III (vorhanden 1 Stück)   19   E-IV
(VRIL I)   (vorhanden 17 Stück)   84   (Schumann)

Empfehlung:
Beschleunigen von Abschlußerprobung
und Produktion „Haunebu II"
+ „VRIL I"

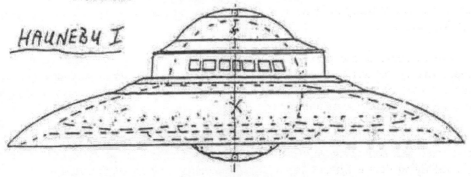

HAUNEBU I

The earliest non-fiction assertion of Nazi flying saucers appears to have been an article which appeared in the Italian newspaper *Il Giornale d'Italia* in early 1950. Written by Professor Giuseppe Belluzzo, an Italian scientist and a former Italian Minister of National Economy under the Mussolini regime, it claimed that "types of flying discs were designed and studied in Germany and Italy as early as 1942". Belluzzo also expressed the opinion that "some great power is launching discs to study them".

Unfortunately none of this German technology was able to be fully developed before the end of World War II. They simply ran out of time. And I suspect the United States was fully aware of how far along they were in their progress. It was likely one of the motivational factors to ending the war quickly by using the nuclear bomb. The U.S. couldn't afford for Germany to finalize their designs and create a "Wunderwaffe" or superweapon using alien technology.

Isn't it obvious why the United States elected to recruit so many Nazi scientists as part of Operation Paperclip, officially authorized by President Harry Truman in August 1945? It gave them a massive head start in the development of a secret space program, in comparison to their adversary at the time – the Soviet Union. The Americans possessed the hardware (spacecraft), and the engineering knowledge of German scientists who had at least seven years experience working on advanced extraterrestrial propulsion systems.

Mars Base Observed

Over recent years there have been many claims that a base on Mars has been observed. Researchers maintain that it remains hidden through some type of shielding technology. For some reason this shield sometimes is shut down allowing the base to be observed for brief periods of time. However, it has never been shut down long enough to allow it to be filmed or photographed.

It was reported that an amateur astronomer claimed to have identified a human (or alien) base on Mars. David Martines noticed a mysterious rectangular structure that appeared on the Martian surface while searching the planet using Google Mars, a new map program created from compiled satellite images of the planet.

It is a video of something he discovered quite by accident, and was released widely across the internet on June 5, 2011. Martines nicknamed it "Bio Station Alpha," because he assumed that something lives in it or has lived in it. A screenshot of the video is shown below.

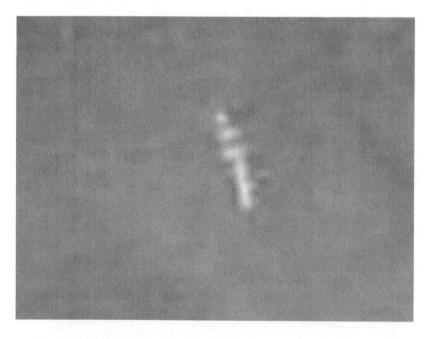

He listed the coordinates as 49'19.73"N 29 33'06.53"W. The object is over 700 feet long and 150 feet wide. It looks like it is a cylinder or made up of cylinders, and appears to be painted red, white and blue. It definitely looks out of place when compared to the surrounding Martian surface features and terrain.

Did Martines really find evidence of alien life, or a secret Martian base, as he and some researchers mentioned earlier in this book have claimed? Or is it simply a glitch in the image caused by cosmic energy interfering with the camera, as claimed by mainstream scientists flocking to debunk this discovery?

The video clearly shows a structure having perpendicular angles. The chances of nature being able to create so many perfect 90-degree angles are very remote and highly unlikely. Because of this, there is a strong possibility that this anomaly is artificial in construction. Whether it is a Mars base is another question entirely.

UFO Crash Retrieval and Recovery Teams

There are three reasons for establishing elite response teams worldwide to recover crashed UFOs.

1. To recover extraterrestrial bodies and hardware, with the intention of reverse-engineering the hardware to develop our own spacecraft utilizing this alien technology.
2. To recover foreign hardware and technical intelligence from other countries.
3. To hide and further protect the existence of terrestrial spacecraft designed as part of a top-secret black budget space program.

It has been common knowledge for some time that the U.S. military/Air Force has specially trained response teams prepared to act on a moments notice anywhere in world to retrieve crashed UFOs. Project Moon Dust and Operation Blue Fly are clear proof of this. Moon Dust is a specialized part of the U.S. Air Force's program to locate, recover, and deliver descended foreign space vehicles.

Blue Fly is a unit established to facilitate expeditious delivery to the Foreign Technological Division (FTD) of Moon Dust and other items of great technical intelligence interest. Many prominent and highly credible experts and eyewitnesses, including former high-ranking military officers and intelligence employees, have come forward to verify this. The release of "Special Operations Manual SOM1-01" (photo below) in 1994, detailing the classified government program created for managing crash retrieval operations, is yet further confirmation.

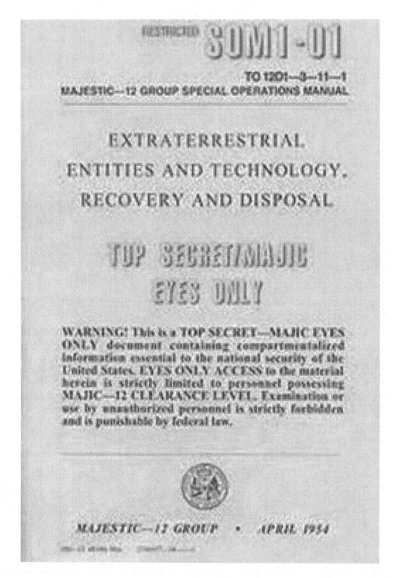

These crash retrieval teams are given the highest priority at all times regardless of their apparent rank or status. No person has the authority to interfere with team personnel in the performance of its duties by special direction of the President of the United States.

In addition, these teams sometimes travel internationally to perform crash retrievals. In most cases these special teams are led by a civilian who takes charge of the crash retrieval operations despite the presence of high ranking military personnel at the scene.

Official documents released through the *Freedom of Information Act* indicate the following activities:

- On December 9, 1965, a three-man team was sent to recover an object of unknown origin reported downed in Kecksburg, Pennsylvania. Witnesses state an object was recovered while the Air Force says nothing was found.
- In August 1967, an object described as a satellite crashed and was recovered in the Sudan under Project Moon Dust. The description on the DIA (Defense Intelligence Agency) document released by the State Department does not fit that of a satellite.
- In 1968, Project Moon Dust recovered four unknown objects in Nepal.
- Also in 1968, a dome-shaped object with no identification marks was retrieved underwater off Cape Town, South Africa. The metal object had been subjected to extreme heat and showed no signs of corrosion. NASA determined it was made of almost pure aluminum and stated that the NASA analysis of the sample and photographs "does not otherwise provide a clue as to its origin or function although it is possible it is a space object of U.S. origin."
- In 1970, Project Moon Dust investigated a metal sphere that fell "with three loud explosions and then burned for five days" in South America. It had "ports" which had been melted closed.
- A May 1970 State Department document describes a fallen, unidentified object in Bolivia, depicted in the newspapers as metal and egg-shaped. The Department expressed a desire to assist the Bolivian Air Force in the investigation. "The general region had more than its share of reports of UFOs this past week," the document noted.

All the documents on the above events represent raw, unprocessed field intelligence data. The public, however, is not privy to the final determinations of these investigations. Where are the finalized intelligence products? Where are the recovered fragments?

Project Moon Dust and Operation Blue Fly have recovered objects of unknown origin. Physical evidence in the possession of the U.S. government could shed light on the secret space program as would nothing else.

In 1982 a special operations group was established after consultation with then President Reagan, and Secretary of Defense Weinberger in co-operation with a secretive group within the DIA (Defense Intelligence Agency) following reports that UFOs, some with living or dead EBE (extraterrestrial biological entities) occupants, began inexplicably crashing in Alaska, northern British Columbia, Yukon, Ohio, Arizona, northern Mexico and also internationally in Norway, Africa, Argentina, Colombia and Brazil.

These events were investigated whereupon crash debris and EBEs were retrieved using existing Special Operations Forces (SOF) such as the 1st Special Forces Operational Detachment-Delta (1st SFOD-D-Delta Force) and other high level, vetted for security clearance Combat Engineering Teams.

Initially, these teams were based in and designated only for Areas of Operation within the Continental United States and the country and territories of Canada.

It wasn't until the large ($291 billion) 1987 Fiscal Year Defense Budget was passed, did President Reagan sign a Classified Department of Defense Directive allowing the formation of multiple teams based domestically and in foreign nations that had the local authority to act in a co-ordinated manner without oversight or interference from any other U.S. intelligence agency or Department of Defense (DOD) department other than the President, Secretary of Defense, Chairman and Vice Chairman of the Joint Chiefs of Staff and the Presidential appointees overseeing and directing the retrieval teams.

Initially all team members were vetted and selected from then current Delta Force operatives and the vetted Defense Intelligence Agency (DIA) personnel until 1988 when specialized and heavily vetted operational Combat Engineering types, Transport & Logistics Support personnel and Biological & Medical Evaluation and Measurement & Signature Intelligence personnel were added to aid in the effectiveness of Alien Entity and Technology retrievals.

Specialized HumInt (Human Intelligence) from the DIA and NRO (National Reconnaissance Office) Imaging & Analysis personnel were also added later to document and analyze immediate Areas of Operation that allowed the forensic-level recording and preservation of immediate evidentiary and scene analysis data at crash or contact sites to aid the tracking of global crash and contact cases and to predict future areas of interest & operation – and again this was on a global basis.

The recovery teams, while using all available intelligence assets within any usable and available DOD group and operatives from within the NSA, DIA & CIA, were designed to be completely autonomous from those groups and used the secrecy of the compartmentalization that is intrinsic to such intelligence assets to allow no external group access to or the ability to make sense of all available information & gathered intelligence data from the recovery teams.

In most cases, external personnel were given specific sub-sets of data to work on but were never able to see the entire picture and thus could not obtain a clear overall and objective overview of the alien entity and technology recovery program.

In late 1989 and early 1990, President Bush signed another DOD Directive allowing vetted personnel to be transferred and assigned from the NSA, DIA and CIA and from current Special Forces directly over to the recovery teams in one of four operational Global Recovery Centers based in Maryland, California & Nevada, Australia and

England that were tasked with the co-ordination of logistics and personnel to allow the rapid covert recovery and transport of alien entities and technology back to specific "Holding and Evaluation Centers" located within the United States.

Each team is sub-divided into two assigned specialties:

(1) EBE-RT (pronounced as Eee-Bert) Extraterrestrial Biological Entity Recovery Team

(2) ETECH-RT (pronounced Eee-Tek-Are-Tee) Extraterrestrial Technology Recovery Team

They are assigned two very different tasks which have very different logistical and intelligence support assets behind them.

EBE-RT teams are tasked with the observation, engagement and, if necessary, recovery of extraterrestrial biology which can include living or dead alien beings and any alien fauna and other living or biological-based artifacts or environments. Specific protocols dealing with rules-of-engagement, protection and prevention of disease & infection are outlined to and followed by all team members on a continuous basis.

Other protocols for initial & continuing contact, infiltration and survey of facilities, bases and quarters were also created and tasked to each singular recovery team which was then allowed to build up an experience database that is then disseminated to all other recovery teams on an ongoing basis.

While containing specific and experienced subject matter experts, these recovery teams were tasked much like EMT (Emergency Medical Team & Ambulance Personnel) which is to, as quickly as possible, recover alien biologically-based items, fauna & entities and bring them back to the United States for further observation and analysis.

The ETECH-RT teams have a slightly different directive which is to, as quickly as possible, recover any hard technologically based items such as spacecraft, undersea craft, facilities, clothing, infrastructure, gear, goods, devices, weapons, or any other type of hard-technology items in a secure and clandestine manner for further evaluation by specifically assigned laboratories and test facilities based in the United States mainland. These teams usually have no interaction with alien entities other than to obtain information that would allow them to recover and transport hard goods and devices back to the evaluation centers.

It sounds very much like the ETECH-RT team's mandate in recovery operations would be perfectly suited in helping to conceal and further protect the existence of terrestrial spacecraft designed as part of a top-secret black budget space program.

So why is there such a keen interest in the recovery of UFO wreckages? Why the need for the government to establish elite recovery teams around the world? Why is the government so quick and eager to collect these fallen objects? Is it because the wreckages belong to extraterrestrial craft? Or could it be because some these craft happen to belong to the United States, and not extraterrestrials – part of a top secret back budget space program?

Could it be that these downed spacecraft are actually fully functional or perhaps experimental terrestrial ships built by using reverse-engineered technology acquired from crashed extraterrestrial spacecraft? Granted that part of the reason behind these recovery efforts is related to national security – not wanting our top secret technology to fall into the hands of a foreign nation. But, based on the evidence presented throughout this book, couldn't another logical reason be to maintain a cloak of secrecy over an elaborate "black budget" space program that was responsible for development of high-tech space vehicles here on Earth? From what we have learned don't you think that there is plenty enough to hide?

Admittedly the original intention of this retrieval program was to recover extraterrestrial technology. However, once this alien technology led to the development of copycat Earth-based spacecraft it necessitated an ongoing need to recover failed man-made experimental and prototype models as well as any additional "accidents" which might have occurred along the way. That would account for the top-level (under special direction of the Presidential) urgency and attention which this project receives.

"It is better to remain silent and be thought a fool than to open one's mouth and remove all doubt."

– Abraham Lincoln (1809-1865)

Chapter 7

Summation

In this book we have examined the following facts supporting the existence of a secret space program:

- Following the end of World War II the establishment of, not only the mainstream conventional space program which came to be known as NASA, but also a parallel space program using Nazi scientists and recovered alien hardware and advanced technology.

- Expert and eyewitness testimony from many highly credible sources within the scientific, military and intelligence fields detailing specific events that occurred and spacecraft designs relating to such a program.

- Information obtained from 97 NASA and U.S. military computer systems which revealed a list of "Non-Terrestrial Officers" containing names and ranks of U.S. Air Force personnel who are not registered anywhere else. It also contained information about an off-Earth space fleet and ship-to-ship transfers, but the names of these ships were never noted anywhere else.

- The allocation of black budget funding (all without any Congressional oversight or approval) in the tens of billions of dollars for covert projects involving high-tech spacecraft and weapons technology.

- Observations and accounts from Apollo astronauts of a lunar base, mining activities being conducted on the Moon, and of unusual spacecraft which came within close proximity to the Apollo spacecraft.

- Photographs and images from the Moon and Mars showing spacecraft (either crashed wreckages or fully operational), structures, buildings and possibly even bases.

- Wernher von Braun's warning to the world of an upcoming announcement that a fabricated and contrived alien attack was to be orchestrated by those who are in control of this space program, in order to justify increased spending and development of the secret space program's weapons and technology systems – in essence the weaponization of space.

The starting point for the rise of a secret space program can be traced back to the end of World War II. This time saw a rogue group of renegade Nazis with control of vital advanced technology and physics being allowed to re-locate to the United States to join forces with American scientists and, under the watchful eye and protection of the U.S. military, continue their research and development. This was the beginning of the emergence of a secret space program. The pieces of the puzzle were being assembled. Recovered alien technology and the brightest minds of the time (including Nazi scientists) came together in the United States in 1945 in the form of Operation Paperclip. And the most amazing part of it all was that this was orchestrated and sponsored by the United States government.

In response to the Soviet space program's launch of the world's first artificial satellite (Sputnik 1) on October 4, 1957 the United States officially formed NASA on July 28, 1958. From that point onward NASA was to be nothing more than window dressing for the real space program – one which was highly classified, driven and controlled by the military through a black-budget world, and in possession of highly advanced extraterrestrial technology.

The Library of Congress adds roughly 60 million pages to its holdings each year, a huge cache of information for the public. However, also each year, the U.S. government classifies nearly ten times that amount – an estimated 560 million pages of documents. For those engaged in political, historical, scientific, or any other archival work, the grim reality is that most of their government's activities are kept secret.

This makes it extremely difficult to the layperson (or anyone for that matter) to really find out the truth. And this, my friends, is the reason why secrecy has always been, and will always continue to be a prerogative of the powerful elite.

The world of secrecy has run away from us, beyond the ability of free citizens to examine and critique. When we trace the evolution of this secrecy, we find it hard to pinpoint just when things went wrong. This has been going on for a long time.

I often refer back to the *Brookings Report* of 1961 in my books for this single document is clear evidence that the government were, at some pont, contemplating an announcement to the world of extraterrestrial life. The *Brookings Report* was simply an initial attempt to "test the waters". This document has now become the driving force behind and reason for the secrecy.

Many researchers have come to the conclusion that the secret space program is at least many decades more advanced than what we are led to believe. Some even put estimates (thanks in part to alien technology obtained through reverse-engineering) as far out as over 1,000 years more advanced than present day technology. Secret space stations, travel via time viewing, bases on the Moon, Mars, Jovian and Saturn moons, extrasolar planets, FTL technology, particle beam weaponry, subterranean bases, sub-oceanic bases, inter-dimensional travel, and matter manipulation are just some of the technological advances possibly achieved.

Why keep all this incredible technology hidden from us? The short answer is to retain and build a power and control base by a slowly evolving shadow government; a general immaturity of the human race to accept or be able to deal with it; and the implications of integrating this technology into the current global economic structure without damaging it.

Such breakthroughs mean attractive ground floor investments, significant profits, and less-than-zero motivation for revealing the "goose that lays golden eggs." What is the benefit (if any) for announcing these secrets to the public? But let us take the scenario even further.

What if even greater breakthroughs of understanding were achieved – a better source of energy, a functioning electro-gravity propulsion system, or a biotechnology that eliminates certain diseases, or stops the aging process?

There is no doubt that breakthroughs of that type would be blocked from reaching the outside world. A new source of energy, especially if it were "free", would effectively destroy the petroleum industry, while certain biotech developments would threaten the pharmaceutical industry. These are two of the largest industries in the world.

Major breakthroughs would also threaten to destabilize society and challenge the structure of power. Low-cost and portable energy, as implied by flying saucers, would revolutionize our world so completely that no one can truly imagine what the world would look like once it became available. The same can be said for technologies that might enable people to live for hundreds of years longer.

Perhaps the motivating reason for keeping this knowledge of advanced technology secret is that we, as a society, are not ready. Those in decision-making positions have determined that our civilization has yet to achieve the level of maturity and sophistication not to abuse this knowledge.

Another consideration in their reasoning would no doubt be the impact on the global economy by introducing such advancements in the energy and biotech fields. How would we deal with massive unemployment in these primary industries and the "trickle down effect" into secondary industries? This factor alone holds massive economic implications.

I believe that this breakaway group (shadow government) would be reluctant to share with the rest of humanity what is going on. Their own reality is probably so far beyond our own, they may rightfully ask, how is it possible to educate the rest of us without causing a worldwide psychological meltdown?

This "Black World" exists with, essentially, an infinite amount of money to play with and an incredible amount of secrecy within which to perform what they do and really no oversight.

I am curious, when the existence of extraterrestrial life is officially acknowledged by world governments and formally announced, what the skeptics and debunkers will say. What will their reaction be? What will be the explanation for their relentless blind, uneducated, bigoted criticism? Will they actually take ownership and accountability for their gross incompetence? Will they finally admit to their embarrassing failure in analysis and that they totally "missed this one"? Where will they run and hide?

They will probably look to direct blame away from themselves and their own ineptitude. No doubt this will be the context of their response: "This is not the time for laying blame – humanity must all stand together as unified against this threat from outside of Earth."

There will be no apology, tribute or gratitude for those pioneering individuals who had their lives ruined – who spent their lives being ridiculed and discredited and who sacrificed their careers and, in some cases, lives in pursuit of the truth. Where is the solace for those people and their families? The critics will be finally exposed and end up appearing as either totally ignorant or pathetically spineless – one or the other.

If the skeptics had been able to read and interpret the data, information and evidence as many of us had, there would have been a wider public acceptance and a louder voice to demand the truth at a much earlier time. If nothing else, this would have made such a profound announcement (the revelation of extraterrestrial life) less difficult and the transition for society, while still difficult, a little smoother.

"Judge a man by his questions rather than his answers."

– Voltaire (1694-1778)

Appendix A

Who Owns the Moon?

According to the *Treaty on Principles Governing the Activities of States in the Exploration and Use of Outer Space, including the Moon and Other Celestial Bodies,* the Moon is unclaimable. The treaty has so far been ratified by 100 United Nations member countries, including the United States.

The 1967 *Outer Space Treaty* was considered by the Legal Subcommittee in 1966 and agreement was reached in the General Assembly in the same year (resolution 2222 (XXI). The Treaty was largely based on the Declaration of Legal Principles Governing the Activities of States in the Exploration and Use of Outer Space, which had been adopted by the General Assembly in its resolution 1962 (XVIII) in 1963, but added a few new provisions.

The Treaty was opened for signature by the three depository Governments (the Russian Federation, the United Kingdom and the United States of America) in January 1967, and it entered into force in October 1967. The *Outer Space Treaty* provides the basic framework on international space law, including the following principles:

• The exploration and use of outer space shall be carried out for the benefit and in the interests of all countries and shall be the province of all mankind;
• Outer space shall be free for exploration and use by all States;
• Outer space is not subject to national appropriation by claim of sovereignty, by means of use or occupation, or by any other means;
• States shall not place nuclear weapons or other weapons of mass destruction in orbit or on celestial bodies or station them in outer space in any other manner;
• The Moon and other celestial bodies shall be used exclusively for peaceful purposes;
• Astronauts shall be regarded as the envoys of mankind;
• States shall be responsible for national space activities whether carried out by governmental or non-governmental entities;
• States shall be liable for damage caused by their space objects; and
• States shall avoid harmful contamination of space and celestial bodies.

Further information can be obtained by visiting the website of the United Nations Office for Outer Space Affairs (UNOOSA).

Appendix B

White House Denies Existence of Extraterrestrials

Is there really other life in the universe outside Earth or will it all remain a mystery? On November 8, 2011 the White House issued an official answer in response to two online petitions (containing more than 17,000 signatures) that requested the government "formally acknowledge an extraterrestrial presence engaging the human race" and "immediately disclose the government's knowledge of and communications with extraterrestrial beings".

On September of 2011, the White House launched "We The People," an initiative in which the Obama administration officially was to respond to any petition that received more than 25,000 signatures within 30 days. The petitions asserted that extraterrestrials exist on Earth and that the government had gone to great lengths to hide that information.

How did the government respond? Phil Larson, who worked in the White House Office of Science and Technology Policy, officially stated, "The United States government has no evidence that any life exists outside our planet, or that an extraterrestrial presence has contacted or engaged any member of the human race". The official White House response also stated that "there is no credible information to suggest that any evidence is being hidden from the public's eye".

One questions remains: Why did the White House respond to these petitions when they were short 8,000 signatures? There were other petitions that did not get a response concerning same-sex marriage, Keystone XL Pipeline, and the Electoral College. At the time of this posting, only the Electoral College petition had more than 17,000 signatures. It had gained 19,082 signatures, and the White House hadn't issued a response.

I suppose this demonstrates that the U.S. Government still insists on sticking to its plan of denial and deception – despite a growing amount of evidence to indicate otherwise.

Appendix C

Exopolitics

So what is exopolitics?

Exopolitics is an interdisciplinary scientific field, with its roots in the political sciences, that focuses on research, education and public policy with regard to the actors, institutions and processes, associated with extraterrestrial life, as well as the wide range of implications this entails through public advocacy and newly emerging paradigms.

This definition integrates three different meanings the word "exopolitics" is used in:

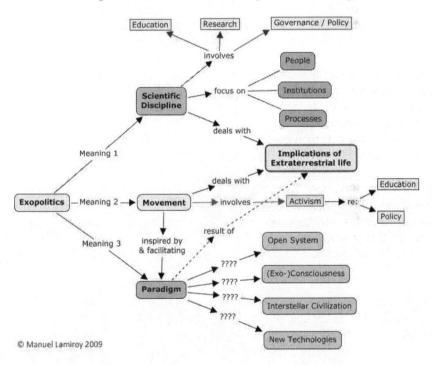

© Manuel Lamiroy 2009

Some older definitions include:

Exopolitics: a speculative branch of political science; is the study of possible contact and relations between humanity and extraterrestrial civilizations. The hypothetical study of political relations between humans and extraterrestrial civilizations.

Michael Salla, founder of the Exopolitics Institute, provides two complimentary definitions:

• The study of the key individuals, institutions and political processes associated with extraterrestrial life.
• The study of the political implications of the extraterrestrial presence on Earth.

Alfred Webre invented the word "exopolitics" and described it as "the study of political process and governance in interstellar society".

Appendix D

A Guide to Scientific Explanations for Anomalous Discoveries

Over the years mainstream science has come up with some very creative and humorous explanations for anomalous discoveries here on Earth and throughout our Solar System. However, their standard "go-to" textbook explanations have not changed. These tired old explanations are dragged out of the closet and used when no other logical explanation is possible.

Here are the main explanations used:

• Natural Rock/Geological Formation – NASA uses this extensively to explain anomalous figures, archaeological artifacts or features photographed on the Earth's surface and underwater, on the Moon and planets in our Solar System which appear artificial in origin.

• Differential Weathering/Erosion – used to explain anomalous structures (pyramids, buildings, monoliths, or statues) photographed on the Moon and planets in our Solar System.

• Genetic Mutation – used when an unknown/anomalous condition or discovery (human speech, bipedalism, or the existence of certain inconsistencies in the evolutionary timeline) cannot be explained.

Appendix E

Bibliography and Credits

Acknowledgement

Special thanks to various articles, publications and websites courtesy of Wikipedia, Association for Research and Enlightenment (A.R.E.), Science, The Spectrum newspaper, The New York Times, ScienceWatch, The American Journal of Science and Arts, Scientific American, CNN, Time Magazine, Associated Press, United Press, Discovery News, The Antarctic Sun, Society for the Advancement of Education, USA Today, Science Daily, Newsweek, Washington Post, U.S. News World Report, Science Frontiers Online, National Geographic News, The Dinosaur Interplanetary Gazette, Quest Magazine, BBC News, Hamilton Advertiser, The Binary Research Institute, Nexus Magazine, American Anthropologist, U.S. Geological Survey, Skywatch, Il-Mument, American Encyclopedia, The London Times, Los Angeles News, Los Angeles Herald, American Antiquarian, The Nevada News, The San Diego Union, California Mining Journal, The UK Guardian, PloS One, The Cleveland Herald, The Victoria Advocate, Seattle Post Intelligencer, U.S. National Research Council, LiveScience, New York Tribune, Fort Wayne Daily Gazette, The Hartford Times, The Union Medicale, Denver Colorado Tribune, The Daily Sentinel, Near Eastern Religious Texts Relating to the Old Testament, Archaeology of the Bible, U.K. Telegraph, Associates for Biblical Research, S8int.com, About.com, Pretoria News, The Assam Chronicle, The Morrisonville Times, West Wales ECO Center, UFO TV, NASA Earth Science Enterprise Data Center, ABC News Nightline, Smithsonian.com, Atlantis Rising, World-Mysteries.com, Crystalinks.com, Los Angeles Times, Pravda, Taipei Times, Hindustan Times, Space.com, Space Daily, Nature News, UFO Digest, The Planetary Society, Encyclopedia Britannica, Life Magazine, The Enterprise Mission, Marsanomalyresearch.com, SERPO.org, FarShores.org, AboveTopSecret.com, MMMGroup.com, Wired.com, The Media Research Center, American Antiquity, Christian Science Monitor, Boston Globe, The Australian, ScienceNOW, NewScientist, The Santiago Times, UC Berkeley News, History.com, Sentientdevelopments.com, Reuters, CBC News, Der Spiegel, Xinhua News Agency, Herald de Paris, Alternate Perceptions Magazine, Spaceflightnow.com, Aviation Week & Space Technology, The Society for Scientific Exploration (SSE), FOXNews.com, Indo-Asian News Service, Solar System Research, Icarus, exopolitics.org

I would like to extend a sincere debt of gratitude to the following authors and researchers for their pioneering work on many of the subjects discussed in this book: Albert Einstein, Stephen Hawking, Charles Darwin, Robert J. Oppenheimer, Nikola Tesla, Dr. Carl Sagan, Ron Wyatt, J. Harlan Bretz, Lloyd Pye, Sir William Matthew Flinders Petrie, Edward Leedskalnin, Dr. Zahi Hawass, Heinrich Schliemann, Colonel Percy Fawcett, Richard Milton, Mary Leakey, Robert Ballard, William Ryan, Percival Lowell, David Adair, Admiral Richard Byrd, Dr. Carl Baugh, James Churchward, Dr.

Immanuel Velikovsky, Daniel Ruzo, Graham Hancock, Robert Bauval, Mark Lehner, Professor Charles Hapgood, John Anthony West, Dr. Robert M. Schoch, Adrian Gilbert, Zecharia Sitchin, Erich Von Daniken, Edgar Cayce, Michael Cremo, Dr. Richard L. Thompson, David Childress, Richard Milton, James Nienhuis, Critchon Miller, William Henry, Dr. Brian O'Leary, Dr. Tom Van Flandern, David Flynn, Bob Frissell, Richard C. Hoagland, Richard M. Dolan, Christopher Dunn, Dr. Frank E. Stranges, David Icke, Patrick Geryl, Rene Noorbergen, Michael J. Oard, Joseph P. Skipper, Mike Singh, Jay Melosh, Dr. John Brandenburg, Harrison Schmitt, Andrew D. Basiago, Dr. J. Allen Hynek, Col. Phillip J. Corso, John Maynard, Albert M. Chop, Harland Bentley, Dr. Edgar Mitchell, Neil Armstrong, Buzz Aldrin, Scott Carpenter, Eugene Cernan, John Glenn, Gordon Cooper, James McDivitt, James Irwin, Alfred Worden, Dr. Jerry Linenger, James Lovell, Victor Afanasyev, Yevegni Khrunov, Major General Vladimir Kovalyonok, Maurice Chatelain, Karl Wolfe, Yevgeny Arsyukhin, Donna Tietze (Hare), Dr. Pierre Guerin, Victor Marchetti, David Froning, Dr. Richard Boylan, Col. Steve Wilson (USAF ret.), Command Sergeant Major Robert Dean, Norman Bergrun, Ben Rich, Henry Deacon, Dr. Carol Rosin, Dr. Steven Greer, Clark McClelland, Dr. Gilbert Levin, Chandra Wickramasinghe, Dr. Mark Carlotto, Ronald R. Nicks, James Erjavee, Captain John Lear, Robert M. Collins, Dr. Michael Wolf, Sgt. Clifford Stone, Dr. L. Parker Temple, Dr. Michael E. Salla, Franklin Spinney, Warren Botz, Jack D. Pickett, William Cooper, Phil Schneider, Don Phillips, John Walson, Ingo Swann, Dan Sherman, Dr. Robert Wood, Major Kevin Randle, Stanton Friedman, Brian Josephson, Iosif Shklovskii, Alex Collier, John Lash, Nigel Kerner, Dr. Francis Crick, Sir Fred Hoyle, Jeremy Narby, Michael Harner, Dr. Peter Gariaev, Dr. John E. Mack, Professor John McPherson, Dr. Arthur Horn, Professor Paul Davies, Professor Derek Bickerton, Steven Pinker, Brad Harrub, Bert Thompson Ph.D., Ph.D., and Dave Miller, Ph.D, Philip Lieberman, Terrance Deacon, Jean Aitchison, John McCrone, Michael Corballis, Carl Zimmer, Noam Chomsky, Carl Wernicke, Werner Gitt, Johannes Muller, John Skoyles, Dorion Sagan, John W. Oller, John L. Omdahl, Suzette Elgin, M.A. Nowak, George Gaylord Simpson, Leonid Ksanfomaliti, Farida Iskiovet, Commander Mark Huber, Sgt. Willard Wannal, Major Wayne S. Aho, Dr. James Hurrah, Christopher C. Kraft, Dr. Farouk El-Baz, John O'Neill, Paul Hellyer

References

Evidence of Lost Ancient Civilizations: Case Closed, Joe Szostak, 2009, PublishAmerica

Riddles of the Past: Solving Mankind's Ancient Mysteries, Joe Szostak, 2010, PublishAmerica

Mankind's Origins: The Hidden Secret Revealed, Joe Szostak, 2011, PublishAmerica

Our Martian Ancestry Exposed, Joe Szostak, 2012, PublishAmerica

The Cosmic Bloodline, Joe Szostak, 2013, PublishAmerica (unreleased)

The Terran Directive, Joe Szostak, 2016, Amazon Publishing

Creatures of the Goblin World, Jerome Clark and Loren Coleman, 1978, Clark Publications, Chicago

Lost Cities of North & Central America, David Hatcher Childress, 1994, Adventures Unlimited Press, Kempton, IL.

The Anti-Gravity Handbook, David Hatcher Childress, 2003, Adventures Unlimited Press

The Mystery of the Olmecs, David Hatcher Childress, 2007, Adventures Unlimited Press

Forbidden Archaeology, Michael A. Cremo and Richard L. Thompson, 1998, Torchlight Publishing

Human Devolution: A Vedic Alternative to Darwin's Theory, Michael A. Cremo, 2003, Torchlight Publishing

The Hidden History of the Human Race, Michael A. Cremo and Richard L. Thompson, 1999, Torchlight Publishing

Fingerprints of the Gods, Graham Hancock, 1996, Three Rivers Press

Supernatural: Meetings with the Ancient Teachers of Mankind, Graham Hancock, 2007, The Disinformation Company

The Message of the Sphinx: A Quest for the Hidden Legacy of Mankind, Graham Hancock and Robert Bauval, 1997, Three Rivers Press

Orion Mystery, The: Unlocking the Secrets of the Pyramids, Robert Bauval and Adrian Gilbert, 2001, Arrow Publishing

Serpent in the Sky: The High Wisdom of Ancient Egypt, John Anthony West, 1993, Quest Books

Voyages of the Pyramid Builders, Robert M. Schoch, 2004, Tarcher

Voices of the Rocks: A Scientist Looks at Catastrophes and Ancient Civilizations, Robert M. Schoch, 1999, Harmony

THE 12TH PLANET, Zecharia Sitchin, 1991, Bear & Company

Shattering the Myths of Darwinism, Richard Milton, 2000, Park Street Press

Technology of the Gods: The Incredible Sciences of the Ancients, David Hatcher Childress, 2000, Adventures Unlimited Press

Maps of the Ancient Sea Kings, Charles Hapgood, 1979, Turnstone Books

The Giza Power Plant: Technologies of Ancient Egypt, Christopher Dunn, 1998, Bear & Company

Bones of Contention: A Creationist Assessment of the Human Fossils, Marvin L. Lubenow, 1992, Baker Books

Cloak of the Illuminati: Secrets, Transformations, Crossing the Stargate, William Henry, 2003, Adventures Unlimited Press

The Phoenix Solution, Alan F. Alford, 1998, Hodder & Stoughton

Buried Alive: The Startling Truth about Neanderthal Man, Dr. Jack Cuozzo, 1998, Master Books

The Orion Prophecy: Will the World Be Destroyed in 2012, Patrick Geryl, 2002, Adventures Unlimited Press

Lost Star of Myth and Time, Walter Cruttenden, 2005, St. Lynn's Press

Secrets of the Lost Races: New Discoveries of Advanced Technology in Ancient Civilizations, Rene Noorbergen, 2001, Teach Services

The Complete Pyramids: Solving the Ancient Mysteries, Mark Lehner, 1997, Thames & Hudson

The Secrets of the Mojave, Bruce Alan Walton a.k.a. "Branton", 1999, Creative Arts & Science Enterprises

Ancient Near Eastern Texts Relating to the Old Testament, James B. Pritchard, 1955, 2nd ed., Princeton: Princeton University

Life and Death of a Pharaoh – Tutankhamen, Christiane Desroches-Noblecourt, 1963, World Books

Dark Star: The Planet X Evidence, Andy Lloyd, 2005, Timeless Voyager Press

Frozen in Time: The Woolly Mammoth, the Ice Age, and the Bible, Michael J. Oard, 2004, Master Books

Climate Confusion: How Global Warming Hysteria Leads to Bad Science, Pandering Politicians and Misguided Policies that Hurt the Poor, Roy W. Spencer, 2008, Encounter Books

Invisible Residents, Ivan T. Anderson and David Hatcher Childress, 2005, Adventures Unlimited Press

Montezuma's Serpent, Brad Steiger and Sherry Hansen Steiger, 1992, Paragon House Publishers

The Rainbow Conspiracy, Brad Steiger and Sherry Hansen Steiger, 1994, Pinnacle

Worlds Before Our Own, Brad Steiger, 2007, Anomalist Books

The Sirius Mystery, Robert Temple, 1998, Destiny Books

America's Ancient Civilizations, A. Hyatt Verrill and Ruth Verrill, 1953, Putnam

Genesis of the Grail Kings, Laurence Gardner, 2002, Fair Winds Press

The Structure of Scientific Revolutions, Thomas S. Kuhn, 1962, University of Chicago Press

Proposed Studies on the Implications of Peaceful Space Activities for Human Affairs, The Brookings Institution, 1961

The Hidden Records, Wayne Herschel and Birgitt Lederer, 2005, Hidden Records

The Cygnus Mystery, Andrew Collins, 2007, Watkins

Earth Under Fire: Humanity's Survival of the Apocalypse, Dr. Paul LaViolette, 1997, Starlane Publications

The Monuments of Mars: A City on the Edge of Forever, Richard C. Hoagland, 2002, Frog Books

Timeless Earth, Peter Kolosimo, 1968, Bantam Books

Terra Non Firma Earth, Dr. James Maxlow, 2006, Terrella Press

Worlds in Collision, Dr. Immanuel Velikovsky, 1950, Paradigma Ltd.

Earth in Upheaval, Dr. Immanuel Velikovsky, 1955, Paradigma Ltd.

Noah's Flood, William Ryan and Walter Pittman, 1997, Simon & Schuster

The Martian Chronicles, Ray Bradbury, 1950, William Morrow

The Origin of Species, Charles Darwin, 1859, Signet Classics

Intelligent Life In The Universe, Carl Sagan and I.S. Shklovskii, 1966, Emerson Adams Press

The Cosmic Connection, Carl Sagan, 1973, Anchor Press/Doubleday

Broca's Brain, Carl Sagan, 1980, Ballantine Books

Cosmos, Carl Sagan, 1985, Ballantine Books

Ring-makers of Saturn, Norman Bergrun, 1986, The Pentland Press

Alien Rapture, Edgar Rothschild Fouche and Brad Steiger, 1998, Galde Press, Inc.

The Catchers of Heaven, Dr. Michael Wolf, 1996, Dorrance Publishing Co.

Hyperspace, Michio Kaku, 1995, Anchor Publishing

Prehistoric Europe, Philip Van Doren Stern, 1969, W.W. Norton & Co.

A Contribution to the Physical Anthropology and Population Genetics of Sweden, Lars Beckman, 1959

In Search of Adam, Herberdt Wendt, Houghton-Mifflin, 1956

The Ascent of Man, J. Bronowski, Little, Brown & Co., 1973

X-Raying the Pharaohs by James E. Harris and Kent Weeks, Charles Scribner's Sons, 1973

The Illuminatus! Trilogy, Robert Anton Wilson and Robert Shea, 1983, Dell

The Symbolic Species: The Co-Evolution of Language and the Brain, Terrence Deacon, 1998, W. W. Norton & Company

The Cambridge Encyclopedia of Human Evolution, Stephen Jones, Robert D. Martin, and David R. Pilbeam, and Richard Dawkins, 1993, Cambridge University Press

Up from Dragons, John Skoyles and Dorion Sagan, 2002, McGraw-Hill

Gods of Aquarius, Brad Steiger, Berkley, 1982

The Song Of The Greys, Nigel Kerner, Hodder & Stoughton, 1999

Life Itself: Its Origins and Nature, Dr. Francis Crick, Touchstone, Simon & Schuster, 1982

Life from Space, Sir Fred Hoyle, Simon & Schuster, 1982

The Cosmic Serpent, Jeremy Narby, Jeremy P. Tarcher/Putnam, 1999

Humanity's Extraterrestrial Origins, Dr. Arthur Horn, Silberschnur, 1994

Eve Spoke, Philip Lieberman, W. W. Norton & Company, 1998

The Seeds of Speech, Jean Aitchison, Cambridge University Press, 2000

From Hand to Mouth: The Origins of Language, Michael Corballis, Princeton University Press, 2003

How the Mind Works, Steven Pinker, W. W. Norton & Company, 1997

The Wonder of Man, Werner Gitt, Christliche Literatur-Verbreitung, 1999

Mankind, Child of the Stars, Books 1 and 2, Max Flindt, Fawcett Books, 1974

X-Raying the Pharaohs, James E. Harris and Kent R. Weeks, Charles Scribner's Sons, 1973

You Are Becoming a Galactic Human, Virginia Essene and Sheldon Nidle, Spiritual Education Endeavors, 1994

Earth Under Fire: Humanity's Survival of the Ice Age, Paul A. LaViolette, Bear & Company, 2005

The Gods of Eden, William Bramley, Avon, 1993

About the Author

Joe Szostak is an author, researcher, and alternative historian.

His previous books have included **Evidence of Lost Ancient Civilizations: Case Closed (2009), Riddles of the Past: Solving Mankind's Ancient Mysteries (2010), Mankind's Origins: The Hidden Secret Revealed (2011), Our Martian Ancestry Exposed (2012),** and **The Terran Directive (2016).**

These books deliver an important message by offering a unique perspective into mankind's earliest origins and the theory that an advanced ancient civilization once existed upon the Earth prior to recorded history.

The Other (Secret) Space Program is the latest episode yet. It offers compelling evidence in support of the existence of a covert space program, operating outside of the mainstream of government and NASA and funded through a black operations budget.

Each book in this thought-provoking series while intended to stand alone, is best appreciated and enjoyed in the pre-arranged sequence listed above.

Joe Szostak is Vice President of a manufacturing and distribution group of international companies based in Ontario, Canada.

His professional background and formal education are in Business Management, Engineering and Manufacturing. He has held senior executive positions throughout his career and has also worked independently as a consultant dealing with business acquisitions and mergers.

He has been a science enthusiast since his teens and has developed a personal interest in the research and study of science, history, ancient civilizations and the theories involving mankind's origins.

His wide-ranging exploration of these subjects and desire to deliver an alternative perspective, to what is offered by mainstream science and history textbooks, has led him to undertake these writings.

Joe Szostak and his family live in Ontario, Canada and the Treasure Coast of South Florida.

Made in the USA
San Bernardino, CA
01 March 2020